SINNERS' RETREAT

Maximus Mucho

SINNERS' RETREAT

First published 2014
First Edition
Copyright © 2014 Maximus Mucho
Editor: Inamorata Mucho
Cover art by Prickly Pear Works

Maximus Mucho has asserted his right under the Copyright, Designs and Patents Act 1988 to be identified as the author of this work.

ISBN-13: 978-1505575569
ISBN-10: 1505575567

THE EXCLUSIVITY

The hotel was sexy and amazing.

It was a shining white mirage located on the edge of a brown, rocky cliff, with kilometer upon kilometer of white sandy beaches stretching out to either side below.

In front of the hotel the blue ocean stretched out seemingly endless.

The impressive and towering hotel was two hundred feet tall, making it one of the largest structures in the country where it was built, and completely covered in imported, white marble.

The Italian architects had designed the grand hotel in what they called an Imperial Roman Column-style, but to most people, the massive hotel most of all resembled a giant fork with a broken off handle that had been driven into the ground, perhaps in anger by Poseidon, on the edge of the cliff. The fork's teeth consisted of seven giant square columns that narrowed slightly in towards the open, shared ground floor where the lobby was situated.

On top of the columns there was an amazing, shared roof-terrace with a large lounge area, bar and swimming pool. A gold, wave-shaped railing with glass inserts enclosed the whole terrace.

The hotel's closest neighbors were kilometers away, and the rooftops of their houses were only barely visible in the far distance from the roof-terrace.

The location for the hotel had been strategically chosen by the owners and investors to make sure that their wealthy guests at all times would be spared from seeing, or in any way having to relate to, the country's poor inhabitants.

Below the roof terrace, in between each of the fork's arches, large wind turbines had been installed.

According to the hotel's brochure, on windy days, the hotel could be completely self-sustained with electric power solely by the use of the turbines.

Unfortunately, for the time being, the turbines weren't functioning like they were supposed to. No matter the wind force, the wind just didn't seem able to make them start running. The most obvious reason was of course that the turbines' exterior design had been prioritized ahead of their technical interior's functionality. This somewhat minor issue, according to the hotel's administration, had for the grand opening been solved by the installment of engines inside the turbines, providing the guests and on-site reporters with the illusion it really was the wind making the propellers run.

In between the seven massive columns containing the hotel's luxurious guest rooms and suites, large glass elevators had been installed to cater to the guests' comfort needs meanwhile offering a combination of breathtaking and dizzying views.

On the hotel's façade, a decorative, spiral staircase was clinging to each of the columns. They were all locked off to prevent unauthorized use, but were still a part of the hotel's fire escape plan.

On the hotel's seaside, offering to lead the hotel's sun and bathe-hungry guests down to the white stretch of beach below the steep cliff, there was a glass elevator and a broad, decorative, spiral staircase on each side of the hotel.

The record costly advertisement campaign for the hotel, with romantic and exotic pictures of male and female swimsuit models and the fabulous views from the terrace, was run on every front-page of any significance around the world. A fit six-pack against the sunset and a bouncy breast in profile against a sunrise was always a sure way to sell vacation dreams to any potential guest.

Operational-wise, the exquisite hotel was nothing less than a technological wonder. Among other, the newly developed, highly advanced A.I system that had been installed just before the grand opening was one of the hotel's most reputed attractions.

All the hotel's VIP suites had been set up with their own, individual artificial intelligence, allowing for each room and the staff to better accommodate the guests, and to the greatest extent possible satisfy all of their, both conscious and unconscious, desires.

The suites' AIs were all programmed to register and analyze everything about their guests' behavior, response patterns, personal preferences, habits and daily routines as well as their food, drink and any other substance intake.

All the suites' individual AIs' were controlled by and reported back to a joint main control unit, that the hotel's IT responsible, tech nerds simply referred to as "The Almighty".

The Almighty was placed in a regulated atmosphere down in the hotel's basement, and was, in addition to re-analyzing and interpreting the individual analyzes and readings sent back from the suites' AIs, also set up to monitor and screen all other activity taking place on and around the hotel's premises by the aid of surveillance cameras and a variety of strategically placed, high tech sensors and filters.

Through air filters The Almighty would anatomize the contents of the air the guests and staff exhaled, while through filters in the hotel's drainage system, it would sample hair, mucus and other bodily waste matter.

Finding pheromones, testosterone, estrogen and drawing conclusions from their levels, while monitoring blood pressure, bodily temperature and heart rate would all help "The Almighty" sort out what type of persons were staying and working at the hotel. One of the attractions of the A.I was that the VIP suites would name themselves sometime during the first days of their guests' stay based on the information "The

Almighty" gathered about their personalities. The machine had been built by using cheap labor and even cheaper parts from some underdeveloped country and its sole purpose was to help pamper more privileged humans. It would of course in addition to naming the suites after the owner's personality learn the temperature they preferred the rooms to be, what they liked to eat and it could, based on the information it gathered, even give them advice on how to improve. Recommend food that was good for a person with a heart condition or a special shampoo if someone was suffering from dry hair. "The Almighty" would use the internet as its source of finding solutions to the needs of the hotel's guests.

From the hotel's main control room a number of different advanced systems could be activated, either by the tech support working there or by the "Al Mighty" itself, for the entertainment and comfort of the guests. This included underwater speakers that would attract dolphins to the hotel's beach, sea temperature control to regulate warm current flows around the beach area to adapt the sea temperature, and a wave generator capable of generating small to large surf-able waves in certain areas of the beach should there be a request from any of the guests to do some surfing. Strategically placed lighting on the beach and in the sea would in the evening and at night illuminate the whole area in addition to the artificial reefs and create the picture perfect surroundings for the guests. The hotel's interior looked as if it had been decorated by Marie Antoinette employed by the British royal family in anticipation of a great celebration.

Each of the hotel's exclusive rooms had a minimum of three window sides and a balcony facing the sea offering magnificent views.

In all of the seven columns there were two rooms on each floor, apart from on the top floors where the extraordinary and special VIP suites had the complete floor to themselves.

Having bought the piece of land the hotel was built on for a surprisingly low amount, the German owners had spared no expenses when it came to the appearance of the hotel. The style throughout was so pompous it would have given even the style-conscious Hercule Poirot an erection if he ever visited it.

The hotel was built exclusively for the upper of the upper classes, and of course anyone else who could manage to afford staying there.

With the endless blue ocean and its tints of sparkling lights as a background, or as the foreground, the hotel resembled a fairytale creation.

Long before its impressive opening, it was already a favored photo object. Travel magazines made numerous articles claiming it to be the number one hot spot to vacation - if you could afford it, that was.

The construction of the hotel had just finished its final stages, and the hotel began waiting in an atmosphere of virgin elegance for its first guests to arrive.

Everything was perfect!

Except, maybe, for the small, practically unnoticeable crack in the ground, or perhaps one should rather call it a tiny gap.

The tiny gap, which was so small it was virtually impossible to spot with the naked eye, ran all the way from the security booth right outside the hotel entrance and continued alongside the avenue all the way down to the avenue's end.

For the moment it seemed as the tiny gap was waiting in peaceful harmony together with its surroundings.

☐

VIPS

Mubasher Muhjadra was relaxed. He was in fact so relaxed he hadn't bothered going over to the medicine cabinet to retrieve some Viagra, or even been bothered calling his personal house doctor to bring some to him. One of his mistresses was desperately trying to work up an erection on him. He watched her struggling while lying casually on top of his silk draped bed.

She was one of the pretty ones, he admitted to himself, and he took great joy in her obvious discomfort in failing to please him. Because he was such a great and good leader, he kind of wanted her to succeed, but that meant either walking all the way over to the medicine cabinet in the bathroom, or having to call someone, and both scenarios just seemed like too much work for the moment. To have the young mistress quit what she was doing and get her to retrieve the pills was absolutely not an option.

The young mistress tried working on him with her mouth, but it just made his penis more slippery, and then the friction was gone, and she ended up struggling even more with using her hands.

Mubasher quickly realized she'd made a mistake with his royal penis and decided she should be replaced. She was just too clumsy to be the mistress of a successful ruler of a nation, even if she did have the beauty. There were plenty of beautiful women to find out there. Next time he saw another one suiting his taste, he would point her out to his guards. Picking his new mistresses like that was often more fun than shopping. How she ended up at his disposal afterwards he didn't give a second thought. He was the great leader, and he could, deserved and should do whatever suited him at any given moment. He would give this failing mistress to his guards so they could have their way with her for as long as they wanted. You didn't become a successful and enduring dictator without taking care of the people who took care of you. That was something his father had taught him before he had him overthrown.

Mubasher for a moment stopped paying attention to how the mistress was failing with his penis and glanced around the room at the gold plated eagle statues, the gold plated bed posts, the gold plated walls and the gold framed painting of himself being the most active he could remember having been for a long time. The picture showed him sitting on one of his mother's favorite horses. He couldn't remember its name. He was wearing a uniform designed by one of his mistresses. It was made from the finest of fabrics, in a deep purple color, with gold decorations, and to complete the outfit, a white hat, almost like a cowboy hat, with feathers in. He remembered the feathers had come from a bird called a bald eagle, but how could a bald eagle have feathers, and if it didn't have feathers how could it be a bird? He didn't bother thinking about it anymore. Reaching out with one arm and gripping a gold bell he called for one of his personal servants. When the servant arrived he ordered him to take the mistress away and deliver her down at the guard's barracks, and then to have his bathtub filled with water.

Having the bed slightly elevated when installed in this, one of his favorite bedrooms, had been pure genius, and of course his very own idea. That way he could see some of the yard outside his summer palace without having to get out of bed.

Mubasher took great pride and joy in his own geniuses, and lately it seemed he'd excelled in coming up with great ideas. He thought about his stand-in. The head of his guards had suggested he should have one in case someone made an attempt on his life. At first it had seemed like a totally illogical idea. Why anyone should ever want to kill him had been way beyond his capability of understanding, but when he'd had some time to think about it, he'd supported the idea completely. The last few months he'd even started regretting not having arranged the stand-in set up a long time ago. Now, he had time to do whatever he wanted, which for most of the time involved lying down on his back while being served by his different servants and mistresses. His stand-in now carried out practically all his tasks, in fact he performed all his public duties and even some of his more personal ones. Currently, the stand-in was somewhere in the mansion posing for a new painting. The duties involving pleasure, he executed all on his own. This was an excellent arrangement. He truly deserved it, and anyone in the same position would've done the same. Of course no one else could, he being a powerful dictator, and they… well. He wasn't actually sure who they really were. They were probably his people - the word: his, being the foremost thought in his head.

Mubasher felt relieved and relaxed as he slid down from the bed and entered directly into the gold-plated bathtub his servants had rolled out and placed next to it. He ordered them to bring him some Viagra, another bottle of champagne and, of course, a new mistress. In the tub, the extent of his own genius surprised him yet again. His mother's funeral was coming up. Well, not the actual funeral, as that had already been, but the public commemoration. He'd been trying to put off thinking about it ever since the date had been set. It would doubtlessly be incredibly boring and exhausting. He would have to receive a number of greetings and condolences, in addition to most likely having to be in an upright position for the majority of the time.

Mubasher smiled as his new mistress was shushed in through the gold framed doors, because of his ingenious thinking his stand-in would attend his mother's commemoration. He felt as if a weight had been lifted of his shoulders, and life was currently good. He studied the mistress, she was indeed a new one, and if she was as good as she looked he would spend a couple of more days in bed while all the stressful commotion was taking place. He called his servant over to instruct him to make the arrangements with the stand-in, meanwhile the new mistress started working on his penis. This time his penis reacted, and, totally ignoring the fact he'd just swallowed two Viagra together with half a bottle of his premium champagne, he assumed it was all due to himself and his elevated mood from ingeniously solving a potentially stressful task.

Later, maybe sometime next week, he would have his chauffeur drive him around in the capital in his new Bentley so his people could see he cared about them enough to not only take part in his mother's commemoration, but also make inspection tours in the city. He could combine the publicity friendly drive with looking for a replacement for his newly lost mistress.

☐

Fernandez Golden Ball Gomez was having a bad day. Actually, it had been a bad week. Yesterday he'd had to beat up his new wife, and that of course always meant some sort of trouble afterwards. He really thought the beating hadn't been all that bad. He'd only casually slapped her around in the living room for a little while, but obviously she bruised easily. He still felt she'd brought it on herself. She'd practically openly disrespected him by making fun of him in front of two of his friends, and then she hadn't even apologized when they got home. That he'd lately been having re-occurring dreams about her making love to one of his friends while he watched, in addition to the drugs and drinking that had been involved, had probably made him even angrier

The actual problem that made Fernandez's day and week bad was related to him, just a couple of weeks earlier, divorcing his old wife. Or, more to the point, she'd divorced him after claiming to have been repeatedly abused and beat up in the relationship. During the stressful divorce he'd also beat up one of the referees at a soccer match he'd been playing, but that had of course been the referee's own fault. At least from Fernandez's point of view.

The divorce, and of course the bashing of the referee, had made the top news in most countries where absolutely anything slightly related to soccer was regarded as among the most important of news, and that again was in most countries in the human world.

He'd become much more famous because of the two beatings than by anything he'd ever achieved on the field in a match.

The split picture with his old wife after one of his beatings on the one side, and him almost trampling on the referee's head on the other, had made numerous front pages. But neither of those incidents were the reason for his bad day or week, and nor was his new wife's black eye which she at all times made sure to cover up behind big, dark sunglasses.

Fernandez's PR consultant did cost a bundle of money, but she was worth it. Fernandez Golden Ball Gomez had risen from the negativity in the press by asking publicly about forgiveness, and then explaining it all by telling the saddest stories about how he, himself, had grown up with an abusive father and mother, and how he'd been helplessly introduced to drugs after a sports related accident. Most of it had of course been made up and edited by the PR consultant, but the reporters and public had consumed every single thing he told them with an almost endless thirst. Soon after, he'd received several new offers from other, bigger soccer clubs, and life had been even better than before. Then, when he one evening had happened to throw a beer bottle in the face of another guest in a bar, and several of the other guests had stepped forwards and claimed he'd first been provoked, life had suddenly started to make sense. He was talented, he was young, and people agreed with what he did. At least, that was how he viewed the situation. The guest, who'd been in the receiving end of the bottle throwing, had simply been paid off with a forgiving and silencing amount, and he, even thought he'd been extremely annoying, neither had anything to do with his bad day or week.

Last weekend Fernandez had re-married. His new wife was a semi-famous bikini model. During the wedding his PR consultant had tipped the paparazzi on where the wedding was taking place. This had of course also been a wish from his side, for him, all publicity had been a good publicity. But, during the wedding one of the paparazzi had taken some pictures where it appeared as if he was starting to go bald on the top of his head. The paparazzo who'd taken the pictures had renamed him Golden Bald in the pictures' headline; Fernandez Golden Bald Gomez. Obviously he'd been furious when he saw the new nick name and the pictures. The honeymoon had ended up with him taking drugs while drinking heavily, and then finally, when neither had helped to heal his bruised self-esteem, he'd beat up his new, model wife, and finished the beating by whipping her with the bikini he'd ripped off her. The public, so far, had no knowledge of him beating up his new wife, and his PR consultant had advised him it should remain that way. It was too early, and the incident was just too close to his previous incidents, she'd explained. She'd advised him that he and his new wife should extend their honeymoon, and spend the remainder of it somewhere secluded where his wife's bruises and cuts could heal unnoticed.

He deeply hated the fact he was starting to go bald, but the extended vacation, on the other hand, didn't bother him at all. After all, his PR consultant had found a brand new, top of the class, luxury hotel for them to stay at.

Fernandez was becoming increasingly angrier as he sat searching the internet for hair growth products. Most of the products he'd found seemed to originate somewhere in Asia, and was evidently made from so-called endangered animal species, which probably just meant the products were extremely special and difficult to obtain.

Somewhere behind him his new wife's mobile rang, and he listened suspiciously when she came out of the bedroom and answered it. Did it look like she was covering for the sound of the voice talking to her? Was she making fun of his hair loss, or maybe it was his friend calling her to set up a sex date behind his back.

Two new e-mails ticked in to his account. The first from a reporter asking him for an interview regarding the pictures taken at the wedding, and the other from some Asian company answering him that the hair growth product he'd requested was difficult to obtain, but that he could be on their waiting list. Both made Fernandez even more furious, but then an alarm set off on his mobile and reminded him he had to go to the bathroom to take his daily dose of steroids.

☐

Gunther Schmadt was sitting behind his desk in his office.

The office was dominated by a strong smell of sweat. The powerful smell would surprise anyone who visited the office for the first time, or that is; anyone who didn't know the owner.

The office was large enough to contain a small African refugee camp, including the cows they probably didn't have. That was, if they could have managed to stay there withstanding the way it smelled.

The enormous size of the office in theory made it highly unlikely for one man's sweat to be able to dominate it, but it was simply a regular case of: you have to know the man to understand.

The wooden desk occupying the center of the office was so enormous it would easily have made any skeptic understand how deforestation was a problem. Most people who saw the desk concluded that the office, as well as the building containing the office, could only have been built around the desk. The single thing really making the desk seem made for any human was the owner, either sitting behind it, laying partially on it, or standing next to it hitting it with his fists.

Gunther, called Big Gunther when he was around, and most often Burger Gunther when he wasn't, was a giant of a man. Not the tall and muscled type of giant, but a surprisingly fat one. But, despite of Big Gunther's impressive physique, it was still the strong smell that dominated his office.

Gunther had just had to fire one of his secretaries. Not the young, new one with the big boobs that used to skate around outside his office on roller-skates during her lunch breaks, but one of the old ones. He shifted irritably on his great mass of blubber behind his desk. The chair screamed in protest and the desk was punished by sweaty hands pounding on it. He needed to go to the toilet and was waiting impatiently for someone to change the toilet paper. He wanted the soft deluxe type of paper, and currently the toilet was only offering semi-soft paper rolls.

"What is this?! Am I living in some poor developing country?!"

Gunther shouted and several times more pounded on his desk. For tax reasons in addition to easy access to cheap labor, Gunther's factory was located in East Germany. But, despite the lower labor costs in East compared to in West Germany, it now seemed he was being punished for his choice of location by the lack of accessibility to soft fabrics. He was certain this toilet paper issue was never a problem in West Germany. At least, he'd never experienced the problem there. His large-breasted secretary roller-skated passed his windows, but with his increasingly pressing need to take a shit he wasn't even horny at the moment. Anyway, he still managed to decide he would also today grab her boobs and play with them before the day was over. She really did have a pair of great breasts, and squeezing them comforted him. Once he'd seen some kind of soft ball that one could squeeze as an anti-stress exercise on the TV-shop channel. He'd thought the ball was one of the most stupid things he'd ever seen, but after he'd started squeezing his secretary's breasts he understood the ball better. Breasts would nevertheless always beat balls.

Where the fuck was that new toilet paper?

Gunther's phone started making its ringing sound. It was the Porsche dealer. His new car was ready to be picked up. "Pick it up? Fuck you! I expect service when buying my cars from you. Bring it to my office, now!" He hung up the phone and shouted once more for an update from anyone regarding the toilet paper situation. Outside his secretary rolled by again, and her breasts made their slightly hypnotic movements.

The secretary looked through the office windows at her boss. She hated him. Her breasts were bruised and sore. She tried her best to find another job, but because of the current economic situation in East Germany it wasn't the easiest place to find new employment at the moment.

The secretary fantasized about using some kind of poison on her breasts. The poison would unquestionably very soon end up on his hands, fingers and eventually, inevitably, in his mouth. Somehow it seemed like absolutely everything sooner or later ended up there. She'd seen him eat - undoubtedly all of his employees had seen him eat, and at one time or another they'd all ended up with some food remains from his eating on them. His way of shuffling the food into his mouth left everything, that didn't make it down into the evidently bottomless, pink hole, splattered out all over his shirt and other objects unfortunate enough to be anywhere within his proximity.

Sometimes he would also make her lick his hands and suck his finger while he was playing with her breasts. If she decided to use poison one day, that would of course make her taste the poison herself, but it might just be worth it...

Thankfully, he was taking his son on some deluxe holiday soon. Maybe she could manage to find some other job, any other job, before he returned?

Inside his office Gunther shouted and pounded at his desk again.

Some minutes later he sat on the toilet. He was sweating profoundly and felt as if he was about to give birth to a, so far, unknown, giant creature. It had become evident his rectum didn't have the same great patience that his mind had. If the rectum hadn't been a part of his body, he would have fired it immediately for having let him down. He cursed his rectum and it trumpeted loudly in return as a protest, showing its defiance to him.

Gunther pulled out a couple of sheets of toilet paper and then rubbed them between two of his fat fingers. It wasn't close to as soft as he preferred, but maybe his rectum deserved it this time? He became even angrier with his employees and his rectum when he realized he simply wouldn't stoop to the level of using toilet paper of such low quality. The coarse paper would only end up hurting him and make him sore.

Gunther's anger soon turned to be directed solely towards his employees. After all, his rectum normally did a fantastic and impeccable job. Comparing what he ate with other people's food intake, his rectum did a three rectums' job, at least. Gunther shouted for new toilet paper. It was fucking unacceptable and intolerable. Clearly, East Germany was a lot less modern than what he'd expected. He grabbed the toilet paper roll and threw it in anger out through the gap between the door and the ceiling. To make matters even worse, as his rectum had loudly made his insides emptier, he'd now started getting hungry.

Gunther struggled to move about on the toilet seat trying to see how much he'd actually produced. It was a lot, even if he only managed to see a little of it. For a moment he also thought he caught a glimpse of his penis, but then his stomach again swayed in and covered the view.

The huge amount of shit, going straight to waste, irritated him. That was why he a few years ago had gotten large septic tanks installed in his factory. Over a month he'd gathered a great load of shit in the tanks from all of his employees and, of course, from himself, and then he'd tried to sell the produce to farmers as a fertilizer product. Nobody had wanted it, and he'd begun hating the new East Germany. In the old days you could make money on practically anything, and the customers were never so picky. He'd then tried to sell the produce to some Arabian and African countries. He'd argued that the shit, which he'd named: Der Naturliche Dunger, would transform any desert or dry area into an oasis. But, his sales effort had been for nothing, nobody in any other countries had wanted the product either, and now, the specialized containers he'd bought to transport it in, were standing right in the middle of his factory yard, as one of his few reminders of bad business. The name: Der Naturliche Dunger, was written in big, bold letters on the sides of all the containers. Every day when he arrived at work he would see the containers on the parking lot, but any day now, he would find a solution on how to use them. Otherwise, soon everything would have dried out and he wouldn't need a solution at all, and he hated the fact that he might end up with having to give the shit away for free.

Where the fuck was that toilet paper?

Gunther had raised the prices on all the food in the factory canteen after the Der Naturliche Dunger no-sale incidents, and it had soon made up for his losses in the shitty affair, but the thought of it all still made him agitated. He used the agitation as a motivation for a final push and emptied himself with a loud grunt and liberating rectum burp. Someone made a strangled, sobbing sound on the other side of the toilet door, and a new, extra super soft roll of toilet paper was pushed in through the gap beneath the door and stopped by his feet. He dried himself, and then he went directly from the toilets to go look for something to eat and someone to fire. He'd just had a new chef flown in from a restaurant in France to work in his kitchen at the factory. The chef was excellent, even if there did seem to be some problems with getting fresh and high quality ingredients delivered. Nevertheless, Gunther's stomach was soon filled with specially made gourmet dishes.

Later, in his office, with his stomach content and his hands busy groping his secretary's breasts, Gunther decided he would replace more of his secretaries with other, more big-breasted ones. He also wanted a bidet installed in the toilets and a large stock of extra soft deluxe tissue toilet rolls. There was no point in being the boss if one couldn't have everything picked from the top shelves.

Gunther relaxed by squeezing the secretary's breasts, in almost the same way as the presenters had squeezed the ball in the TV commercial, while he thought about his upcoming vacation.

Gunther's son, **Jurgen-Gunther**, was playing with his nanny. Yet again she'd had to collect him from the elementary school he was attending. It seemed Jurgen-Gunther had once again eaten all the food belonging to some of the other children in his class, and then he'd started playing some sort of bomber plane while throwing stuff at his teacher.

The nanny had several times tried to talk to the boy's father regarding his misbehavior, but most often the conversation had ended up with the boy's father fondling her breasts, while he seemed proud and amused by what his son had been doing. The nanny had given up trying to make the boy's father realize anything, and then she'd also given up trying to teach the boy any manners. Now she just collected him every time the school rang, and then let the boy eat and play whatever he wanted. In the meantime she was trying her best to find somewhere else to work.

Currently, the boy was sitting on the floor with a combination of snot and chocolate cake all over his face, while he played with his plastic machine gun. The nanny looked at her watch. She hoped the boy's father wouldn't be late, and that she would manage to get out of his house before he grabbed hold of one of her breasts. Jurgen-Gunther shouted for more chocolate cake.

☐

Zhang San Wang Wei was in France visiting a small city called Saint Raphael. He'd been sent there by his American employer to quickly learn some French cuisine before the competition started. Wei was a fast learner, and he was now sitting at one of the restaurants down at the marina eating some kind of ice-cream, chocolate sauce, whipped cream and pastry mixed dessert. The dessert was too sweet, too ice- and whipped-creamy and too buttery for his taste, but obviously it was very popular among the locals, just as any other kinds of sweets also were in France.

The American company he was working for had made him travel extensively as part of his preparations to be a judge in the competition. "You need to experience the food locally to better understand and to be able to evaluate it correctly," they'd said as he got the job.

He looked at the other tourists sitting at the tables around him in the restaurant. He didn't want to be a judge in a cooking competition, but for the moment it seemed to be the only way for him to get a taste of the western decadence he so terribly wanted.

Wei had been prepared ever since he was a child to someday take his share of the luxury that had become almost a standard in so many countries but his own.

He made an attempt to eat the rest of the sweet, buttery, ice- and whipped-cream mess on his plate, and thought about his father. His father had been working in what he now knew the westerners would have referred to as a sweat suit factory back home in China. The factory he'd been working in had produced and delivered mainly tights to what seemed to be a majority of Caucasian people in mostly Caucasian countries. His father would every weekend borrow a pair of tights from the factory, and during Sunday morning breakfast he would hold them up in front of Wei and his brother. "See these tights! You both need to work much harder if you're ever to succeed in a world where the owners of these are the successful ones! Can you two imagine the muscular bodies tights like these are designed for?" His father would say before grabbing one leg of the tights, and pulling at one side of it and his mother at the other, to show the two boys just how much the tights could stretch and how big they actually were. "The people using these must have a lot of muscles and be really fit to fill these pants! You boys really must exert yourselves if you're ever to gain their respect and want to be treated as their equals, and if you someday want to have what they have of luxury possessions."

Of course, the reality was a very different one, as Wei soon discovered when he arrived in a Caucasian dominated country and saw the tights' true users for the first time. He'd never dared telling his father the truth about what type of people who were usually wearing his precious tights.

Wei watched as two severely obese, tights-wearing women wobbled past him, and then, shortly after, a fat man with walking sticks came walking the other way, also proudly wearing a pair of tights. The fat man entered the restaurant where he was sitting, and leaned his walking sticks against the bar as he ordered himself a milkshake.

Wei turned away from the fat man and instead looked over at the restaurant next door where he couldn't help but stare at the folded fat on the two obese women's behinds as they had stopped to read the menu outside. They were probably also out to get themselves some milkshakes. How these people could be so comfortable in their tight clothing and use it as everyday casual wear, was beyond his understanding. They all displayed such confidence through their appearances and the way they behaved it almost shocked him. It also made him envious. There was no misunderstanding that their upbringing had been quite different than the one he'd experienced.

Wei's father was, and had always been, a very strict man. One time he'd surprised him and his brother playing with a pair of his home-lent, educational tights. He and his brother had squeezed inside each their tight leg and jumped around the house. When his father had seen them he'd been furious and spanked them, and then he'd made them work in the factory for one week to pay for the tights, even though the pair hadn't been damaged in any way by them playing with it.

Observing the fat women and the man in their tights Wei now understood far better the quality and endurance of the fabric, and also how his and his brother's playing couldn't possibly have damaged the product.

His father had nevertheless cut the pair of tights they'd been playing with in two pieces, and then he and his brother had been handed one half of the tights each. Later that day his father had nailed the tights legs above each of their beds as a lesson, to permanently remind them of Caucasian muscles and of the consequence of playing with things that weren't toys or things to be played with. His father's example had worked and he and his brother had learned their lesson. His brother had ever since the incident been working out hard every single day of his life and was now a successful weightlifter. The last he'd heard was that he might be a candidate for the Olympic Team.

Wei hadn't been able to build muscles the same way as his brother, so he'd instead been directed into a career as a chef. "People wearing these kinds of tights have to eat a lot, a lot of healthy food!" His father had said, so Wei had become a chef specialized in healthy food. Both he and his brother had worked harder than anyone he knew to achieve their father's goal.

Wei had found work in Singapore. His mother was Japanese and his father Chinese. It had sometimes been complicated when he was growing up, but later in life it had seemed to make things easier. In his first job as a chef he'd been a success, and was predicted to have a great career in front of him. Healthy food seemed to be almost an in-between the meals snack to the tights-wearers, so they could have a better consciousness when they drank their milkshakes, or ate some, or rather a lot of, not so healthy food.

But, after a while the financial situation had changed. People began claiming they could no longer afford eating healthy food, and Wei had found himself looking for work. As a specialist on healthy food, and with a partially famous brother, at least in Asia, he soon got a position where his job was to find positive health reasons to why people should buy different types of foreign, imported food. He would look through the products' ingredients, and then write a short, often very short, recommendation based on whatever he could find of healthy ingredients used in the product. It had all felt bogus, and there had never actually been any truly healthy way to present the products. But, then an American company trying to get into the Asian market suddenly offered him a position as a judge in a cooking competition. The company's PR department had suggested that by making him a judge, his endorsements of their products would carry more weight later. The competition would undoubtedly make Wei's name more valuable, and maybe even just a little bit famous. Wei, who lately had started to feel inferior to his popular brother, accepted the job offer without any hesitation.

Wei glanced around the restaurant once more as he swallowed the last spoonful of the dessert. At the restaurant there were at least three women he desired. He then looked down the street, and parked nearby he could see five cars he wished was his. He wanted it all! Life would be so much better if he only possessed all the wonderful things he'd seen others have as he travelled around doing background research for his new job.

He'd seen pictures of the magnificent kitchen where the cooking competition was to be held. He wanted to own that kitchen, and he also wanted to own the hotel the outstanding kitchen was located in. The pictures of the luxurious hotel in the brochure had looked amazing. When looking through the brochure he'd craved so much to be a guest there that he'd almost forgot that it was exactly what he was going to be, one of the exclusive hotel's special guests.

Wei opened up his lap top and began searching for news about Olympic teams.

☐

Flavio Balducci had been with many women, but they'd all had the same problem. Not that he'd been aware of it at the time, but the problem was that none of the women had been men. It had been a depressing period of his life. Then he'd started being exclusively with men, but a new problem had presented itself. The result had been an even greater depth of depression. For the moment he was so depressed he was even considering going back to having sex with women.

Flavio was the most famous singer ever of romantic, Italian ballads. He made Julio Iglesias appear like a rude choirboy in a rock band. At least, that was what most of the critics claimed. His silky smooth voice and the tones he could master had the unlikely ability to make women have an orgasm. Women, not men, and that was why he was now so desperately depressed by lust.

Flavio had been famous for almost two decades while he lived inside the closet heterosexuality represented to him. Then one day he'd held a concert in Asia, and afterwards one of the females in the public had sued him for not having an orgasm during his concert. It had been the first time someone sued him after a concert, usually, at least all the females in the front row seats were happy customers. Some evil critics had of course claimed there were fakers among the public, but no one had ever sued for not being satisfied during a concert before. Soon after the lawsuit it had been revealed that the lady who'd sued him actually had a penis. The incident should have stopped there, but instead it had triggered a lust inside Flavio. He'd given into his natural, but previously unnoticed, attraction to men instead of women. His PR consultant had advised against it since most of his fan base was female, and said it might influence his record sales negatively, but Flavio felt he'd made enough money, and his newfound lust had easily won over the consultants greedy arguments.

Soon the closet doors were wide open and Flavio was a liberated homosexual, but still something was missing in his life. No matter how much he sang he couldn't manage to bring any of his male lovers to an orgasm by using his voice. His voice was his one great gift, and by employing it he'd been able to have any women he'd ever not really wanted. If he could only do the same with men, of course, it being slightly different since he really wanted all of the men, but just the thought of it drove him almost crazy. His intense desire to be able to sing to any man and give him an orgasm, even if he was a heterosexual, was almost unbearable.

Of course, the way Flavio had come out of the closet hadn't been exactly how his PR consultant had envisioned or planned it. At the time, he'd been staying at a luxury hotel in Rome with his latest male lover, a beautiful young man who'd also been his private chauffeur to the latest of his concerts.

Flavio's thoughts jumped for a moment to the video that had been spread on the internet.

The cleaning woman on his floor at the hotel in Rome had passed in the corridor outside his room and heard him singing. She'd been an eager fan, and, like practically everyone else, she was of course also the owner of a mobile phone with a camera. She'd silently unlocked his door and pushed open a small gap so she could record a short sequence of him singing to show her friends and family. But instead, the scene she'd actually ended up immortalizing on her recording ensured her whole retirement and a new house by the beach in the Amalfi area. On the film, Flavios' lover had been resting naked on his back on the suite's sofa with his legs spread wide apart, in a position looking as if he was about to give birth. Between his legs, as if he was receiving a child, Flavio had been sitting crouched down while singing in his most melodious voice into his young lover's elevated rectum.

The cleaning woman's mobile camera had had an impressively

high resolution, and both the picture and audio quality of the recording had been remarkable. The camera's quality had in fact been so good that the branch had noticed a slight increase in its sales after the incident became public. That was the single, positive thing that had come out of the whole affair, and none of it had benefitted Flavio.

His young, male lover had of course become a celebrity himself after the incident, and he'd more than willingly shared his story with the media several times afterwards. He'd claimed that Flavio, in fact, hadn't been able to give him an orgasm at all, even when they'd had conventional sex, and further, that Flavio had tried to sing to his balls after having had him shave them, evidently in an attempt to achieve a better resonance effect, and when that hadn't worked, he'd tried singing directly into his asshole.

Other pictures, and among them some of Flavio using his lover's penis almost like a microphone, had also suddenly surfaced on the internet. It had all been private pictures he'd never expected to be shared. But soon, the media was all over the fact that Flavio, the famous womanizer who'd given thousands and thousands of women orgasms, wasn't able to give a single man, not even the man he was in love with, the special pleasure of an orgasm.

Flavio deeply felt it had all been handled quite rudely by the media, even the rumors about his reluctance to give his lover a blowjob in case it could damage his throat had been loudly discussed in public.

Flavio now had a new young lover. He suspected a lover of his money, but that really didn't matter to him. He was motivated by pure lust to hang on to the young man, either until he achieved giving him full orgasmic pleasure, and by that satisfying his own ego, or until he almost died trying.

Flavio looked at his new lover and imagined him naked, maybe naked on a secluded beach… Perhaps some days away from all the press and stress were exactly what they needed for him to succeed in giving his new lover an orgasm? He'd read an article about a new and supposedly amazing hotel that was just about to open. The article had been accompanied by some pictures of a delicious and fit man in a sunset. He could still remember the pictures in detail. Flavio decided he would immediately book a suite at the luxurious hotel for himself and his lover.

Flavios' latest lover looked at Flavio standing over by the window where he seemed to be pondering about some of life's greater questions. He was lying comfortably stretched out in bed while waiting for Flavio to confirm that he was going to book a room for them at the new hotel he wanted to be seen at.

His plan was to stay together with Flavio until he was as famous as his last lover had become. Already, the relationship had begun boosting his up-until now, going nowhere, career. He'd just been offered a job as the ring-card man at some major female boxing matches, and even though he was a homosexual, he was quite sure he was going to manage sleeping with at least some of the female boxing stars if there was any sexual pressure to do so, or if it looked as if it in any way could help boost his career further. Some of them were really butch, at least more butch than Flavio.

Flavio's new, young lover really wanted to go to the new, exclusive hotel, if for nothing else, than to be able to update his online social status to saying he was there.

☐

Mugade Magada was having a bad day, which was strange because normally it was everyone else who had the bad days, not him.

Mugade had made himself rich, powerful and respected, or maybe more feared than respected, but to him, the latter was one and the same. All the people around him, those who were normally having the bad days, would of course not have called it respect, but fear.

Mugade had recently decided that his respectful people should start calling him Lord Mugade Magada. Behind his back, most of the fearful people called him Warlord Mugade, and had Mugade himself known about this, it would have made his day even worse.

Lord Mugade didn't deal in weapons, or, at least, not in weapons exclusively. He actually preferred drugs, and most of his acquired wealth so far came from his drug dealing business. But, being an entrepreneur, as he considered himself to be, he would want his share of the money wherever money was being made, so another part of his money came from his numerous internet companies, most of them based in Nigeria. They were continuously sending out e-mails to rich Western and European countries. In addition, he also had a foot inside the human trafficking business, and that brought in another chunk of money to his accounts, but not much. He actually earned so little on the trafficking business compared to his other dealings that he most often viewed the business as plain charity work.

Lord Mugade was spending some of his bad day talking to one of his advisers.

"So why can't they bring more drugs on each trip? This is a step down from ass balloons. I wanted this to be a step up, not a step down!"

"This isn't my fault, Mugade! The women-"

"Lord Mugade!"

"The women, Lord Mugade, are simply too thin to carry any more drugs. It was you who wanted to use models, and models are very thin."

Lord Mugade stared angrily at his employee, No. 2. He'd started calling him No. 2 after having been inspired by a movie where the boss had simply called his employees by the number referring to their importance in the company. Was No. 2 trying to blame him? He'd killed many people for much less, but he suspected No. 2 of somehow being correct this time. "Look. Look at her! She can carry more cocaine than any ass-balloon-woman." Lord Mugade had a picture of Pamela Anderson on his lap top screen when he turned it around to show No. 2. "Pamela Andorson. I told you I wanted Pamela Andorson models!"

As if he had difficulties understanding where exactly he was supposed to be looking, No. 2 bent forward and looked closely at the Pamela Andorson woman his boss pointed at. "Boss, I agree with you. Pamela Andorson could carry much cocaine, but she's old time model. New time models are much skinnier. Adele, who did the last trip to Amsterdam, seriously hurt her back, and now she needs to use back braces and won't be able to do any more trips for a long while."

This wasn't what Mugade wanted to hear. He had several buyers waiting for new shipments. "No. 2, then we should begin using fatter models. Start using other types of models!"

"Well, Boss, now we're using catwalk models. We could try bikini models?"

Mugade looked distasteful at his No. 2, as if he'd suddenly developed white skin, or told him that he had Ebola. "No, we need strong models that have strong backs, not any fat or skinny models. We need sexy and strong models! Models who are fit. Yes! Fitness models and bodybuilder models!"

No. 2 looked at Mugade as if he was the brain of Einstein. "That's why you're the boss-man, Lord Boss-man!"

Mugade had just been considering whether or not to shoot him, or at least have him shot by someone else, but now changed his mind. No. 2 was a good soldier-adviser, even if he was incapable of doing any thinking on his own. Obviously, he was then probably not such a good adviser anyway, but he still was an okay soldier who usually did as he was instructed to do, and that was a quality Mugade appreciated. "No. 2, my vacation is coming up in six weeks. I want you to see to it that my daughter gets the maximum load possible for the vacation. They must be the best! Remember, this is a business.

I will of course continue to do business, even on my vacation – as you know, I never sleep. So, No. 2, I tell you again; these must be the very best! I'm going to show them to a potential, new business associate, and if they're not good enough, I'll hold you personally responsible. If you fail me in any way, I'll make you into my No. 5, or maybe do something even worse to you.

No. 2 looked at Mugade. "Lord Boss Mugade, why No. 5, man? I think No. 3 would be fairer."

Mugade stared back at his No. 2. How did he dare question his sayings?! "That's because No. 3 and No. 4 can't be moved up or down, they're too valuable where they are in the organization." For the moment Mugade couldn't remember exactly what No. 4 was doing, but No. 3 was in charge of running his operations with the false profiles on his dating sites, and it was big business. "Just don't fail No. 2, and we don't have a problem! I won't have you making me look stupid, or failing in getting this new contract. This could lead to a lot more business for me." Mugade sent No. 2 his most intimidating Lord-Mugade look, and finished almost as an afterthought; "Also, she's my daughter, so she's of course precious. Make sure the operation and packaging are of the very best quality." He then sent No. 2 away, leaned back in his chair and re-arranged his feet on his desk.

He studied the picture of Pamela Andorson on his laptop for a while. If she'd been black, she would have been perfect! He thought and stared out his office windows. He hated Cape Town, but he loved his office and the modern building it was in. It was all power and façade. Eventually he picked up his phone to make arrangements for his upcoming vacation meeting. It was always a long and tiresome procedure involving his people talking to the other man's people, and the exchange of information only on a strict need to know basis until they actually met each other. This new, potential, business associate represented such a vast and promising, new field of customers to his business that he, himself, had to be the one who took the meeting. Otherwise, he would have just had one of his numbers do it for him. He would have to get the promising, new contact to agree on meeting him at the new, luxurious and, according to the media, best hotel ever built. That way, he would be able to mix the business with some pleasure.

Mugade was in the middle of his yearly process of wife changing, so he wouldn't bring with him any wife on the vacation. Each spring he would have his old wife replaced by a new one. What happened to the old ones, he really didn't know or cared about, none of them had made any real impression on him anyway, and none of them had given him any sons. All he had was one daughter from some wives back, Ophelia Posh Victoria Magada. She was the one who would accompany him on the vacation. He was proud of his only daughter, but he was more proud of his own capability of using her for business purposes. He both could and had made money on practically anything he'd ever come in contact with.

Mugade focused on his computer again. It was time to choose the faces of some new male models. One of his companies would use them on its European dating sites to lure horny, white women into relieve themselves of some of their money. He hated this part of his work, the looking at men, but he didn't trust any of his numbers to do this part of the operation without him. He would later finish by selecting female models for the horny, white men. That was by far the more enjoyable part, and he worked through the males faster by having the females as a motivation. Maybe there was also a potentially new wife for him somewhere in the stack of photos?

Mugade's daughter, **Ophelia**, had just said goodbye to her friends after having done some shopping in preparation for her upcoming vacation together with her dad, when her mobile rang. It was one of her father's employees. She thought his name was Ngade, but she'd only ever heard her father call him No. 2. He called her claiming to have good news. It seemed her father had finally agreed to her getting the new breast implants she'd been wanting.

Ophelia wasn't sure what sort of business her father actually was in, it was all kind of shady, but she really didn't care as long as she had lots of money at hand, and she always had. Recently her father had also got involved in the surgical business, and she'd jumped at the opportunity and started asking him for bigger breasts. Now, No. 2 confirmed that her father had given the go-ahead for her operation, and he asked if she could come to their newly built and recently opened clinic the next morning. Then they could have the operation done in good time so her breasts would be healed and ready for any wanted degree of exposure by the time of their vacation. She, of course, instantly confirmed she would be there, and then she turned around to go and exchange the new bikini tops she'd just bought into some in larger sizes.

Now, if only her father would also give her the new car she wanted, life would get even a little better. She really felt she deserved a new car, the old one was already one year old, and it felt dirty and used.

The next morning, after having had to drive her old car to the clinic, Ophelia felt she deserved the largest breast implants possible. No. 2 was afraid of contradicting Mugade's daughter, but he was more afraid of Lord Mugade himself, so he just confirmed whatever the agitated young woman demanded, and then he called his boss when she was under anesthesia, but before they began the operation. Lord Mugade instructed him to have the doctor install the biggest load possible that would be safe, but also pretty to look at. Ophelia ended up with two times 280 grams implants. That meant she could carry a total load of 560 grams of cocaine, and, even if one withdrew some grams for the liquid solution the powder was dissolved in, it still amounted to at least half a kilo of cocaine.

When she woke up from the anesthesia, Ophelia felt she'd been framed. The implants were much smaller than what she'd asked for and wanted, but her father seemed unshakable regarding their size, and the vacation was now too close to do anything about it.

Regardless, Ophelia decided the discussion was far from over. She would just have it with her father sometime during the vacation.

☐

Johan Torgerson was being as quiet as he possibly could. He was laying on his back in bed, looking at the love-bat there it stood casually leaned against the wall, only partially hidden behind the bedroom door. The small gap in the drapes allowed just enough light into the bedroom to make the head of the bat glisten in the dimness. Johan cursed himself. It was his own bad performance at closing the drapes that now made him able to see the result of his wife's lovemaking. Normally, he took great care to close the drapes tightly to make sure the room was completely dark before they went to bed so he would be spared such sights. Seeing his wife make passionately love to his baseball bat, before she finally calmed down and went to sleep, was a highly disturbing sight. He just knew he would have to work-out extra hard this evening before he, himself, would be able to get any sleep. The fact that it was all nothing but his own fault, didn't help a bit on his mood.

His wife, Dagmar, most often just called Dagny, was now entering her rem sleep. After her loud sex noises the night had suddenly become strangely, but blessedly, quiet. Now, the only sound that could be heard was the farting noises coming from her folds of fat as she moved and turned beside him, occasionally accompanied by her actual farts. He still didn't feel safe that she was in a heavy enough sleep for him to begin his workout, so to pass some time he turned his attention back to his abused bat in an attempt to try to forget the sounds and the smells that was now starting to fill the room.

Johan had known that his wife was of the modern and liberated kind when he'd met her. It was actually one of the things about her he'd first been attracted to, but that was forty kilos and almost twenty years ago. Next to him Dagny suddenly farted almost violently. He found some pleasure in the fact that she in her fatness had developed almost proportionally. As Dagny over the years had only increased in size, her sex toys had only grown larger, and the sound of her farts had only become louder. Well, he couldn't exactly actually remember her farting volume really growing. The farts had at one point just suddenly seemed to exist and be part of her. If fact was that she'd been a farter all through their relationship, they had to have been of the silent type in the beginning, or he might have been so in love at a time that he hadn't noticed them. However unlikely that now seemed to him.

Johan kept staring at the love-bat. It was still glistening there it stood nonchalant leaned up against the wall. He felt like it was grinning at him. It was Dagny who'd placed the bat there after finishing her loud and awful lovemaking. The routine seemed to take longer and longer each evening. He wished he believed Dagny had placed the bat almost behind the door out of some kind of respect to him, but he knew she'd only put it there because it didn't fit in her bedside drawer. It really was all, his fault. He'd been the one to bring the baseball bat into the bedroom in the first place. Albeit, it had to be said that he'd put it beneath the bed, and he'd only thought of it as a protection against possible burglars. He should have known, taken into account his knowledge about his wife's ever increasing appetite for sexual pleasure, that it was a mistake to do so. It really was sad because he'd made the bat himself at school. It had been his favorite baseball bat.

The first time Dagny had made love to the bat he'd felt nauseated and almost physically in pain. It hadn't only been because he'd witnessed his wife's appalling lovemaking, but also for the sake of his poor baseball bat. Later, he understood that he'd possibly been feeling some kind of symptoms of abuse, so he searched the internet to find out more, and to see if there perhaps existed an internet site that helped people who'd had their possessions raped or violated in some way. He'd found one site dedicated to raped teddy bears, but the site hadn't seemed to reflect any regrets or remorse in any way. It had rather appeared to be a site for people who were turned on by stuffed animals, and it had ended up being of little help to him.

Johan focused on the baseball bat again. He wished it at least could have been still kept underneath the bed, but Dagny had been quite strict in regards to where it could be placed. She'd made it very clear that she didn't want any dirt or dust bunnies on it. He'd actually found it to be quite strange, because she'd never seemed that preoccupied with the other things she usually pleased herself with. She'd also argued that the bat was no longer meant for violence or defense, but only for love, she called it her love-bat. He felt a bit unwell just by the thought of it.

After a few minutes longer Johan got quietly out of bed. He went around it and over to where the bat was standing. He looked down at its glistening head and shaft. That she'd made such a point of not getting it dirty when she obviously didn't even bother to wipe it clean after what, according to the noises, could only have been a successful lovemaking session, made him regard her as being even filthier than he'd done before. She was too fat to do any vacuuming or household chores anymore, and he was busy trying to avoid being at home, so their whole house was in bad need of some cleaning. He blamed her. In the bedroom, he anyway wasn't able to do anything except pulling the curtains closed. The memories and fear of what was taking place there every evening had done that to him. That he now, evidently, wasn't even able to draw the curtains completely close together anymore, was really just a sign of how far he'd come in his revulsion to both her and the room itself.

Johan knew exactly what he had to do next. He composed himself and reached down and picked up the bat. He was careful to grasp it low by the end of the handle first, and then he felt his way slowly with his other hand until he had a good, two-handed grip. There was no way of knowing how large part of the bat had been actively participating in his wife's lovemaking, but considering the noise and the movements he was expecting the worse. It turned out that, despite his fear, he could use his two-handed grip on the bat without it sticking to his hands.

Johan almost tiptoed over to where Dagny was lying in bed. He felt over-precautious. She was making as much noise as a mid-size national celebration when the horn sections of the marching bands were tuning their instruments in unison. He took a deep breath of air and immediately paid the prize when he drew in some of her noisy fragrance. The nasty smell made him even more nauseous, but he still lifted the bat high above his head, so high that his arms began shivering and his muscles ached from the stretching. Then he swung the bat forcefully down.

Johan had a lot of experience. He'd practically been doing the exercise every night for the last four months. His precision had improved, and he felt pride in the fact that he now was able stop the bat closer and closer to Dagny's head. This time he realized he'd actually managed to hit the bat so close that it could only be centimeters left between it and her head. He could see her wispy hair wave away every time the bat came down and went up again. Up and down, up and down, harder and faster, harder and faster. He could feel how the aggression and frustration slowly released its grip on him. The built up tension caused by his wife's persona gradually gave way to a more relaxed feeling. Still, he had to continue doing it for almost half an hour before he felt satisfied. It seemed as the better he got at the exercise, the longer it took.

He wouldn't think of drawing any comparisons between his wife's use of the bat and his own, even if the fact was that it made them both sleep better.

Johan had noticed that he'd gotten in much better shape after he'd also started to sort of exercise with the baseball bat. Even Dagny had mentioned he looked better when she'd one day seen him through the gap after he'd forgotten to completely close the bathroom door. When she'd said it, he'd panicked. For a moment he'd thought she was making a move on him. Totally out of the blue, after months without any sexual relations between them, she'd maybe wanted to have sex with him again, but thankfully nothing more had happened. The morning after the incident he'd studied himself more thoroughly in the mirror, and he'd had to admit that she'd been right. His upper body had seemed more muscled and toned than ever before. It had been too bad he couldn't use the bat with his legs, but instead he'd gone out and bought himself a bike. After having bought the bike and felt how his leg muscles also had started to develop, he'd started using tights everywhere he went.

Johan made the last few strokes with the bat extra fast and hard. He finally felt finished and went quietly over and placed the baseball bat back by the door in the exact same position he'd found it. Then he also went to bed exhausted after having had his own round with the love-exercise-bat.

The next morning Johan got up early and before his wife, as usual. He did this out of consideration to himself. In the last six months he'd only overslept one time, but the sight of his wife leaving the bed naked had haunted him to such a degree that any doctor, anywhere in the world, would have subscribed him happy-pills for the next ten years just by hearing him cough once. He would much rather get out of bed early than give a doctor writer's cramp. Not out of consideration for the doctor, but because of his own, egotistical, mental well-being.

Today, it nevertheless looked to be beautiful morning. He could barely distinguish it through the small gap in the curtains. What he then noticed in disgust was the trail, obviously left by his wife's juices that ran up and down the curtain, like a dirt track up the back of a cyclist who'd been cycling in water and rain through a very heavy storm without a mudguard on his back wheel.

Dagny woke up with the sun shining in her face. It was typical of her puny husband to get even sloppier in relation to the curtains. Yesterday there had been a gap between them, and now they were completely removed. She'd suspected that Johan had left the gap in the curtains on purpose so he would be able to witness her erotic lovemaking with Batsy. The name, she'd thought of just as she was about to fall asleep the night before. It made her feel like she could have been making love to a part of Batman. Not the new Batman, but one of the old, more male-like Batmen. Frustrated, she felt how her horniness from thinking about wet, hot lovemaking with Batman became surpassed by her increasing irritation with the curtains and her no good husband. He would probably come up with some poor excuse for why he'd removed them, something lame about needing to wash them or something. She could clearly see, by the way torn pieces of curtain fabric were still hanging in some of the rings on the curtain rod, that he'd just carelessly pulled them down, as if he'd been in a great hurry to have them removed.

Sometime during the night she'd briefly woken up and noticed him standing almost bent over her. Most likely, he'd been so agitated and horny by seeing her sensually masturbating with Batsy, that he'd wanted to study her naked body in the shine of the moonlight. It had sounded as if he was masturbating. He'd probably gotten the idea after seeing her doing it earlier. What a coward and poor excuse for a husband and man he was, jerking off next to her in the dark like that when he thought she was sleeping. She was of course way too sexy and attractive for him, so she'd pretended to still be sleeping while he kept on at it, and shortly after she'd stopped pretending as she really fell asleep again. Nevertheless, Johan had given her something mysterious to ponder about. How had he been able to pull down the curtains without waking her up? She knew she was practically soundless when she slept and she always woke easily. And, also, why did it seem like the hair on the right side of her head had become fluffier and more voluminous than that on the left side?

Even though he felt proud because he was potentially one of the fastest ever to ride a bike, at least among the ones within his age group, Johan was cursing. He'd retrieved his bike from the garage, and after having quickly taken a picture of himself posing in tights in front of his bike, and then shared the picture on his Facebook page, and then, after having logged into an app that would tell his friends how far he would be cycling today, he was now pedaling like a maniac towards an interior boutique that, according to his iPhone, sold curtains. Monitoring the map's directions on his iPhone holding it with one hand and steering with the other, proved to be a small challenge, and he decided he would buy a holder for the iPhone so he could have it mounted on his steering wheel. Maybe he could find a holder that matched his helmet and made him look even more professional. He already had a helmet camera that was adjusted so it would record footage of his thighs as he cycled.

Johan hoped the shop he was going to had thick curtains, really thick curtains. Maybe they had something similar to the curtains that were used during World War ll, some kind of blackout curtains? He would have to ask them.

Johan had achieved good speed on the bike, and he felt he could have easily joined in the Tour de France or a similar race, and that he maybe even could have won, or at least managed a highly regarded position somewhere among the best participants. He looked down at his thighs and felt a satisfaction about how they almost seemed to continue to grow as he watched them. If his wife developed proportionally, so would he! He looked reluctantly up from his thighs to watch where he was going. If he ever got the chance he would probably win the Tour de France. Norway had some of the best cyclists in the world. But, now, what he really needed was some new curtains. The thought of not having any curtains in the bedroom scared him into going even faster on the bike. He began feeling the same burning sensation in his legs as he'd experienced in his arms in the beginning when he'd started using the baseball bat. It had to be a good sign, showing that his exercise was really having an effect.

Johan arrived at the boutique, and after having thoroughly locked his bike outside the windows so he could see it from inside, he entered. Norway had both the best bike thieves and the best police in the world. But, the police was often busy doing other things than investigating bike thefts, so they strongly advised you to always lock your bike.

Inside the interior boutique a young, worried, female shop assistant tried to guide the middle aged, exhausted customer in wide circles around the fabrics on the display tables.

Pearls of perspiration were dripping from Johan's nose, and streams of sweat were running down the inside of his growing thighs and legs. A small pond of sweat would gather underneath him if he stood to long in the same spot. He noticed the young woman's eagerness, and the way she looked at his body could only mean she thought he was sexy, and he couldn't blame her. He saw his reflection in the window as he checked that his bike was still safely locked outside, and he had to admit, he really did look sexy in tights.

The shop assistant found some new curtains for him, the thickest they had, in an amazing speed. Johan looked at her again. He deserved something better than his wife. He would have to leave her as soon as their vacation was over, maybe he could even tell her during the vacation? Shit, how could I've been so stupid? He thought as he received the new curtains. The last thing he wanted was to go on a vacation with Dagny, but the tickets had been bought under pressure from their marriage counselor a long time ago. As he left the store he decided to google what type of workout facilities the hotel offered.

The hotel where they were spending their vacation was brand new and reputed to have been built for only the wealthiest of people. They had booked a suite at the luxury hotel after having invested in yet another apartment in Oslo. It was meant as a celebration, not of their marriage of course, even if that actually hadn't been so bad at the time, but again, it had been their marriage counselor who'd intervened and suggested they should go away to celebrate their participation in the seemingly never ending success story that was Norwegian real estate. The rest of the world's real estate markets had crashed, but Norway was special and different, and they had both thought a celebration in honor of their own excellence had sounded like the perfect idea. Johan still thought the idea was a good one, except he should have been going with someone who deserved him, someone like the young and fit girl working in the curtain shop. He wondered if Dagny would bring the baseball bat. Regardless, the hotel was most likely equipped with excellent exercise machines so he would be able to have effective, full upper body workouts while they were there either way. Was it even allowed to bring a baseball bat on a plane?

Dagny was sitting at home by the kitchen table. Shit, how could I've been so stupid? She thought as she once more looked through the brochures from the fantastic hotel. She couldn't see too little of her husband, and now she had to go on a vacation with him. The expensive booking had been done a long time ago, and, even if she hated him, there was no way she was going to let him go on his own. She looked down at the picture of the impressing silhouette of the hotel. The picture had been taken in sunrise, and the pillars of the hotel casted long and impressive shadows. Some crumbs from her breakfast cake fell down on the picture, and as she was brushing them away she thought she could see a sexy looking man doing gardening in one of the smaller pictures. Dagny licked her lips and decided she would google what type of food they served in the country, just in case she should pack some Norwegian food along with her clothes. She looked at the man doing gardening again and thought that she could, and maybe even would, seduce him. Norwegian women were enormously popular in foreign countries, she'd recently read about it in the local newspaper. For a moment she considered if she should bring Batsy along just to be sure, but, most likely, she would be so popular among the men at the hotel that she wouldn't need it.

She'd decided she would leave Johan, maybe even during the vacation, but before she left him she would have to have a serious talk with him about his nightly masturbating perversities.

Dagny went over to the kitchen counter and fetched herself another piece of breakfast cake.

SUPERVISIONS

The hotel's manager was **Miss Joselyn Hardfakk**. She had the reputation of running any business she was head of in a strict almost military fashion. Nobody actually knew quite how many businesses before had had the pleasure, or perhaps rather the displeasure, of being under her strict command. What, on the other hand, was known to everybody was Miss Joselyn Hardfakk's background as a former fitness athlete, although, nobody really understood how that in any way qualified her to now being capable of running a large, exclusive hotel. But, she also had a reputation for having very sharp breasts, and that, among other rumors surrounding their use, claimed she'd used them to elbow, or maybe rather breast, her way into many of her different managing positions. If there was any truth to any of the rumors, or the use of the breasts, only Miss Joselyn Hardfakk herself really knew.

Joselyn drew a deep breath of air and pointed almost accusingly with her breasts at the other hotel employees. They were all gathered in the hotel's reception area, and she was standing composed in front of them with a cool and sexy posture, preparing herself to say a few words to boost their moral before the hotel's very first guests would start to arrive.

Joselyn's grandmother had been Asian, and she'd inherited some of her grandmother's physical features. The suit she was wearing was a tight fit that brought attention to, among other body parts, her successful and ambitious breasts. She had never slept with anyone, even if she'd slept with a lot, to gain her career. She knew very well about the rumors concerning her and her breasts, but she wasn't bothered by them, and that they involved some of her body parts she only saw as an advantage. The truth was that being a former fitness competitor, she actually often missed some of the focus on her body.

Joselyn inspected her staff while she thought about what she

43

wanted to say to them. She wasn't at all impressed by what she saw. Still, a couple of the male staff did look potentially suitable to have sex with at some point. But, all in all, as so-called professionals, supposed to be the groomed staff at the probably best hotel in the world, they definitely had a thing or two to learn. They all stood gathered like a bunch of schoolchildren on a field expedition to the local zoo. She walked between them and made them stand in lines together with their colleagues working at the same stations. That at least gave them some appearance of being slightly more organized.

If nothing else, their uniforms looked new and clean, but she was disappointed to see that some of her staff didn't have the right body shapes to carry their uniforms in the sexy, fashionable way they were supposed to. She made a mental note on which they were, so she could replace them as soon as possible. She felt they had all had ample time to prepare both their minds and bodies for their work at the hotel. To at this point not be fit enough to carry the uniform, were to her just as bad as not having learned their duties properly.

Most of the hotel staff was occupied with either watching Joselyn's breasts, or trying their best not to watch them.

"Stay sharp," Joselyn said. "Our first guests are arriving tomorrow morning. As you all know, the owners' decision was that only the suites were to be booked for the hotel's first open weekend in a test of both the hotel and us working here. I will accept absolutely no negative incidents happening because of any deficiencies from your side to perform your tasks. There will be no acceptable excuses for negligence of any kind!" She stared hard at them all. "And remember, in addition to our suite guests, we'll also be servicing the twenty chefs participating in next week's televised cooking competition. They'll be staying in some of our ordinary rooms, and they'll be using the weekend to get accustomed to the kitchen area and develop some chemistry amongst themselves before the show starts. The chefs are all to be treated as guests, but of course they should be prioritized second to our suite guests. Now, are there any questions?"

Most of the hotel staff, except the ones who would have direct contact with the guests, didn't have the best knowledge of English, but their service-smiles would have made any pure breed English imperialist proud, and probably made him immediately order another cup of tea.

Joselyn felt satisfied and drew another deep breath, again showing off her sharp breasts, as she sent the staff one last, hard stare. Then she sharply, almost military like, pirouetted around and walked out. The majority of the male staff watched her ambitious and almost aggressive bum as she with firm steps left the room to head back to her office. Then they went to their stations to do their final preparations. Some of the female staff tried copying Joselyn's pirouette, as they too, slightly quicker than the men, left to go to their stations, but all failed.

When she entered her office Joselyn just reached seeing a couple of the female staff trying to copy her pirouette on the surveillance monitor, and she instantly decided they would also have to be replaced. Not for copying her pirouette, but for failing to do the pirouette properly. If they didn't have the self-discipline to control their own body and looks, how could they be able to perform their other tasks with any excellence?

THE INCHECKABLES

They came from the greatest country in the world, and Johan felt a strong sense of pride as he majestically handed the two red passports to the concierge behind the reception desk.

"Ah, so you're Swedish?" The concierge said as he received the passports.

"No, no! We're from Oslo, it's in Norway," Johan said, clarifying that he in fact was from the world's best country, and therefore a very special guest.

"Ah, yes, Norway, that's the capitol in Sweden, right? Or is it somewhere in England?" The concierge smiled at Johan.

"No, no, we're the country with oil and sport."

The concierge looked at the guest in front of his desk. It was always strange to meet people who seemed obsessed with their own nationality. And what did the guy mean by them having oil? Wasn't he aware of how much oil the country he now was in, in fact, delivered around the world?

"We're from Norway." The sweaty guest dressed in some kind of tight underwear pants kept saying the same thing over and over to him as if he was presenting a valuable gift, and afterwards he just stared at him as if he was expecting him to applaud or something. The concierge just stared back at the guest, not sure what to say further.

Then, suddenly, the Norwegian shouted; "You know skiing!? Like Bjoorn Daehlii!" And then he followed up by swinging his tights dressed ass up and down while moving his arms as if he was masturbating two very well-endowed men standing on each side of him.

"Oh, you meant that Norway! Oh, yes, a great country, truly great! Welcome to our hotel, Sir, it's always a special pleasure to meet people from your country. Here are the keys to your suite. Just walk straight up to the elevators, and then the elevator, or elevators that connect with your suite key will automatically open for you. Your suite's internal artificial intelligence will have named your suite by tomorrow morning. You'll find cold welcome drinks over in the lounge area, if you would be so kind to wait there for a moment, and one of our bellboys will come shortly to help you with your luggage."

The concierge briefly considered if maybe he should google Norway later, but then he remembered the site he was currently downloading his porn from and instead went back to thinking about boobs and asses.

Dagny hadn't noticed Johan's skiing demonstration over at the reception desk, or anything else for that matter. She'd been busy looking out through the doors leading to the hotel's sea front, in a hope of maybe catching a glimpse of the handsome gardener from the picture in the brochure. She'd thought a lot about how the foreign men would be throwing themselves at her during the vacation, and had put on a quite revealing flowery, summer dress for the occasion.

After Johan had received the keys for the suite he turned around to go and find Dagny.

Special, I'm special! People all over the world always like Norwegians. Johan felt like he was on top of the world and his mood was brilliant as he walked through the lobby towards the lounge area. It all changed instantly when he caught eye of his wife's white, fat body looking like it was about to explode out of her over-stretched dress. He decided he would try to avoid her as best he could until he found the opportunity to tell her he was leaving her.

Dagny felt interrupted and annoyed as her husband came over to join her. The fact that he didn't even seem capable of waiting alone for their luggage help showed just how much he depended on her, also, he looked idiotic in those sweaty tights and that football shirt.

The two Norwegians waited expectantly in silence for their special service luggage carrying treatment.

Mugade marched up to the reception desk and aggressively hit the desk-bell on the counter. The concierge, standing only about two feet away, made a small jump and quickly came over.

"My name is Mugade. I have reserved your biggest suite!" Mugade spoke in such a low voice he was almost whispering, and the concierge had to bend forward and lean over the counter to be able to understand what he said. It made Mugade smile. He loved when people had to struggle to please him.

"Ah, yes, Sir, welcome! Of course, you have one of our top suites." The concierge smiled politely and talked extra loud.

"One of your top suites?! I specifically ordered the biggest and best one!" Mugade was no longer whispering. He was angry. He wanted the biggest and best suite, or no suite.

"Sir, we have seven top suites. They're the best suites in the world, and each of them is unique in its own way."

Mugade looked like he'd just found out that someone besides himself had diluted a shipment of cocaine. Hadn't he already agreed to meet the new and potentially lucrative business associate at this specific hotel, he would have cancelled his reservation immediately. "It better be the most unique of them all!" He said with an angry voice.

"Here are your keys, Sir. I'm certain the suite will satisfy your every need." The concierge handed Mugade the keys with a Colgate white smile and then called over the bellboys.

While her father was checking in, Ophelia was waiting next to their luggage trying to see if the bellboy's hands were clean enough to touch her Gucci's. She'd expected her new pair of breasts to be the focus of anyone they met during their journey to the hotel, and that she by now would have started feeling slightly annoyed by all the attention they'd got. Instead it had seemed like most people they'd met hadn't noticed them at all, and it had made her mood turn quite sour. It was a clear sign that she'd gotten way too small implants, and it was all her father's fault. If they didn't fulfill her attention expectations down at the beach either, her father would definitely have to buy her a new car, and not just any new car, but exactly the one she wanted.

Ophelia's mood rose a little when the bellboy seemed to

fumble with her luggage as he picked it up because he was distracted by her body. But, his distraction was obviously because of her body in general, and not particularly because of her breasts, so it didn't really change anything when it came to her decision regarding the car. At least his hands appeared to be clean.

He appeared to be almost gliding over the tiled floor as he approached the reception desk. On his way, he briefly stopped by the boys who stood ready to carry the guests' luggage and looked them over. They were young, attractive and seemed to have wirily muscled bodies. Flavio let his eyes rest a little longer on the youngest of them. With a noticeable sound he licked his upper lip, stinging his tongue a little on his new, thin moustache. He'd recently started growing the moustache in a hope it might make his lover feel a pleasant tickling sensation on his balls when he pretended to give him a blowjob, or maybe more precisely; when he played around in his groin area. Flavio continued his gliding walk and finally ended up in front of the concierge.

"I am Flavio Balducci," he said in his most melodious voice and tried to glance back over his shoulder at the two bellboys to see if either of them responded to his voice or his name. That none of them seemed at all affected made him want them even more.

"Ah, Dear Mr. Balducci! Your suite is of course ready for you. Here are the keys to your special suite." The concierge handed over the keys to Flavio. "The specials you pre-ordered have been placed in the minibar, and the fruit baskets are all filled with bananas, just as you requested."

Flavio had always liked bananas best of all the fruits. He believed they kept his voice tuned, and the shape of them was just nature's way of showing that it could produce delicious perfection. His lover wouldn't arrive until sometime in the evening, as he was currently learning how to hold a card while seductively walking in small circles.

Flavio thanked the concierge and instantly became horny when he turned around and noticed that it was the youngest of the bellboys that had picked up his bags. He followed the young bellboy with eager steps towards the elevators and then asked him if they perhaps couldn't use the stairs instead. Flavio was looking at the bellboy's ass as he asked, and he was already imagining how his tight, young buns would look in front of him walking all of the stairs, all the way up to his suite.

The concierge, who'd accidentally overheard Flavio's question, came over and said politely; "Sir, I'm afraid your suite is on one of our top floors, and it will just take too long for the bellboy to walk up all those stairs with your bags. I really need him down here when our next guests arrive. You're of course welcome to use the stairs yourself, but he needs to use the elevator. Also, there really is a spectacular view from the elevator that you might appreciate."

Flavio felt as if someone had attached a chastity belt on the boy, which would have given almost the same result as what had just happened. He composed himself and followed the frightened bellboy into the elevator while he once more licked his upper lip.

The hard sound of shoes with special heels was heard by the concierge as they crossed the lobby floor. He looked up and saw a man in slightly elevated shoes approaching his desk in speed. The man looked agitated and in a hurry.

"I'm Zhang San Wang Wei," the man said in a tone as if he was daring the concierge to question both his identity and his presence at the hotel.

"Of course you are! We've been expecting your arrival and your suite is ready for you. Your suite is in the fourth tower, Sir. I'll have a bellboy here to help you bring your belongings up in a minute."

Wei looked suspiciously at the concierge. Was the fourth tower as good as the other towers? Had the other guests had to wait for the bellboy to help them with their bags? The concierge stood and smiled at him. Had he smiled that way to the other guests? Wei tried to read his smile, but found it difficult to interpret. Was there something slightly patronizing about the way the concierge smiled at him?

"If you would like to sit down while you wait I can have something to drink brought over to you?"

Wei glanced around the hotel lobby. There were comfortable seating areas with small sofas and lounge chairs spread about in the large hall. The ground and first floor of the hotel was one enormous, open hall, with the columns containing the guest rooms and VIP suites built on top of it.

Wei looked at the concierge again. "I will sit over there!" He pointed as if he was claiming possession of one of the seating areas facing the seaside.

"You can sit wherever you like, Sir," the concierge answered still smiling.

Wei marched over to the seating area and sat down while he kept a keen eye on the reception area to see if any of the other guests arrived, and if the concierge would smile and treat them in the same way he'd been treated. Perhaps someone else came and they wouldn't have to wait for their luggage to be carried to their rooms?

The big, black car from the hotel's transport service that had just stopped in front of the hotel's entrance elevated itself some inches in relief as Gunther excited the vehicle. It continued to elevate, and then it suddenly became its normal height when his son also climbed out. They both left their doors ajar, and then they started moving, rolling together like some large tidal wave towards the hotel entrance.

The chauffeur closed the open car doors behind them before he removed their luggage from the trunk. Then he watched as they approached the entrance and hoped none of the other guests would be unfortunate enough to try exiting while the two of them were in the process of entering the building. Both Gunther and Jurgen-Gunther were wearing Hawaiian style shirts, and to the chauffeur they looked most of all like a large section of a rain forest during a tropical storm.

Apart from the squinting, seemingly highly focused, Asian man sitting in a sofa in one of the seating areas, Gunther could see few other guests in the hotel's lobby area. The Asian guy seemed to be extremely occupied by him, or, actually, by the whole reception area in general.

Gunther had wobbled his way across the floor to the reception desk and now faced the concierge. His son had stopped by a table in one of the seating areas, where he'd fallen down in a large chair and begun eating from a snack basket while waiting for him. Gunther felt how he got hungry by seeing his son eat, and grabbed an apple from the fruit basket on the reception desk. Then he re-decided and helped himself to some drops instead. The apple he'd taken a bite of he got rid of by just putting it back in the basket.

"I have a reservation." Gunther threw his heavy credit card on the reception desk. The card made a different noise than most other cards would have made when it landed. It was the sound of a card bearing a noteworthy amount of credit. The card had landed face down, as if it had been instructed by its owner to do so.

The concierge looked down at the name on the card without touching it. "Mr. Schmadt, welcome! Your suite is ready, and here are your keys." The concierge looked like he was about to continue, but was interrupted by Gunther.

"Izt the kitchen open? I would like room service."

"Yes, of course it is. Here you are, Sir." The concierge found a menu and handed it to him. "You will of course also find both a computer terminal and a regular menu to order from in your suite. Or, if you prefer, you can call our suite attendant, or you can even address your suite's A.I."

Gunther wasn't listening to what the concierge was saying. He was reading the menu, and his fat finger left a trail of grease from the French fries he'd eaten in the car as he slid it down from one dish to the next in the menu as he read through it.

The concierge moved discreetly a little further down behind

the reception desk and messaged both the bellboys once more. Fortunately, the bellboys soon arrived. One was fresh from his break, while the other seemed somewhat terrified, as if he'd just seen someone's penis somewhere he hadn't expected to see it, or something similar. The concierge sent the scared bellboy over to Mr. Wei, and the other one outside to retrieve Mr. Schmadt's luggage.

Wei tried to sort out if he'd received the best or the worst of the two bellboys. He felt his bellboy seemed a bit more jumpy, and definitely more tired, than the one the newly arrived guest had got.

A new guest entered the hotel. He was very fit, but at the same time he appeared tired, or maybe more well-used, as if he'd decided to stonewash his pants, but forgot to take them off before he did so. Behind him an attractive, blonde woman followed.

The man walked casually across the floor, with an attitude as if he owned the hotel, and making one of the bellboys having to jump out of his way as he passed. It had almost seemed as if the man had wanted to confront the bellboy in a weird, walking version of the game of chicken to see who would step out of the way first.

The man came up to the reception desk and placed both his hands on the counter. The knuckles on his right hand were sore and had some small cuts.

"I have a suite, name's Fernandez!"

The concierge looked at him. "Ok, Sir, if I could just have your last name?"

"Don't you know who I am?! I thought this hotel had some class! Are you making fun of me? You want me to come behind that desk?"

To the concierge it looked as if the man was about to jump over the reception desk, and he considered calling security.

"Gomez, the last name's Gomez." It was the attractive woman standing behind the man who spoke. The man immediately turned around, looking like he was about to say something in protest, or maybe even slap the woman. She seemed to shrink as he faced her.

"Fernandez Gomez, yes, here you are. You're in one of our best suites, and I'm so sorry for the inconvenience caused by asking your surname!" The concierge hurried to say, and the man turned back towards him, but still looking like he wanted to slap someone hard.

Fernandez snapped the keys out of the concierge's hand before he gave his wife a brusque nod directing her to follow him as he headed for the elevators.

Fernandez's wife was a little disappointed that her husband hadn't slapped her right then and there in front of everybody. It could have been the final scoop she needed before she divorced him. She'd practically been able to see the front pages of the papers in front of her when she thought he was about to slap her. An incident like that would have made her instantly famous, and then she could have used her pre-fabricated story about her life of struggles, which now also included abuse, to propel her career. Maybe she could even become one of those motivational speakers? Getting paid to travel around, being admired and regarded as a clever woman, while speaking to her audience about how her surroundings had made her make all the wrong choices, but that it had all made her so much wiser than she'd been before?

She followed Fernandez towards the elevator, knowing his temper, it was just a matter of time before she would join the famously intelligent group of star society.

Miss Joselyn Hardfakk had stopped by to visit the reception on one of her many inspection rounds. "Are all the special VIP guests checked in?"

The concierge confirmed, but Joselyn would of course control the guest-list herself to make sure it had all been done correctly once she was back in her office.

"We have no more VIP guests on the list that we're expecting, unless you count a friend of one of the special guests who'll be arriving sometime this evening. The next ones to arrive are the chefs. They're supposed be here in a couple of hours. All their rooms are ready, but we're still waiting for the deliveries of their special food supplies."

Joselyn looked at the concierge. He actually seemed to be slightly intelligent, and he did have kind of a sexy appearance. Maybe she should offer him a raise? A sexual one? Maybe sugared by the offer of a career move sometime afterwards? That she, herself, had never slept her way into a new position didn't mean she didn't offer the opportunity to others. The concierge was unsuccessfully trying not to focus on her breasts. A short silence occurred while Joselyn was thinking and the concierge was trying the not focusing.

A sudden noise interrupted the silence; "Miss Hardfakk? Miss Hardfakk! We have some trouble with the Dolphin Attraction System." Joselyn turned around to face the voice that had interrupted her thoughts. It was the tech support guy from the hotel's control room. To her, all the tech guys looked like nerds. She suspected them of just sitting in front of their computers eating potato chips while masturbating to some virtual online fantasy when they weren't busy. But, she wasn't bothered by it as long as they didn't do it at work, and, of course, as long as they also actually did their work satisfyingly.

On the hotel's roof terrace, a few of the guests had showed up to relax and wait for the dinner to be served. Meanwhile they enjoyed their welcome drinks, or just regular drinks, anything with alcohol really.

Gunther had brought Jurgen-Gunther up to see the view, and, hopefully, to find some pre-dinner snacks. Both Gunther and his son felt warm and sweaty being directly exposed to the hot sun on the terrace, and sweat had already begun gathering in the folds of their fat. Then they'd discovered the big swimming pool running all the way along the sea side of the terrace. Along its edge it had a glass-fence, making it appear to go on forever. Jurgen-Gunther immediately started nagging about taking a bath, and Gunther was easily convinced into taking a dip. They didn't bother spending any time on taking off their Hawaiian shirts, but just went straight for the cooling water.

After having made an enormous splash as he jump-fell into the pool, followed by his son's smaller, but still impressive splash, Gunther and Jurgen-Gunther were floating lazily around in the middle of the pool.

Some water had splashed all the way over to the lounge area and hit Mugade's suit jacket. At first he'd been staring angrily at the fat, obnoxious man floating in the swimming pool, but then, as he continued watching him, his stare turned more focused. The fat man clearly showed that he possessed some ruthless authority. It could mean he was working within some of the same areas of trade as himself. Could this be the man he was supposed to meet at the hotel?

Mugade had brought his daughter up to the roof terrace to have a drink and maybe sort out who his contact at the hotel could be. He didn't have a name or description of the man yet, but he was supposed to receive it shortly on his mobile. Still, he hated the waiting. It felt like he was losing money every second, all the while contact hadn't been made.

Gunther hadn't paid any attention to how he'd created a small tsunami by his way of entering the pool and had he noticed, he wouldn't have cared. For the moment he was carefree floating about in the pool on his back while his son was swimming in circles around him pretending to be, according to what he could hear him say when he occasionally surfaced his head to draw a breath of air, a successful, German, World War ll submarine.

Jurgen-Gunther's grandfather had been a submarine captain during the Second World War, and he'd told his grandson all the heroic stories of his life several times.

Gunther was proud of his father, as well as of his son, but now the most important thing on his mind was that he had to pee. Scheisse! He thought, and looked around. It was urgent. Jurgen-Gunther was still swimming around him, but he couldn't see anybody else close by, nobody else was in the pool anyway. There was one guy, maybe Scandinavian, standing over by the bar with some girly umbrella drink, and looking as if he was hitting on the bartender by the way he was swinging his arms back and forth while moving his tights dressed ass up and down in the same rhythm.

Then there was a large African man, who clearly was pretending not be envious of how well white people could swim. Gunther had heard his father tell stories about how black people lacked the skill to be good swimmers. Together with the man there was a young African woman. She appeared to be busy texting or playing with her mobile, but it looked like she was struggling with her breasts being in the way, as if she wasn't used to having them there. He felt an urge to feel her breasts, but what was pressingly more important at the moment was his need to pee. He quickly concluded that the people over by the bar were all too far away to see anything if he was to relieve himself in the pool.

Gunther peed, and as he did so, he also involuntarily farted. To his submerged son it had approximately the same effect as World War ll sink mines; the submarine was forced into surfacing.

"Papa! Explosion! Eine grosse Unterwasser-Bomben!" Jurgen-Gunther shouted.

"Shh! Be quiet son!" Gunther tried hushing his son to shut up, but he had to admit to himself that the fart had been unexpected and quite forceful.

"Aber die farben?!" Jurgen-Gunther continued and pointed at the area in the water surrounding him. He looked down and saw it too. All the water in his immediate proximity had turned into a shade of purple, and he soon realized that the colored area surrounding him was still expanding. Truth be told, he had peed quite a lot, and the purple colored water would undoubtedly soon be covering such a vast area of the pool that it would become visible to the other guests. Jurgen-Gunther obviously felt that the colored water was intimidating and was about to start swimming away. He reacted instantly and quickly grabbed his son's foot and pulled him back into the center of the purple colored water. He then continued to pull Jurgen-Gunther in circles around himself so it would seem the colored water somehow originated from him.

His father's foot-pulling made Jurgen-Gunther shout and scream in-between gulping, spitting and splashing purple water all over the place.

Through the splashes Gunther could see the bartender and the Scandinavian guy come rushing over to the edge of them pool to see what was going on.

"It's nothing! My son, I'm afraid he had a very small accident!" He almost shouted at them as he pulled Jurgen-Gunther, still by the leg, towards the pool ladder, leaving a jolly trail of purple behind in their wake.

"Nein! Es war eine grosse Unterwasser-Bomben!" Jurgen-Gunther shouted as Gunther hoisted him out of the pool.

"My son plays a submarine game," Gunther said explanatory as he hurried passed the bartender and the Scandinavian guy and then continued pulling Jurgen-Gunther towards the elevator.

Gunther was annoyed and hungry, mainly hungry.

Down in the basement of the hotel "The Almighty" hummed with satisfaction in its computer core. It seemed it was already getting an ample amount of collectables from its guests that would help in determining their personalities.

Johan had treated himself to some delicious umbrella drinks to celebrate the beginning of his vacation. Perhaps a few too many, he had to admit. Well, actually, he'd really started his holiday celebration with red wine on the plane, or, rather, he'd started with a couple of beers at the airport before takeoff. Anyway, he was now in an excellent mood, and he smiled friendly at the German man who was dragging his son passed him while he wondered if maybe he should applaud? Norwegians were excellent at applauding. But, the German seemed in a hurry to leave, so instead he turned around and asked the bartender; "Did you see the 15 kilometer cross-country skiing yesterday?"

Mugade watched as the fat man left with his little pisser of a son. Fuck, that has got to be the guy I'm meeting, he thought. Only a real hard-ass would behave that casually about an incident like that. The man had the looks and behavior of someone who was used to be in control. He would have to approach the man later, as soon as an appropriate opportunity presented itself. For now, he had to explain to his daughter that it might be necessary for her to show her breasts to someone.

As far as he knew, Ophelia was aware that he operated within some shady business areas, but nothing as serious as what he really was involved in. She also didn't know that her new breast implants were filled with liquefied pure cocaine. Ophelia thought he was dealing, among other things, in real breast implants, so explaining to her the need to show off her new attributes to an important business associate shouldn't be too difficult.

Mugade smiled as he turned towards his daughter and got her attention. It would probably cost him that new Mercedes she'd been nagging him for, but compared to what he would make landing the deal with this new associate representing new markets in new parts of the world, the cost of buying her a Mercedes amounted to a bird-shit in space.

Down at the beach some of the hotel's other guests were busy testing out the sunbeds and checking the water temperature.

Dagny had noticed that Johan had headed for the roof terrace, and had immediately decided she would rather go down to the beach to let the hot sun caress her beautiful body there and maybe even go for a little swim. At least she would find out if there were any sexy men working in the beach area, or, if she was lucky, maybe even the gardener from the brochure would be somewhere around down there.

She'd put on her new, flowery, two piece bathing suit with ruff borders which had been specially acquired for the vacation

Dagny peered eagerly around the beach area, but could neither spot the sexy caretaker nor anyone else who would qualify to have his way with her. The only ones at the beach were some of the other hotel guests and a skinny woman working in the beach bar. Out of the corner of her eye she watched as one of the guests, another really skinny woman, lit herself a cigarette. That someone in their day and age were still ignorant enough to be smoking was way beyond her understanding. The skinny woman would probably soon get deep wrinkles as a result from the smoking, if she didn't have them already.

Dagny went down to the water and took a swim, or it was more like a walk with water reaching up to her navel, before she chose one of the sunbeds closest to the bar and laid down, just in case a handsome, male bartender would show up there.

She looked down at her legs and shook one of her calves, relieving herself from a combination of sweat and water. It resembled a hairless bulldog shaking itself after a bath, but to Dagny it was female perfection, the round curves of a voluptuous, mature woman.

The sun was still baking hot and Dagny figured she'd probably not acclimatized yet. Sweat was pouring out of her body, as if she'd sprung a serious leak of the size that could have sunk the Titanic.

Fernandez's wife had sat herself down on a sunbed some meters away from the bar after having been for a swim. She'd chosen a bed in the shade to get out of the sun. Not because she didn't like the sun, but she might have washed off some of her sunblock during the swim, and she didn't want to risk getting any wrinkles from overexposure to the sun.

Fernandez's wife lit herself another cigarette. She'd been chain-smoking ever since she got out of the water. It was mostly because she was restless waiting for a certain text message on her mobile. Discretely she watched how the fat woman a few sunbeds away from her was sweating in the sun. The sweat just seemed to be pouring out of her, like someone had been wearing spiked shoes and run across a waterbed. The fat woman was probably not concerned about getting any wrinkles from the sun. Most likely she would just compensate and fill the wrinkle out by eating some more unhealthy snacks or something.

Fernandez's wife put out yet another cigarette in the sand next to her sunbed and thought she would have to remember using another sunbed the next day if she was going back to the beach. Cigarette butts in the sand like that were really disgusting.

Fernandez had seemed busy when they'd arrived in their suite. He'd wanted to take a shower and then maybe go up to the roof terrace for some business calls. What type of business calls he was supposed to be taking she'd no idea, and frankly didn't care about, she was just happy he was busy with something so he didn't bother her.

She checked her mobile phone again, how long should it take before her manager-lover answered after she'd sent him a picture of her breasts? She was more annoyed by his inertia than hurt by it.

As the sun shifted its position in the sky, the two women at the beach changed between the different sunbeds as one tried to avoid the sun and the other tried catching it. Fernandez's wife kept decorating the sand around her sunbeds with cigarette butts while Dagny left behind small ponds of bodily fluids on hers.

Wei was standing by the railing at one of the cliffs above the beach area. He'd been standing there for a while observing the people down at the beach. His uplifted mood after having experienced that the bellboy carrying the luggage to his suite almost treated him with respect, or it could have been fear - even if it had seemed the boy was already scared of something before he'd carried his luggage, had completely disappeared after he'd went for a walk around the hotel's perimeter. Viewing all the luxury, these people, the hotel guests, were probably always surrounded by when they went on their vacations had made him realize how insignificant and poor his previous vacations had been.

Now, Wei was watching the sexy, slender, blonde woman with the long legs down at the beach. Her looks and the way she behaved by constantly checking her mobile told him she was very popular. Some sunbeds away from her, a fat woman was laying. She had the body of a successful sumo wrestler, and it made him think about a sumo wrestler he'd known at school and how he'd always been with, and probably still was together with, women who looked like the popular, long-legged, blonde woman.

Flavios' lover was sitting in one of the chairs on the suite's balcony only wearing a speedo. His body was glistening with oil, and Flavio, who was sitting on the chair next to him, looked at him with an almost pleading look in his eyes. Together they had oiled down his lover's body, before taking some picture of him to email to the organizers of a female boxing match who'd wanted to see how he looked. Flavio's lover had even carried around some brochures they'd found in the suite above his head as he'd performed the walk he'd learned about the room while Flavio took the pictures. The photo session had made Flavio horny, and he was about to suggest that they should have some sex.

Meanwhile, the sun had begun fast descending and made a beautiful show of leaving that none of the guests were paying any attention to. Most of the guests that weren't already in their suites, now went there to get changed and prepare for dinner.

Back in her office, after having sent divers out to replace the non-functioning underwater speakers, Joselyn pulled her short pencil-skirt up around her waist, sat down in her chair and placed her legs on the big mahogany desk. The idea of pulling up her skirt she'd got from something she'd seen on TV where a guy had taken off his suit-pants so they wouldn't get wrinkled when he sat down. She wasn't really all that concerned about her skirt getting wrinkly, but she liked to sit and look at her own legs. Seeing her well-muscled thighs made her feel strong and attractive, and the cooling evening breeze coming in through the office window felt smooth as it stroke across her legs.

Joselyn retrieved her pad and began looking over the list of guests that had checked in. That stupid and slow working concierge, she thought and stared angrily at the pad. There had to have been made a mistake, none of the suites' names were available yet. It could be that the suites' A.I system, "The Almighty" or whatever stupid name it had, required more time to interpret the guests' personalities, but it could also mean that someone, and it could clearly be blamed on the concierge, had activated the system too late.

Joselyn concluded she both could and would blame this on anyone she chose to. That lazy unfocused concierge, she thought as she made her final choice on who she would blame. Nonetheless, she was still turned on by the thought of having sex with him, and now, as she was viewing her own thighs, they were turning her on even more. The positive thing was that she wouldn't need to offer the concierge a raise in exchange for sex. Now, he risked losing his job on the basis of something he really could be blamed for, and that would probably make him even more allegeable for her preferred kind of sex. She would have him go down on her while she occasionally strangled him with her thighs.

Joselyn smiled as she called the reception desk to tell the concierge to come to her office. She then called the nerdy tech guy in the control room to have him start the welcome firework display as the sun had just set.

The great welcome firework display was set off from two small, strategic and discrete placed barges in the sea in front of the hotel.

As it began, most of the guests went out onto their balconies and watched in excitement.

The rockets raced with their fire trails behind them high into the dark night sky, before they exploded in a multitude of magnificent shapes and a spectrum of different colors.

The thundering noise from the explosions soon made most of the guests withdraw and go back inside again to rather watch the display through their windows instead. Inside the loud sounds was muffled and more tolerable.

The display was certainly a beautiful spectacle to look at, and it made all other none human creatures tremble in fear of human's superiority and power for miles away. Birds flew disoriented around, some crashing into the hotel's façade while others suffered heart attacks. Down on the ground, all kinds of land animals fled for their lives.

As the rock-ground beneath the hotel vibrated from the largest of the explosions, the hotel itself shifted ever so slightly, but completely unnoticed by anyone.

Dagny was watching the grand display and feeling special. This was all for her. Well, maybe for the hotel's guests, but she was most certainly one of them.

Gunther had seen much better firework displays before.

Mugade decided he would start having firework displays whenever he made a successful deal.

Fernandez was irritated and angry because the noise from the fireworks was disturbing his phone sex with his mistress. He was on the roof terrace using his hand to cover his right ear while trying to hear his mistress through the phone on the left. She was currently whispering dirty words to him, which he only found to be annoying and interrupting, in-between the heavy panting that really was all he wanted to hear.

Wei was looking at the fireworks and feeling almost violated. Didn't these people appreciate that it, in fact, was in his part of the world fireworks had been invented? They should out of respect have much smaller displays of it than the ones they had back home in Asia.

Flavio was busy pretending to suck his lover's dick out on their suite's balcony. Not wanting to risk damaging his vocal cords made him seem almost shy when being in a face to penis situation. He found it difficult to interpret if his lover was being pleasured the way he wanted him to be.

Flavio wanted to ask if his newly grown moustache was tickling him the way he hoped it would, but the thundering firework explosions, and the fact that he almost had a penis in his mouth, made any kind of conversation slightly complicated. Instead he continued nibbling a bit on the sides of his lover's penis, but when he noticed in the sudden light of one of the large explosions that his lover was more focused on watching the fireworks than paying attention to him and his new moustache and what he was doing with it, he lost some of his motivation.

The hotel and its surroundings plummeted into an unnatural silence after the last of the fireworks had finished, and while the guests were making themselves comfortable in their suites and preparing themselves for the hotel's first dinner.

Down in the hotel's lobby area the silence lasted only for a short while. Behind the reception desk a new concierge had just arrived. She was actually supposed to be working the night shifts, but today she'd been called up and asked to come in early. Evidently, the day time concierge had been called into Miss Hardfakk's office on a very urgent matter.

The new concierge was soon busy sorting out the accommodation for the twenty chefs who'd just filled up the reception area after having arrived at the hotel by bus.

In the capital of the country where the hotel was located, silence was nowhere to be found. A loud riot had broken out among the people.

Mubasher exited the elevator on his mansion's roof terrace. He walked all the way around the large swimming pool, and then he crossed the dance area with its strategically placed stripper poles, before he reached the edge where he would be able to see the riots with his own eyes. The walk across the roof terrace had been exhausting, but it was his people after all, and he felt he had to make the effort to see for himself what was really going on.

It had actually been one of his advisers who'd informed him about the ongoing situation. Not having really believed in what he said, Mubasher had reluctantly agreed to journey all the way from his chambers up to the edge of the roof terrace to get the information confirmed or rejected.

Now it was confirmed. His people were really rebelling.

From his roof terrace Mubasher had a view both of the huge city park, the Tranquility Garden of Everlasting Happiness, as well as the streets around it and the majority of the nearest city areas.

Already a huge number of people were flocking together in the park. Some of them had gathered in circles and were chanting loudly in unison.

The number of people crowding in the park rapidly increased, and soon they began spreading out into the streets and further into the center of the capital. Not long after, reports about small incidents of violence and cars being overturned and set afire, began coming in. Then the capital's radio tower was overrun, shortly followed by the same being the case for the State run TV station, and suddenly it seemed like the whole capital was in a state of complete havoc. Meanwhile, reports about similar incidents taking place in other cities in the country had also begun streaming in.

Mubasher had felt worn out just by looking at all the activity taking place down in the park and the surrounding streets. His military advisor-general had advised him to urgently send his troops into the capital to suppress the rioters, but he'd felt reluctant. If he was to do so, it would mean that he would later have to appear in different public settings where he would most likely have to make speeches, and that all meant a lot of work, even if someone else wrote the speeches for him.

Mubasher sighed loudly and wished he could have used his stand-in for all of it. His only problem with that was that it seemed it had been his habit of using his stand-in that had been the small spark igniting the whole riot in the first place. In addition, now he didn't even know where his stand-in was, and first finding him, and then using him to cool things down again, would probably only entail even more work. That was, if his people found out...

Rumors said there had been some observant participants at his mother's commemoration who'd noticed that he'd used a stand-in there, and that they'd shared the information on an internet site called Facebook. The news had travelled fast and lead to one of his former mistresses emerging. She'd claimed that he'd actually been receiving blow jobs while the commemoration was taking place, and then the riots had really accelerated.

All the fuss going on made Mubasher feel exhausted, and he'd decided to follow one of his advisers' recommendations to leave the city for a few days. All the necessary arrangements had already been made, and he was now just having a short rest before the probably tiresome ride to wherever it was he was going. They would leave the mansion late at night and arrive at the destination early the next day. He only hoped it was a place of quiet luxury.

How his people could be so ungrateful towards him was a complete mystery. He'd even recently placed a new gold statue of himself, only for their pleasure, at the very place where the riots had started. The thought of how hard he'd had to pose for the picture the sculptor had used to make the statue by, made him feel, if possible, even more exhausted. They were truly all so ungrateful!

His advisor had also specified that he couldn't be driven in his new, gold plated Rolls Royce. For safety reasons he would instead have to be driven in the old, black Mercedes. According to his advisor, his people might be offended by his gold covered car if they saw it. He frowned and then closed his eyes. The seats in the Mercedes were really not as comfortable as those in the Rolls Royce.

Still, a couple of days away on vacation were probably exactly what he needed and deserved. He just wanted the riots and protests to go away, and if they didn't, he at least wanted to be so far away when he gave the order to use military force, that the noise from gunshots and explosions wouldn't disturb his sleep.

The new concierge was in the middle of checking the chefs into their assigned rooms. They were all teamed in pairs of two, representing ten different nations. The cooking competition was to be a well-orchestrated, friendly, televised championship between the ten teams, showing off the hotel's grand kitchen and the dining areas, as well as, hopefully, a lot more of the hotel's other facilities in-between the cooking.

The concierge began at the bottom of her list, handing out the keys to the rooms on the lowest floors first and then continuing upwards.

"You know little lady, I'm a famous, Swedish kock back home in Scandinavia," a tall, blond man said loud to her as he received his room key. "Maybe I can cook you something pleasurable later?"

The concierge felt she was saved by the bell as the reception's telephone started ringing. She politely excused herself to the blond man and answered the phone. Immediately afterwards she seemed to straighten her back in a soldier-like manner that, most likely, would have made Miss Joselyn Hardfakk proud had she seen it, but as she was busy in her office, she didn't.

"Yes, Sir, I understand, Sir," the concierge said, still standing at attention. "Yes, Sir, we've prepared the suite according to your prior demands. No sir, I'm afraid it won't be possible to close off the whole floor and remove the other guests, Sir. But, I can assure you that since the hotel is designed the way it is, he'll feel like he's got the complete floor to himself. No, Sir, he'll be sharing the elevator with one other of our luxury guests. Ok, Sir. I understand, Sir. Then we'll limit the other guest's elevator access. Yes, Sir, this'll make the elevator exclusively his. When will he be arriving, Sir? Tomorrow, midday! Okay, Sir, I'll make sure all the necessary arrangements are made."

While the concierge had been talking on the phone, her assistant had finished checking in the chefs, and they were now loudly relocating from the reception area to their rooms.

After hanging up the phone the concierge urgently sent a message to Miss Hardfakk regarding the newly confirmed, expected arrival of the very, very VIP guest.

☐

FEEDING TIME

Numerous paper lanterns were illuminating the four, small, artificial islands making up the hotel's main outside dining area. The small islands were connected to each other by short bridges, the longest bridge being no more than three meters in length.

The dining islands were each representing one of the four corners of the world, and, normally, when the hotel was fully booked, each island would be specialized and serve culinary delights from their corner. But, since the hotel was only having the suites booked for this opening weekend, only one of the dining islands was being used. Of course, the guests would anyway be able to order anything they would like from any of the four different menus.

Above the wall-less dining islands there where beautiful, overhanging, roofs of vines supported by columns, and the columns themselves were also partially covered by the plants. No music was being played, but the distant sounds of the ocean and the lazy waves crashing onto the beach below created the perfect romantic ambiance.

White, exclusive tablecloths were covering all the tables which were elegantly set with crystal glasses, silverwear, the finest of porcelain, and, of course, complimentary wine and champagne bottles.

On the one side of the dining island there was set up an impressive and bountiful buffet table. The food was both delicately lit and decorated to show off some of what the hotel's kitchen could deliver. The display offered an ample sample of food from all the different menus, but if the guests preferred, they could of course instead order anything they would like directly from the menus.

The hotel itself was also effectually illuminated and it loomed majestically over the dining scene.

In front of the small dining islands, far below the both

beautiful and fearsome cliffs, the open ocean stretched out seemingly eternally in the darkness.

On each side of the dining area there were paths leading alongside the hotel in either direction. At the beginning of both paths there were guest toilets, and next to the toilets there were elevators and staircases leading down to the beach. The path on the right continued past the hotel and ended up at the show and entertainment area, while the path on the left continued and ended up at the fitness and gym center. Overhanging, bright green plants made the pathways in some areas feel almost like tunnels, but it was all beautifully illuminated by yet more paper lanterns.

"Do you have anything mit schweinefleisch?" Gunther asked the waiter loudly. His sweat was running in small streams down around his neck, and his Hawaiian shirt was discolored from the perspiration under his arms and on his back. On the front, the shirt was already smudged with different colored stains from a variety of food that he'd pre-dinner sampled from the buffet table.

"I'm sorry, Sir, but this hotel doesn't serve pork meat."

"Mein gott im himmel! Was is loss mit you people?" Gunther blew his nose loudly into his napkin, and after having studied the result for a second, he then used it to dry the sweat off his forehead. The napkin left a trail of snot just above his left eyebrow.

The waiter pretended not to notice the snot-trail incident and looked anywhere but directly at the fat man.

Gunther lit a cigar and began studying the menu while the waiter waited patiently by his table. The smoke from the cigar briefly covered his forehead, and the waiter gratefully welcomed the smell of the cigar which camouflaged at least some of the stench of the big German's sweat.

"Papa, I want Schweinefleisch!" Jurgen-Gunther practically shouted, partially at his father and partially at the waiter. He then put up a sour face.

Gunther smiled at his son. He had the same strong will, temper and exquisite taste as his father, and he would probably be just as successful in life as well.

Gunther and his son made sure to keep their waiter quite busy throughout the meal.

At a table nearby another waiter was standing and waiting politely next to Wei.

Wei was taking his time ordering. He wanted to impress the waiter and anyone else that could happen to be listening in. Being a chef, he'd read a great deal about how such types of classy restaurants were run, so this was kind of his turf. This was his chance to make anyone and everyone understand that he belonged both at the hotel and among the other VIP guests. Wei finally looked triumphantly up at the waiter.

"I want that fish!" He pointed down in the pond surrounding the dinner island at a large, golden fish.

"Sir, I'm afraid these fishes aren't part of the menu. They're purely there for decorative reasons, and to be seen for the joy and pleasure. If you would like them to come closer so you can see them better, I can find some fish food that you can feed them with? When it comes to the fish we can serve you, Sir, we have a delicious salmon on the menu today that I can strongly recommend. I believe it's from Norway."

Wei looked stupefied at the waiter. "Why would I travel all the way here to feed a fish? Are you asking me to do your job? Do you ask any of the other guests to do your work for you?"

"Ehem, It isn't really my job, Sir," the waiter began answering, but was interrupted.

"You ask me what I want to eat. I told you I want to have that fish for dinner! And then you tell me I cannot eat that fish, but instead I may feed it? That means you're actually asking me to do someone else's job." Wei looked around to see if anybody else were treated as badly as he was. "I want a new waiter!" He said, and then he pointed at the waiter by the fat German's table. "I want that waiter!"

Wei felt stupid and angry, mostly angry. How was he supposed to know that the well-fed fishes swimming all around them wasn't for eating? All fish was for eating, fish was food! At least it should be food when it was placed practically inside the restaurant. Then he became even angrier by the feeling that everyone around him knew more than him.

He felt foreign and different as he waited impatiently for the new waiter.

Johan and Dagny had, more by coincidence than planning, arrived at the restaurant simultaneously, and since none of them really wanted the others' company they seated themselves at one of the larger tables.

The large tables were for those of the guests who wanted to be social and dine together with other guests.

When Johan and Dagny sat down there was already an elegant, Italian looking man seated at the table, and soon after two Africans came and joined them as well.

Flavio had been taken by surprise when the Scandinavian pair had suddenly joined him at what he thought was his private and special, grand VIP table, and then he was even more surprised when yet another pair followed, but he refrained from saying anything. After all, his lover had preferred to stay in the suite, because he'd felt so tired from the journey and their sexual play at the balcony, and rather order room service instead of coming down with him for dinner, so he could use the company.

Mugade had brought his daughter with him down to the dinner, even though he never really felt very comfortable in public areas without his henchmen, his numbers, being nearby. But, this evening, he'd still decided to go down to the dining area in a hope of spotting his potentially new, drug associate there. If he was lucky, an opportunity to approach him might present itself sometime during the evening.

Mugade caught eye of his potentially new, business associate sitting together with his son at a table nearby.

Another couple arrived for dinner at the dining island. It was an angry looking man followed by a blonde, beautiful woman who was wearing sunglasses despite the fact the sun had set hours ago and that the lighting in the dinner area was quite dim.

The couple chose to seat themselves by a table at the edge of the island.

Soon, as a supplement to the complimentary wine and champagne that had already been richly distributed amongst them on the tables, most of the guests had received their additional beverages. Johan had drunk the majority of one of the complimentary wine bottles at his table by himself and had then ordered a beer.

Dagny was completely ignoring her husband's presence at the table. She'd cast her eye one of the busboys and was fantasizing about seducing him.

"We're number one in all sports where you wear tights!"

Johan had obviously had too much to drink and was now trying to start a conversation with someone. Dagny stared at him with a repulsed look on her face before she turned away and instead continued changing between looking horny at the busboy and hungry at the buffet table. She had difficulties deciding what she wanted the most, but then concluded that she first wanted some food and a couple of more drinks, and then, maybe, it was time to show the local boys just how sexy a voluptuous, Scandinavian woman could be? After all, she was on vacation and should allow herself some pampering pleasures, and afterwards maybe someone else would get the pleasure of pampering her...

The hungry look in Dagny's eyes as she approached the buffet table made the busboy hastily retreat from the area. But, Dagny didn't notice, her focus was now completely on the buffet table where she'd discovered some shrimp cocktails bathing in mayonnaise. A second later she also became aware of the display of cakes, which made her reach as close to a running pace as her body would allow her the last few steps up to the table. There she instantly began shouldering the German man and his son who were already attacking the buffet.

Sweaty, white, fleshy arms seemed to work furiously as they dug into the arranged food, and soon large areas of the buffet looked more like there was an alien autopsy being conducted rather than a table set with human food.

Back, over by the large, social table, Ophelia ordered herself a salad while Mugade ordered the most expensive thing on the menu without bothering to read what it was, and totally disregarding the fact that the food, of course, was all included in their stay anyway.

Johan was seated next to the sexy, African woman, while her father was sitting opposite from them.

He was wearing a new pair of black tights and a yellow, red and white sports sweater. It was a copy of some famous soccer player's jersey.

Johan suddenly noticed that his wife was no longer present at the table and turned to face the sexy woman next to him. It was time for him to work some of his charm.

"You look fit. Do you work out a lot? I do! I also bought a very good and very expensive bicycle recently, and I'm thinking of cycling the Tour de France route next year. Sometime during the summer, I'll clock my time and everything." He leaned enthusiastically into the sexy woman as he spoke.

Johan was sweating heavily and a red shade was covering most of his face, it could be from the heat, or, maybe, the strong sun on the terrace earlier, or it might simply be a result of the heavy drinking.

Flavio was very pleased that the Scandinavian man, who was dressed in the tightest and sexiest pants he'd ever seen, had seated himself next to him. When he got the opportunity he tried bending discretely over to get a better look at his crotch.

Ophelia saw the Italian man staring at the sweaty guy sitting in-between them and thought that he'd also noticed the sour smell. The guy really smelled of sweaty crotch. And, no wonder, walking around in that outfit, she thought. Who is this guy, maybe he's Swedish?

Ophelia tried to get the intense, close talking man to

understand that she wasn't the least bit interested in him by looking really bored and not replying to anything he said.

Johan mistook the sexy, African woman's facial expression and silence for interest. She looked as if she was deeply focused and really paying attention to what he was saying, so he continued with less modesty as he saw that Dagny was still busy over by the buffet table. Her broad backside had temporarily blocked the light from some of the paper lanterns, and she actually managed to cast a shade in the dim light as she reached across the buffet table to get to a plate with some kind of pudding. He felt sure she would still be occupied for quite some time.

"Did you see the fifteen kilometer cross country skiing? It was yesterday. Norway usually always wins!"

The eager and sweaty man leaned in even closer to Ophelia, as if he was about to confess something top secret to her.

"But, you know, bad snow can ruin the race for the best, even Norwegians. But, we have the best ski workers, preparers. You know, they butter the skis? Norway even has its own butter-bus! It's the best!"

Ophelia wasn't sure for how much longer she would be able to hold her breath, so she quickly got up and left the table. She pretended to make a call with her mobile as she walked a distance away and sat down alone at a smaller table. Her father didn't even seem to notice that she left as he for some reason was busy staring at the buffet table.

After the sexy woman had unexpectedly left the table, Johan quickly turned around to see if there were anybody else there who might be equally interested in his conversational skills. The African man on the opposite side of the table seemed only interested in the buffet table, but, to his great joy, he found that the polite looking, Italian gentleman sitting next to him, was looking at him with an expectant look in his eyes.

"You know the Preacher's Chair?" Johan held up his mobile and showed the Italian a picture he had of himself on the edge of the mountain. "It's a famous, Norwegian attraction. I went there earlier this year."

Flavio looked closely at the picture and noticed that the Norwegian was wearing the exact same kind of sexy, tight pants as he was now. "Tell me, are you always wearing such beautiful pants?" He asked.

"Oh yes, in Norway, all sportsmen wear pants like these everywhere they go! You know skiing?! Norway is best in skiing!" Johan got up from the table and started demonstrating the same way he'd done earlier in the reception area and at the roof terrace.

Flavio watched with increasing interest and excitement as the Norwegian man demonstrated skiing for him.

"You've heard about North-hug?!" The Norwegian almost shouted at him in-between heavy panting caused by the demonstration-activity, and as he continued to simultaneously move his ass up, down, in and out, all in almost one movement.

Flavio had never heard about such a hug, but he felt quite certain that he might like to receive one. The man was really sending out some strong homosexual vibes, but still, he didn't feel completely sure about where he had the man yet. He could be talking about some ancient, gay, Viking ritual, and even though he'd heard about the Vikings before, he'd heard nothing about their male to male action. Regardless, he decided he would like to learn more.

"Please, tell me more about yourself and the Norways?" Flavio asked when the Norwegian finally seemed to have finished his skiing demonstration and had increased his sweating even more, but at the same time seemed to have calmed a little down.

Johan was excited to have found someone who appreciated his sportsman's skills. He ordered himself a new beer and willingly began telling about the different sports where Norwegians were the best, while he showed the Italian pictures on his mobile where he performed them all himself, at least, almost all of them.

Flavio leaned in and admired all the magnificent pictures of the sweaty, Norwegian man in tights. He'd completely forgotten all about his Foie Gras platter that a waiter had placed discreetly in front of him.

Jurgen-Gunther was shuffling pieces of steak around on his platter with a bored expression on his face. Gunther new he would soon start asking for dessert. Chocolate ice-cream and some kind of cake were usually what he wanted.

Himself, he'd first finished a self-composed appetizer platter, consisting of a taste sample of all the appetizers on the menu, before he'd also eaten the steak. His and Jurgen-Gunther's visit to the buffet table had only been to find some in-between snack all the while they'd been waiting for their steaks to be served.

Having found that the hotel served imported, German beer Gunther had ordered and gulped down liters of it during the meal, and now he needed a toilet. After having ordered an extra-large ice cream portion both for his son and for himself, he left their table to go to the toilet. The amount he'd had to drink, combined with having had to sit and listen to the clucking of the water in the fish-filled ponds throughout the meal, suddenly made it feel urgent for him to relieve himself.

Gunther walked in a wobbly but brisk manner down a small path that was bordered on each side by hedges and palm trees and that almost went in circles around even more small, fish-filled ponds. Those who'd designed the area had obviously thought that the guests who needed to use the toilet would appreciate a long, labyrinth-like feeling walk before they reached their destination. He did not appreciate it! He was in a hurry, and, in addition, his breath had now become heavy, both from the exhaustion of the walk and the feeling of almost being pregnant, as if he any minute could expect his water to break.

From somewhere around the next path corner there was a sound, and suddenly the big, African man stepped out in front of him and blocked the path.

Gunther tried to remember if he'd acted racist in any way, or that was; if he'd acted racist in any way that was not accepted.

He tried to look around to see if there was any way of passing around the big African, but, to not confront the man, the only alternative was to go backwards, and with his ever increasing need to use the toilet, that wasn't an option.

Gunther suddenly noticed that the African's daughter was also standing there. She'd been almost totally hidden behind her large father. He relaxed, and with that he passed a little gas. There was probably no danger as long as his daughter was there. In addition, he'd gotten a glimpse of the toilet door behind the big man, and that also made him slightly calmer.

Out of nowhere, the sweaty man dressed in tight underwear, suddenly came running down the path and pushed his way in-between the three of them while shouting that there was some kind of emergency. They all turned and looked after the man as he continued running down the path in an almost needy way, as if he really needed to pee. Strangely enough, the sweaty guy just ran straight past the door to the toilets, and instead entered into the beach elevator right next to the toilets, where he began desperately pulling at his tight pants. As the elevator doors closed behind him the three of them returned to facing each other again.

Mugade looked at the fat German who'd just farted quite loudly. How he was going to manage working together with such a nasty man was beyond his comprehension. But, then he thought about all the money the potential, new markets for his drugs represented, and with that in mind he tried to smile friendly.

Gunther still felt unsure about the situation, but smiled back at the African.

"I believe we were supposed to meet here. Potentially, we've got a great deal of business to discuss, but first you might want to check for yourself that my delivery system is functioning as promised?" Mugade studied the German's face as he spoke. This had to be his new associate, but the fat man's poker face was hard to read.

Gunther was surprised, but he kept his facial expression neutral while he tried to get a grip of the situation. The only explanation he could come up with was that the large African represented someone who'd heard about his Der Naturliche Dunger, and that they were interested buyers. But, delivery system?

"I've brought my daughter Ophelia, she's carrying a load right now. My system's so safe I've got no concerns about letting her do it. No one will ever suspect a thing. Have a look!" Mugade stepped aside and pushed Ophelia towards the German.

Gunther looked thoroughly up and down the young woman, but couldn't see her carrying anything.

"Show him!" Mugade said to Ophelia, who removed her blouse and took hold of and lifted her own breasts. First she lifted the left, then the right, and then both at the same time.

From Gunther's perspective, he saw nothing but a beautiful, African woman, wearing only a short skirt and a bikini top, who was playing with her breasts, wiggling and pointing them invitingly at him. He stared at her and her breasts in fascination. He'd even briefly forgotten about the toilet.

"Take off your bikini top and show him your breasts naked!" Mugade instructed Ophelia, who in return sent him an angry glance before she closed her eyes and removed her bikini top.

Gunther just continued staring at the sexy woman's breasts, and for a brief moment he could have sworn that he also heard her father encourage him to touch them.

Ophelia felt angry and violated. That her father was in the breast-implant business was one thing, that she could both accept and actually like since it meant cheap and big breasts for her along with a large allowance, but that he would allow the nasty, unattractive man to grope her, made her furious.

She briefly opened her eyes long enough to see that it looked like the obnoxious man was about to reach out for her breasts, so she kept her eyes shut and instead tried focusing on the pair of new, bigger breasts and the Mercedes convertible her father had promised her when they got home.

"Go on, touch them! Feel how natural they are!" Mugade insisted.

Gunther reluctantly moved his eyes from the sexy woman's breasts over to her father's face.

"Listen man, we can't stand here like this all night. Someone else might soon come by, so just feel the breasts, and then we can talk business later. My daughter needs to get dressed again."

Gunther had a numb, horny sensation in his body as he reached out his hand towards the naked breasts in front of him. He cupped the young woman's left breast in his hand before he reached out his other hand. Soon he was busy fumbling with both of her breasts. He squeezed, lifted and closed his hands tightly around them.

Mugade contently watched his new associate's obvious approval of his ingenious delivery system.

Gunther soon fell into his usual, bad habits and began squeezing the woman's breasts harder and harder and pinching her nipples.

Ophelia was about to protest against the rough way the fat man was treating her breasts, but then she became momentarily distracted by what looked like a trail of snot on his forehead. He was the single most repulsive man who'd ever touched her breasts or, in fact, had ever touched any part of her. There was no way he could've been more disgusting.

Gunther was about to put a finger in the young, African woman's mouth when she let out a little scream of pain that brought him out of his almost trance-like state.

"You see and feel? They're of course real breasts in every sense, and as real as such breasts can be." Mugade smiled at the German. He knew he had the man on board as a new associate.

Gunther looked up at the big African. Feeling the young woman's breasts, he'd been reminded of why he'd left his wife. There were just too many breasts to fondle in the world to have a pair of old, nagging and sagging waiting for him at home.

"Izt this regarding the Der Naturliche Dunger business?" He looked questioning at the African, who just stood and stared back at him, and his mouth suddenly felt dry. Then he felt a rushing sensation through his body, and his trip to the toilet became an urgent mission again.

"Very interesting, great breasts!" He almost shouted as he hastily pushed his way past the young woman and her father. Then he ran wobbling down the rest of the path to the toilets.

Ophelia put her bikini top and blouse back on and looked angry at her father.

"I can understand you need to show your business partners the quality of the breasts, and even that maybe some of them need to touch them, but why did this guy have to squeeze them hard and pinch them, and why such a nasty, filthy man? How about gloves? I thought a medical expert would wear gloves!"

Mugade wasn't paying attention to what his daughter was saying. He was watching how the German was rushing towards the toilets.

Shit, I hope he isn't an addict himself, he thought. Working with drugs, it was always a liability if the dealers themselves had the habit. Without exceptions it would sooner or later mean trouble.

"You did good! What color do you want on your new Mercedes?" He asked his daughter.

Mugade and Ophelia walked back towards the dining island while discussing whether white would ever be the new black on cars.

Inside the toilet stall, Gunther was having a volcanic and orgasmic experience all at once. He had a strong erection while he loudly emptied himself.

The thought of the African woman's breasts, the upcoming success of his Der Naturliche Dunger, and the feeling of finally relieving himself on the toilet after it had been really urgent, all gave him great pleasure.

On his way down to the beach, Johan was looking desperately around inside the elevator and occasionally at the view outside the windows. He really needed to pee. Who were stupid enough to place the elevator right next to the toilets?

By accident, focused on his emergency as he'd been, he'd entered through the automatic, sliding elevator doors, and he'd been busy fumbling to pull down his tights, which had been a bit clamp and damp, when the elevator had suddenly started to descend. The elevator's sudden movement had made him almost fall over and raise his drunken gaze, making him aware that he was in the wrong place and not in any toilet at all.

Now he was trying to pull his tights back up again, but it was a struggle. Tomorrow he'd have to do something about the moisture in his crotch area.

The elevator doors opened and Johan stumbled out onto the beach with his tights still only halfway up around his legs and fell nose down in the sand.

Up at the dining island Fernandez was getting angrier by the minute. It seemed all the other guests were being served but him and his wife. He'd tried snapping his fingers to get a waiter's attention, but only managed to make a soft sound. He sent the waiter another angry look, and then he stared fiercely at his new wife. It was she who'd made him put some kind of moisturizer on his sore knuckles, resulting in that he now, of course, had lotion all over his hands and fingers making them slippery, and him unable to snap his fingers. This was all her fault, and he was about to begin telling her how stupid she was when his mobile suddenly vibrated in his pocket. It was a message from one of his mistresses. He looked at the picture and read the dirty proposition she'd written. He then stared suspiciously at his wife. Did she have any lovers she received the same type of messages from? If she had lovers - she probably did! Maybe she received messages like that from his friend? Probably the one he'd been dreaming about having sex with her in front of him.

Fernandez was now almost fuming with rage and had lost his appetite, but, regardless, he still continued trying to get the waiter's attention.

Over by the buffet table Dagny was on her third supply round. She could feel how her ample, natural beauty grew as she was eating. One of the sexy busboys came over and collected one of the empty trays. She smiled at him and giggled girlishly as she took a big bite of a grilled chicken leg. The busboy clearly felt flattered by her attention, he became totally distracted and almost lost the tray as his hands started shivering. The chicken legs tasted excellent. She put three of them on her already bountiful plate, and then she added a couple more before she, with experience, balanced it all back to her table.

Flavio was still sitting at the large table. He stared down at his sorry looking Foie Gras and wondered again how long the Norwegian was going to be gone. He then started thinking about his lover, tired and with a headache, up in the suite, and then about the new beachwear they'd bought for him before they'd left on the vacation. Flavio suddenly realized how much he missed his lover's company and left the table to go to him. Maybe they could find and buy the same style of pants for him like those the Norwegian was wearing?

Wei had finally received his food. It had been served by the same waiter who'd also served the large, German man and his son. He'd had to wait quite a long time for his food to be delivered at his table, apparently the waiter had a lot to do, and he felt some satisfaction about it. That obviously meant that his waiter was the popular one above the other waiters.

Wei picked through the food on his plate with his fork and wondered if he could ask to have chop sticks instead. Now and then he glanced around at the other tables to see if anyone was still staring at him after the fish-ordering incident earlier. When the incident had happened, he'd felt it like everyone in the restaurant had been staring at him, and he couldn't shake the feeling that some of them were still looking.

At the other end of the dining island he noticed the African man and the younger woman coming up one of the pathways and then continuing towards the hotel entrance. He turned his head and stared hard down at the food on his plate. He felt jealous because they'd most likely already eaten their dinner and then they'd probably had a nice stroll around the premises afterwards. At no point they'd had to feel like they didn't belong at the hotel, or that they were misbehaving because of a misunderstanding.

Wei tried to change his focus and instead think about how famous he would become after the TV-sent cooking competition, and how they all would admire him afterwards. He briefly noticed that the fat man in the stained, Hawaiian shirt returned before his thoughts about himself in a worshipped and happy existence took over.

Gunther arrived at his table, but his son wasn't there. Peering around, he spotted Jurgen-Gunther over by the buffet table where he was busy eating eagerly from the dessert section. Gunther watched as his son grabbed a large piece of apple pie and took a couple of big bites before he put the rest of the piece back on the tray at the table, and then how he repeated the procedure with a piece of chocolate cake. Jurgen-Gunther then tried to reach the cheese cake that was placed further back on the buffet table. The boy struggled, his arms were too short, or maybe it was just his already impressive belly that was too big. He was about to start climbing up onto the table just as Gunther arrived by his side.

Gunther had to chuckle, his son really had the go-getter attitude that would bring him great success later in life. He cut a large piece of the cheese cake for his son and another for himself, and then he also added a piece of cherry pie for himself. Afterwards he took another couple of plates and filled them with ample samples of nearly every dessert at the table. They would bring them back to their suite as night snack. Gunther stopped; what if his son wanted more than one piece of something? If Jurgen-Gunther wanted more than one piece it would mean he would be missing one of the types of dessert for himself. To be on the safe side he helped himself to two extra samples of each type of the desserts, of course making sure to avoid the desserts that his son had already taken some test-bites of.

Gunther and Jurgen-Gunther left the dining island carrying several plates of dessert. A waiter came over as they excited and politely informed them that the hotel offered the exact same food on the room service menu, and, if they wanted, he could have the plates brought up to their suite for them.

Jurgen-Gunther didn't want to give away his dessert plates, and Gunther understood him. He'd also already started tasting some of the desserts on the way, and if they didn't bring the plates along themselves, it would be a long, boring elevator ride up to their suite before they would be able to continue their tasting.

Gunther brusquely refused any help from the waiter, and then he and his son wobbling balanced their plates towards the hotel entrance.

Down at the beach Johan had made it out into the water before he peed. The water had made him feel less drunk, and he was now swimming what he considered to be Olympic laps back and forth along the beach. Occasionally he would stop and pull at his tights underwater to try to let some of the urine disappear. After another pair of laps, that in his mind would have probably made him qualify for any professional swimming team in the world, he left the water to stretch out on the beach. But, since nobody could see him doing his stretches, he quickly decided to rather return to the dining area to see if there was someone there still up for a chat. He felt an urge to share how fast he'd been swimming. He'd left his mobile phone by the table, and he would at least share with his friends on Facebook how fast he'd swum.

Wei had finished tasting, or, rather, he'd stopped shuffling the food around on his plate, and was instead observing the clearly successful couple sitting some tables away. The man seemed so experienced in everything he did. He was currently ordering from two of the waiters, and Wei watched his almost aggressive hand gestures as he instructed them with apparent authority. Maybe, if he learned to use the same gestures, he could next time have anything he wanted to eat without an ignorant waiter looking down at him? He almost felt sick when he thought about how his waiter had been explaining to him about the fishes in the pond. It seemed even a common waiter knew more than him about how to behave at an exclusive hotel. On the other hand, he should, since he was working at one.

Wei decided he would fire the waiter immediately, as soon as he'd become rich and successful and had bought the hotel.

He looked over at the successful man's sexy wife and decided he also wanted her. She looked like movie star with her dark shades, her blond hair, slim figure and long legs. Maybe she even was a movie star, or she could be a model? Either way, she would in any case have to be very famous. In fact, they both dressed as if they were celebrities.

Wei suddenly felt uncomfortable in his own clothes. The tailor had promised him that the cut of his suit was one of the latest styles within European fashion, but somehow it didn't feel that way. He'd had the same feeling in the tailor shop when he'd tried it on. The suit had looked very different on him in the test mirror than it had done on Brad Pitt in the picture it had been copied from.

Fernandez made sure to keep an eye on the Asian guy who was sitting some tables away and pretending not to be staring at him and his wife. He'd become aware of his squinting stare only a short while ago. It could be a paparazzo, maybe looking to score a picture of his new wife. The thought of how the public would interpret a picture of his wife wearing sunglasses in the evening made him frustrated and angry. Or, maybe the paparazzo was after something far worse... Maybe he was after pictures of his beginning bald patch? Fernandez lifted his chin so the paparazzo wouldn't be able to get a clear shot of the top of his head.

Wei looked at the man's proud posture. It was so unfair how he'd probably learned how to behave like that by being brought up in a modern, western society. His mobile suddenly vibrated on the table in front of him. He picked up the phone and read the text message. It was from his brother, and was clearly a message that had been sent to several receivers. The text said that he'd made the Olympic Wrestling Team. Wei instantly felt nauseated and left the table to go to his suite.

The unnoticed, incredible view from Wei's table of the dark sea glistening in the moonlight was held company by his almost untouched platter of lobster when he left.

Fernandez watched the Asian guy leave and slowly exhaled. He'd felt a deep anger when the man had reached for his phone to probably begin taking pictures of him, and he'd prepared himself to go over and crush his mobile.

Fernandez just realized that his wife had been talking to him. He hadn't been listening, and for her not to understand that he in fact was busy, just showed how self-obsessed she really was. He turned angry around and faced her. "What? Can't you see I'm busy?" He then asked her to hurry up and finish her meal so they could return to their suite. There could be other paparazzi anywhere out there, they could be hiding in the bushes and taking pictures of him right now. Fernandez lifted his chin even higher and continued to peer around the area.

Mugade had said good night to his daughter by the elevator and had then gone to the night open hotel bar. He was expecting a call about his new business venture in Thailand. At the bar he'd sat down on one of the stools by the counter and ordered himself a Whiskey.

Mugade was busy thinking about how much money he would be earning when his project succeeded in Thailand when the fat woman from dinner came in and sat down on the opposite side of the bar. She immediately started giggling and winking at the bartender. Soon after she was served a pinkish drink with both an umbrella and a stir pin in it, which she immediately began gulping down in big slurps with a straw while she displayed more and more of her mass of white flesh. He looked away as it seemed the woman's dress was shrinking and retracting around her body in an alarming rate, and instead he pretended to be occupied with his mobile phone. He noticed the bartender had started getting the same look in his eyes that he remembered once seeing on some men escaping out of the jungle after having been attacked and chased by a fierce jungle predator.

Mugade tried making a call.

Most of the chefs were snoring loudly in teams of two in their rooms, while the rest of them had fallen asleep on their balconies.

They'd all been drinking hard throughout the flight to the country, and then they'd done their best to keep up the pace on the bus ride to the hotel.

It was hard being a chef. They were the new century's rough sailors. Most previous TV shows had presented chefs as tattooed and with a dock workers vocabulary, and the upcoming cooking competition's organizers had followed the trend when they'd put together their group of chefs.

After arriving at the hotel, the chefs had continued drinking hard in their rooms and on their balconies until they'd finally fallen asleep.

Johan arrived back at the dining island. Behind him, both inside the elevator and leading all the way along the path back to the dining area, he'd left a trail of water mixed with some sweat.

As far as Johan could see, there seemed to be only one couple left at the restaurant. By the way they were sitting intimate and close together at their table he guessed they had to be deeply in love, and maybe on their honeymoon or something similar. He decided they were probably too busy with each other to be able to pay any attention to his story on how fast and long he'd swum, so he retrieved his mobile and left for the hotel entrance.

As he entered the hotel he could see Dagny sitting inside by the bar, so he quietly made his way towards the elevators, still leaving a trail of sweaty water behind. Hopefully, he would be asleep before his wife arrived back in their suite and wanted vacation sex, or found something to have sex with by herself. The thought of Dagny wanting vacation sex, and not having brought the baseball bat with her, scared him into feeling even more sober. He increased his speed and started rushing towards the elevator to get to the suite as quickly as he could.

Inside the elevator Johan relaxed. He could see his reflection in the elevator windows and started to flex his thigh and arm muscles. The blackness of the night outside made the windows into almost perfect mirrors. Of the guests currently staying at the hotel he was probably the fittest man, at least in his age-group, also, he was successful. Of course, divorcing Dagny meant he would lose half of their real estate investments, but it would be worth it. He truly deserved someone better.

Johan turned around and admired his glutes in the window, thinking it was sad no one else was there to see how great his ass looked.

Down in the dining area most of the waiters were sharing stories about how much hair and mucus they'd managed to sneak into the dishes of their obnoxious guests, and who'd had to serve the evening's worst guest. Then they all paused for a moment to watch the man who was making faces and obviously trying to flex his muscles in one of the glass elevators as it rode upwards.

Dagny was sitting comfortably on two barstools feeling sexy and great. She was trying to get some more of the bartender's attention. The man was clearly shy and therefore probably modest when he was around modern, sexy, European women, but he was undoubtedly very interested in her. Across from her, on the other side of the bar, an African man she believed she'd seen earlier at dinner was sitting. She thought he slightly resembled a young and handsome Morgan Freeman, but he seemed only to have eyes for his mobile phone. It could of course also just mean that he was a shy man too…

The bartender was trying his best to avoid the large woman who constantly showed him too much flesh while she licked her lips and made loud slurping noises as she gulped down drink after drink. The only other guest there was a large African man who seemed irritated at his mobile. The bartender decided he would soon close the bar, and if anyone complained, he would claim he'd been feeling sick. He glanced briefly over at the large woman and strongly felt that the small lie could be defended.

Dagny noticed the bartender looking at her and made sure some more of her leg was showing along with her ample breast area. She smiled seductively at him and thought about all the stories she'd heard about foreign men's attraction to curvy Scandinavian women.

The bartender would, nevertheless the claimed attraction, soon close the bar, excusing himself with feeling under the weather.

Dagny sympathized completely with the handsome bartender and would have liked to offer to help him with anything, anytime, anywhere, but instead she only waved sensually at him with a curvy arm connected to a curvy shoulder while whispering; "See you tomorrow, handsome. Hope you feel better then!" Then she slid down from the barstools and left the bar rolling towards the elevators.

The bartender considered if he should call in sick the next day too, but decided he wouldn't. He desperately needed the job, and the rumors of how Miss Hardfakk punished lazy employees, would rather make him be there ten minutes early instead.

The African man left for the elevators while it seemed he once more tried to make a call. The bartender could hear him say hello and start a conversation with someone as the elevator doors closed behind him.

"What the fuck? Where the fuck have you been? I've been expecting a call from you all day regarding Thailand, and then I, myself, instead had to call you!"

The elevator moved smoothly upwards as Mugade listened to his No. 2, then he shouted; "What the fuck do you mean we were muscled out? We're never muscled out. We muscle others out!" He peered around the elevator for something to kick or hit, but then he saw the surveillance camera and let it go as he continued listening to No. 2.

"What the fuck? I've never heard anything about those places being controlled by anyone. Why the fuck didn't we know about this? Fuck! Find out who they are, and then check how the property deal is working out. I don't care if it's the middle of the night, or when their opening hours are! Use one of the fucking useless whores to knock on their doors or something!" Mugade almost broke the mobile phone's end call button as he nearly tried pushing it through the phone. He was severely frustrated. The thought of missing out on the large scale prostitution business in Thailand made him sick. He'd sent down excellent African and Russian prostitutes, handpicked from some of his own operations in other countries, to take over the business. The plan had been to send over more and more of them and slowly take over and control the marked. Now it seemed they'd failed. Evidently, they'd been run out by local girls from all the bars they'd started working in in the Patpong area. How those small girls could muscle out his larger and, most likely, stronger women he didn't know, but he intended to find out. It could be that they all had some sort of special kickboxing training or something. Maybe he needed to give his girls some martial art training? But, that would cost money, and the plan had been to make money, not spend any. Mugade took a deep breath. He really wanted that market. It was just too lucrative to let go of.

As he exited the elevator, he calmed down a little. After all, he still had the surgical facility that he was building there.

He would offer cheap package deals that would include the flight, accommodation and boob jobs during the stay, all at his very own local surgical and recreational facility in Thailand. It had been one of his master plans in the making for a long time. When the women visiting his clinic were operated, they would get his special, liquefied cocaine implants inserted, instead of normal silicone filled ones, and when the women after their recreational stay then returned to their home countries, he would have their special breast implants removed and replace them with ordinary implants as part of his post-operation, special-service follow-up. All without his new drug mules actually knowing they were transporting drugs. It would be excellent. And, even though he would offer his boob-clients very cheap package deals, he would actually also make money on them as well. Of course, that would only amount to pocket money compared with what he would be making from the main drug-implants operation, which would, without a doubt, be a moneymaking machine.

Fuck! Mugade thought as he stopped outside his suite door. He still wanted the money from the prostitution business. The thought of how the men, who were accompanying their partners to his clinic, would have used an excess of their money spending their days fucking his prostitutes, while their wives were having and recuperating from their boob jobs, made him angry again. It should be his money! Those men would never have been there if it hadn't been for their wives getting boobs at his clinic.

Mugade almost felt a physical pain by the thought of the loss of money, as if he in fact was already in business and not currently very early in the process of starting up. He needed to fix this. Maybe by making his No. 2 into his No. 5, and then finding a better No. 2 to do the jobs he entrusted to him. But, first of all, he would need to finish his business with the fat, obnoxious man here at the hotel.

Mugade entered his suite and went straight to bed. A new day meant new ways of making more money. He quickly fell asleep dreaming about being the Lord-King of Patpong.

From her bedroom Ophelia could hear her father enter the suite and then how he cursed irritated until he obviously eventually fell asleep. She lay awake for a while longer as her thoughts drifted between her new Mercedes, how her new breasts would look in her different bikini tops, and which one of them she should be wearing the next day. Come to think of it, she also needed some new pictures of herself and the breasts to post on her favorite, online social community pages. Maybe she should make her father invest in, or perhaps rather buy, one of those internet companies working with social media? Her family owning something like that would undoubtedly make her even more incredibly popular among her friends.

Ophelia fell asleep thinking about how much more visible her breasts would be in a convertible than in a regular car.

Johan was fast asleep when Dagny entered their suite. He'd probably been trying to stay awake to try to have sex with her. She felt satisfied, but still maybe a little disappointed. She'd been looking forwards to rejecting his sexual advancements.

Dagny took a long, relaxing bath and finished by pleasuring herself using the retractable shower head before she went to bed beside her husband. He smelled strong of liquor, sweat and something that resembled urine.

Flavios' lover tried once more to yawn loudly, but it didn't have any effect on Flavio. He seemed determined to tell him absolutely every little detail about the dinner he hadn't been part of, and a guy who'd been there who, according to Flavio, had had the sexiest type of pants ever.

It had been apparent to Flavios' lover for a long time that Flavio always wanted what he couldn't have. He finally resigned, giving up on pretending being tired, and instead turned around and started playing with Flavios' balls to shut him up.

With his young lover fondling his balls Flavio was for the first time in a long time feeling happy, even if he had difficulties getting the thought of the tights dressed Norwegian out of his head.

Wei was sitting in his big bed searching the internet for information regarding how to behave, what to eat and how to dress at luxurious All Inclusive hotels. In parallel, he was also looking for any news regarding the Olympics.

Fernandez wife was showering. She hoped there would be enough hot water to last until she could hear her husband start snoring in the bedroom.

Fernandez was masturbating to one of the pictures his mistress had sent him. For some reason, lately his penis didn't seem to become as hard as it had used to. He'd read somewhere that steroids could have that kind of side-effect, but that just seemed as a stupid campaign from people not knowing anything about true sports. Instead he blamed the lack of erection on the quality of the pictures his mistress had sent.

Fernandez felt how he became angry for not getting a hard enough erection, and because his wife seemed to be showering forever. Exhaustion from the intense masturbation combined with the drinks and drugs nevertheless soon had him sleeping.

When she entered the bedroom Fernandez's wife found her husband holding his penis in one hand and his mobile in the other. She took a couple of pictures of him before she also went to bed, trying to place herself with as much distance in-between them as she could manage.

Gunther and Jurgen-Gunther were, without being aware of it, challenging their air conditioning to work at its maximum capacity. They were both deep in their sleep, meanwhile the air around them was constantly bombarded with different bodily odors.

After they'd gotten back to their suite after dinner, they'd eaten most of their take-away desserts sitting in each of their beds while trying to find a channel in a German language. Not being able to find one, and having finished all their desserts, they'd gone to sleep. Gunther had been in quite a good mood after the breast fumbling, while Jurgen-Gunther was looking forwards to playing submarine and eating more cake the next morning, so the lack of success in finding a German speaking TV channel hadn't bothered them too much before they fell asleep.

In her office Joselyn was smiling. It was late, but the hotel's opening day had sorted itself out nicely. The Dolphin Attraction System had been repaired and was promised to be functioning the next day. The firework display had been perfect, and, according to the reports she'd received, the dinner seemed to have been a success. Also, finally most of the suites had decided on names given to them by "The Almighty". For some reason they all seemed to be in Latin, but she thought they had a nice and classy ring to them and she decided she would perhaps use the internet to translate their meaning the day after.

On her office-sofa the daytime concierge laying naked and sleeping, meanwhile she was walking around the room trying to air-dry her body. They'd had sex three times during the evening, and she'd strangled him with her thighs until he'd fainted all three times. The only thing that had somewhat ruined it for her was that he'd actually seemed to start enjoying it. She glanced over at the sleeping concierge, true, he really had a great body, but, regardless, she would still fire him. She would keep him on throughout the weekend and then replace him with someone else. She preferred it when her victims were staring afraid at her during her thigh use.

The information about the confirmed arrival of their last and very VIP, suite guest, had been a welcome surprise, and Joselyn thought about all the publicity the hotel would receive when she leaked the news about his stay at the hotel to the press.

She bent down and picked up the sleeping concierge's uniform shirt and wiped off the inside of her thighs and her vagina before she got dressed. Then she went over to the sofa, woke him up and sent him away, before she went to her own room in the hotel to get some sleep.

Finally the whole hotel became quiet. Only some deep rumbles could barely be heard from somewhere very far away. Those who might happen to be listening would probably assume it was the sound of thunder. Except, the place very far away from where the sounds originated wasn't at all that far away.

The sounds came from down below, and rather very close.

Gunther was one of the guests who heard the distant sounds. He was up, visiting and manhandling his suite's toilet, and just thought that the rumbling noise was coming from his stomach. Lifting his ass slightly from the toilet seat, he managed to grab the phone mounted on the bathroom wall so he could order some night-snack from the room service menu since all the desserts had been eaten..

OH THY GLORIOUS OF MORNINGS, THOU SHALT NOT SWEAT IT, FOR THOU ART BUT HUMAN.

As the reliable sun quickly and magnificently rose, all the while pouring its warm and life-giving rays over the area, the staff was preparing the hotel for its first full day with guests. Sunbed-boys were cleaning butt sweat and a variety of other different human fluid-stains off the chairs and sunbeds down at the beach and up by the roof terrace pool area. Occasionally they would change or turn over a cushion where the stains just wouldn't come off.

Around the sunbed-boys, the hotel's caretakers were also busy doing their morning chores.

Apparently some of the guests had been walking or taking swims down at the beach before or after dinner the previous evening, and the caretakers were now raking together cigarette stubs, gathering bottles and other not so decorative items, and then shoveling it all down into small pits they'd made in the sand before covering them up with a new and fresh layer of sand.

The outside bar and dining areas were hosed down with water. Liquids, fluids, spit and food leftovers were soon washed away, leaving the tiles clean and inviting for bare and flip flop embellished feet to once again trample on them.

New and empty rat cages replaced the old and full ones inside the bushes and in other discrete areas.

Meanwhile other caretakers were scooping out dead fishes from the small ponds and replacing them with new, and not so dead ones, collected from a large tank in the hotel's cellar. The new fishes weren't as colorful as the other fishes in the ponds, but some sunlight would soon make them more entertainment friendly.

Insecticides were sprayed all around by the hotel gardeners, and then the plants bordering the pathways were showered with water containing small amounts of glossy varnish. This would make them sparkle and look fresh and healthy for any of the guests who would bother to look at them. The varnish was quite an expensive product so it was used sparingly, which was a benefit for both the plants and the animals eating or living on or around the plants since the product was highly toxic, and having dead plants, small animals and insects everywhere would not have been good for the hotel's image.

This morning there were also a surprising number of dead birds lying around on the hotel's premises, but they were picked up in the earliest hours of the morning and thrown discretely away together with the rest of the hotel's waste.

In the hotel's control room the sea current generators were started up to create currents in the water by the beach that would drift away all the litter that had gathered there. The vast and everlasting sea responded willingly, and soon fresh-looking and litter-free water drifted in to replace the outgoing old and dirty.

Joselyn conducted the last part of her morning inspection round by jogging through all areas of the hotel complex dressed in a tight outfit, and making anyone in her path jump away in fear of getting stabbed by one of her breasts or her focused stare. She couldn't find anything that needed to be improved or corrected. It seemed even the unfit ones in her staff had done their jobs. Of course, it didn't mean they would keep their positions anyway, it just meant that her day looked to be easier than she'd expected it to be. Maybe she would even have some spare time on her hands that could be spent indulging in some more office romancing?

The hotel, its surroundings, and its staff, all appeared to be ready to greet its guests a good morning. Down in the basement "The Almighty" had gathered and digested an enormous amount of data from the internet to find names best suited for the hotel's guests and was now in the process of interpreting how to best assist humans with the findings it had made, but it had met some challenges in its task. Since "The Almighty" was an A.I intelligence and not really a robot it had not been implemented with Azimovs "Three laws of robotics", instead it had been implemented with a new legislative law regarding, among other politically correct laws, the environment to help the hotel fulfil the rules and regulations according to the EU. For the moment it was working simultaneously on several items. There were several of the guests with dry hair and a number of other different bodily items of error it could help correct, but at the same time it had noticed an almost genocide like incident with bees and small wildlife around the hotel's proximity. "The Almighty" hummed and searched the internet for solutions to its tasks.

The chefs were all used to having to get up early in the morning no matter how much they'd been enjoying themselves and drinking the previous night, so they were among the first of the hotel's guests to get up. They'd all met up downstairs in the hotel's enormous kitchen to start getting to know each other and the kitchen better.

The cooking competition was set up both as a PR stunt for the hotel, and as a friendly contest between the participating countries to show how well the different nationalities could get along when they got together. The chefs had the time up until the competition's kickoff in two days at their disposal to become friendly.

The organizers and the TV teams would first arrive at the hotel the day of the competition's commencement. Rehearsals had been done separately with all the chefs in advance, and the organizers had felt it would be beneficial for the chemistry between the show's participants, if the chefs got the last days before it all started to interact with each other without the pressure of cameras in their salads.

Therefore, the chefs were now on their own without supervision. So far, they'd been gathered for approximately half an hour, and things weren't exactly going according to the organizers' plan.

The Russian chefs had taken the cooking station closest to the kitchen's stoves and burners' main operation's panel and gas valve. None of the other chefs felt safe with the two Russians in charge of the gas since they both seemed carelessly drunk after having already gulped down a bottle of vodka each for breakfast.

The two Italian chefs had spooked everyone with their knife playing and their posters of Steven Seagal that they'd hung up behind their station. They'd both been telling everybody about how they practiced with their knives, and how they were hoping that the hotel would be taken over by terrorists and that the competition at some point would include a blonde stripper inside a big cake.

The American chefs were in a bad mood because they couldn't find their virgin oil, and because the Arabic participants didn't want to share any of their plentiful supply with them.

The Korean team hadn't said much, apart from threatening anybody who got even remotely close to their station's borders with a pepper spray, and the British chefs had ended up in a dispute about the disposal rights of a small territory close to their station with their neighboring chefs from South America.

The Swedes were busy at their station trying not to get involved with anyone while at the same time still dealing with all sides.

The French team hadn't showed up at all yet since they were still offended by something that nobody could remember if might have happened during the bus ride to the hotel, while the African chefs didn't bother with anything that was going on, they were currently just hanging around by the borders to the cooking stations' area.

Gunther had woken up early. The bed had felt too hard and his stomach was gassy after the night snack he'd ordered from the room service menu. He'd eaten a burger and chips. The hamburger had been a disappointment, but he'd eaten it all the same. He'd just been to the toilet, and the only thing so far meeting his expectations at the hotel was the toilet paper. It was of the softest kind, and using it felt like cuddling his rectum with small fluffs of softness. When the air had cleared a little in-between the rumbling farts, he'd also had to try sniffing the toilet paper-roll because he'd thought that it had smelled discreetly perfumed. He would have to ask one of the hotel staff about which brand of paper it was, he could do it at the same time as he complained about the quality of the hamburger and the bed.

Gunther put on a pair of red, flowery shorts and a Bermuda shirt. The shirt already had ketchup and mayonnaise stains on it from the hamburger, and maybe something else, but he didn't notice. He then went over to his son's bed and woke him up.

"Ich bin hungrig." Jurgen-Gunther said, looking up at his father with sleepy eyes, and then got out of bed. Gunther realized he was also hungry, and shortly after the two of them left the suite in search of some breakfast.

On the door to their suite the name: Gula, had appeared in shining letters on the digital name plate, but Gunther hardly bothered looking at it. Names, unless they were related to something he wanted, meant nothing to him.

Arriving downstairs they went straight to see if the kitchen had prepared the breakfast yet, but it hadn't.

Gunther pondered for a moment about if he should go directly to the concierge and make a complaint about all of the hotel's shortcomings, but beside him Jurgen-Gunther had started nagging him about seeing the sea, so he decided to take his son to the beach for a quick swim instead. Maybe it could help them forget the hunger they were both suffering from while they waited for the kitchen to finish preparing breakfast.

As Gunther and Jurgen-Gunther excited the elevator down at the beach it made a strange sound, but neither of them bothered giving it much thought as they both felt hot, and the sea appeared cooling and inviting in front of them.

Ophelia was on her way out. Her father was still sleeping, and as she passed his bedroom doors, she could hear him snoring loud in-between what sounded like money counting in his sleep.

She exited the suite, and as she tried closing the door quietly behind her she noticed the name: Avaritia, on the door's digital name display. She read it twice before she made up her mind that she liked the name the suite had chosen for itself while they stayed in it.

Ophelia had been one of the few guests to actually read the leaflet explaining about the suites' A.I system. According to what she'd read, the AI system would evaluate its guests for a certain period of time, and then it would choose a name for the suite that was representative of their personalities.

As Ophelia walked through the short corridor to the elevator she wondered if their suite's name had anything to do with the movie Avatar. She'd wanted her father to get her tickets to go to the premiere of the movie, and not just any of the premieres, but the premiere. The thought of how he'd failed in making it happen made her really angry, and she decided she would give him a cold shoulder when she met him later. Maybe then the Mercedes he was going to buy for her could turn into a Bentley.

Ophelia noticed her reflection in the elevator windows as it started descending. One of the small bruises on the side of her left breast was actually so visible it even showed in the reflection in the window. She'd hoped the bikini top she'd chosen would cover all the bruises, but obviously it didn't. The fat German had really left an impression on them during the previous evening's inspection. She smiled to herself; after she'd shown her father the bruises he would definitely buy her a Bentley instead of the Mercedes.

Ophelia exited the elevator, walked through the lobby area and went out at the sea side of the hotel. She walked over to the railing and glanced down at the beach below. There was a large, white creature playing in the small waves close to the beach, and not far up on the beach its mother appeared to be stranded. She leaned out over the railing to get a better look.

Could it be sea elephants? Did they have sea elephants around here? And did sea elephants play around in the water and beach themselves like that? She wondered if she should go back to the suite to get her mobile so she could take some pictures to post on her favorite social network pages. She definitely didn't want to touch the sea elephants, or come to close to them, but a picture from a distance to show off to all her friends would be nice. But, since she'd planned to have a workout before breakfast, she hadn't brought anything down with her other than her body and as minimal clothing as possible to cover the necessary parts of it. She decided she would first go down to the beach to see what kind of creatures the white blobs actually were, and if they really were, among other sites, Facebook sharing worthy.

Ophelia went over to the closest beach elevator and pushed the button. Nothing happened. She tried several times, but it still wouldn't work. A voice suddenly came through a loudspeaker mounted on the wall right next to the elevator doors.

"Madame, is there a problem with the elevator?"

Ophelia looked at the speaker and then around her where she was standing. "Yes, I can't get it to work. How did you know? And who are you?"

"I'm the tech support and surveillance aid, Madame. We have cameras placed in strategic places all around the hotel's premises," the voice answered, sounding a little hoarse.

"Then why did you ask if I have a problem? Isn't it obvious? And don't you have the elevators monitored on your computer so you can see that there's something wrong with them?"

This time there was no reply from the speaker, but down in the hotel's control room the tech support guy had started masturbating as hard as he'd ever done before, all the while he used the most strategically placed cameras to zoom in as much as he could on the sexy woman's breasts. The speaker system was still on since he'd forgotten to turn it off.

Ophelia stared at the loudspeaker, it sounded as if someone was struggling with something. They were probably working hard to get the elevators going again. She waited for a little while, but after hearing nothing more than some heavy breathing from the worker through the speaker she decided she would just take the stairs instead, she could include it as a part of her morning exercise. Behind her as she left she could hear the worker make a loud, almost howling sound, through the speaker.

Fernandez was lying on his back sleeping. He was snoring loudly and traces of cocaine were visible underneath his nose.

In the middle of the night Fernandez had been woken up by the sound of a message coming in on his wife's mobile phone. After having searched her purse and the room for her phone, without any success, he'd snorted some lines of cocaine. He'd wanted to wake his wife up to confront her, but first, he'd laid himself down on the bed to clear his head and rest, and then he'd instead fallen asleep.

Fernandez's wife looked at her husband. He had a two day beard with some cocaine stuck in it. Standing by the side of the bed she took some pictures of him, and then she took another couple where she zoomed in on his beard and the white powder. The cocaine made it look like some of his facial hair was starting to go gray, or rather more white. Fernandez snored louder, then snorted and coughed. She finished with taking pictures. They could either be sent to her lawyer to show his cocaine abuse, or to the media, claiming his hair wasn't only disappearing, but also becoming gray-white-ish. Knowing Fernandez, the media angle about his body hair becoming grey would probably upset him more than if her lawyer got the pictures showing his cocaine abuse. She truly hated him, and she would make sure she'd seriously fucked him over by the time she was finished with him, but in the meantime, she had a career to improve. The bad-boy versus angel-model story never seemed to get old with the media. But still, she would need to stay with him for a while longer, until they'd made a couple of more headlines, before she could divorce him. Her lawyer was already busy gathering evidence, both of his drug- and alcohol abuse and of his violent behavior in the relationship, and preparing it all for the case. Meanwhile, her manager was keeping her continuously updated on how famous her name currently was, and how fast it was getting even more famous as her marriage to Fernandez developed.

Quickly but deliberately she got dressed for some morning exercise. It was critical that she at all times looked her very best should there be any paparazzi around to take pictures of her. Perhaps she ought to give some of them an anonymous call, just in case, and tell them where Fernandez was currently staying and that he was misusing drugs, alcohol and beating up his wife again? She thought about it as she left the suite. Closing the door gently behind her she read the name on the digital nameplate, it said: Ira. The name meant nothing to her, it didn't even sound elegant. She gave it no more thought as her manager, who, in addition to being her manager, also had been her lover ever since she got married to Fernandez, called to excuse why he'd reacted and answered so late to the picture of her breasts. Then they began discussing if it was time to alert the paparazzi, and how close they were to reaching the point where she could divorce Fernandez.

In the elevator, on her way down to the lobby, she saw her reflection in the elevator windows and asked the manager if he wanted a picture of her body. Her hope was that he at some point would leak the pictures she sent him to the media, but she didn't want it to happen until she'd sent him enough of them, showing her body from every possible favorable angle.

Gunther was lying on his back on the beach admiring his son who was bobbing about in the sea, once again playing submarine war. Regularly Jurgen-Gunther would surface to draw some air and shoot at things around him using his fingers as a gun.

Gunther rolled on to his side and looked at his gold Rolex. It was still almost a whole hour until the breakfast opened. He got up from the sand, grabbed his shirt and wobbled over to the closest sunbed to make his wait more comfortable. The sunbed sunk deep into the sand as he sat down on it. Looking around he noticed that there was a beach bar underneath some of the decoratively planted palm trees a little further down the beach. He continued sitting upright on the sunbed and changing between watching his son and keeping an eye on the bar in case someone was working there. Maybe they could get something to eat there while they waited for the breakfast to open?

Gunther retrieved one of his cigars from his shirt pocket and lit it with his gold lighter, but the cigar didn't taste good without anything to drink along with it, so he put it out in the sand next to his foot. He regretted not having brought his mobile with him. Then he could have called the hotel's service desk and had them bring a drink and maybe something to eat down to where he was sitting. He glanced over at the beach bar again. It should have been open, or, at least, it should open very soon. For a so-called luxury hotel to have its guests waiting hungry and thirsty down at beach simply wasn't good service. Gunther's stomach rumbled in agreement with his reflections.

As she got closer to the beach Ophelia was shocked to see that the white creature, which she'd felt more and more certain had to be a stranded sea elephant, suddenly rolled over and got up on two feet. It turned out the blobby creature was actually the nasty man who'd violated her breasts the previous evening. She hoped the man hadn't seen her coming down the stairs and quickly turned around and went towards the other side of the beach. Since she anyway had come all the way down all the stairs, she might as well also add a quick swim as part of her workout for the day.

While Gunther had been focused on watching his son playing in the water and keeping an eye on the bar, the minutes had passed quickly and he hadn't noticed that the early, but still strong, morning sun had already managed to burn his skin, giving it an impressive pink and red color.

Gunther decided he would no longer wait for the bar to open, he was now really hungry. He finally stood up and noticed there were several white lines going directly across large parts of his stomach in the areas where his fat had folded when he sat. "Verdammt!" He looked down his large body and then he looked around at the beach. There were some more planted palm trees not that far away from his sunbed, they were of course to blame for the stripes on his stomach. Some of the branches had had to be covering for the sun. He would most certainly include the matter when he presented his other complaints at the reception on his way back to the suite, probably after breakfast. He shouted for his son to come out of the water and then began walking towards the elevator.

When Gunther and Jurgen-Gunther approached the elevator, nothing happened, even though the doors were supposed to open automatically when someone came. Gunther tried pushing the up button several times, but there was no reaction. Irritated he pushed another button who said speaker, and loud heavy breathing could suddenly be heard. Gunther stared at the speaker and so did his son. It seemed they would have to use the stairs. Gunther looked up the tall cliff wall and regretted ever having come down to the beach and, frankly, to the hotel at all. Then they started climbing the stairs.

Ophelia had only waded in the water. It had been way too cold to even consider going in for even just a short dip. She walked back towards the stairs, and as she passed by the elevator on her way, she could still hear the heavy breathing from the man working to fix it. She glanced up the stairs and got a glimpse of the nasty man and his son being about one third of the way up. She looked down the beach in the direction of the other staircase and was about to turn around and walk all the way over to use that instead, but then she looked up again and made a different choice. The attraction of the opportunity to run fit and light-footed past the two fatsoes was just too great to resist. Ophelia smiled to herself and started running up the stairs.

Gunther and his son were both breathing and sweating so heavily that they had to stop to let their overwhelmed hearts rest for a couple of minutes. Gunther looked down and saw the young, African woman, whose breasts he'd had the pleasure of getting acquainted with the previous evening, come running up the stairs towards them. She was obviously following them. Could it be she wanted him to feel her breasts again? If she offered them to him, he would of course touch them, but what was he supposed to do with his son while he was busy?

Gunther was still working on the dilemma when the young woman, seemingly effortlessly, ran past them. She didn't as much as look at him when she passed. He watched her ass until she was out of sight.

Fuck, women, who could understand them?! Gunther thought, and then he and his son also continued up the stairs, both still breathing and sweating as if they hadn't had any break at all.

On top of the stairs Ophelia turned straight around and ran back down, light-footed and still full of energy she passed the fat guy and his son again.

Gunther and Jurgen-Gunther of course saw the young woman passing them again, but by now they were too out of breath and power to give it a second thought.

Ophelia turned around at the bottom of the stairs and ran back up again, and then she repeated the procedure one more time before she felt satisfied about having showed the nasty pair enough of her superiority. The last time she ran up she almost slipped on one of the steps in a pool of sweat clearly left behind by the fat man or his fat son.

Content with her effort, Ophelia afterwards jogged to the fitness and work-out area.

Dagny had got out of bed early and gone straight down to get something to eat. Arriving by the entrance to the breakfast hall she found out just how early it was. She'd hammered on the doors until one of the hotel staff had come out to explain the opening hours to her. Apparently they wouldn't start serving breakfast in yet another hour, but she was told that she could of course return to her suite and order some room service while she waited.

Dagny turned around and was so agitated when she left the breakfast area that she nearly walked over a boy carrying a bunch of towels. She probed the boy and became horny as she played with the thought about how grateful he would be to get the chance to be with a beautiful, curvy, Scandinavian woman such as herself. How youthfully eager he would be to please her every need. Superbia, she thought, it was what their hotel suite had named itself. She'd read the name as she left their suite. The name had most likely been chosen by the suite's artificial intelligence especially for her. Such a grand name could hardly apply to her husband.

Dagny was still hungry, but she found herself stalking the towel boy through the lobby area as he was clearly heading for the beach. She halted. She should stop by the suite and change into one of her new bikinis if she was going down to the beach. In addition to flirting with the towel boy, maybe there would even be some snacks available down there that she could eat while she waited for breakfast.

As she turned to go back to the elevators, she overheard the large German make a complaint to the concierge over by the reception desk.

"Look at what happened to me down at the beach! Here, look at my stomach!" The German gentleman pulled up his Hawaiian shirt and exposed his stomach to the concierge, who politely leaned forward over the reception desk to look at it.

"As you can clearly see, your palm trees are covering for the sun! You can either make sure they're cut down before beach time tomorrow, or find a more suitable, non-obstructed area of the beach for me and my son!"

The concierge politely promised the German that he would have both the hotel's chief gardener and the sunbed responsible looking into the positioning of the sunbeds in regards to the shades cast from the palm trees.

Arriving at the suite Dagny went straight to the bedroom to find Johan, who for once had slept longer than her. He'd obviously just got up because he was in the middle of getting dressed. Maybe her useless husband could actually be a little useful for once, since he probably was on his way out soon anyway. "Johan, I just heard that some of the sunbeds down at the beach are badly positioned. Go down there and find a sunbed for me, and make sure it's placed in an area of the beach where the sun shines unobstructed. I also want it to be close to the towel booth."

Dagny decided she would take a quick shower before she got dressed for the beach. The thought of the towel boy was still very much present in her mind.

Johan was struggling with his tights. They could occasionally be hard to pull on, but usually, his fantastic potato flour solution; smearing potato flour all about in his groin and butt area, did the trick, but today, in the humid climate, they regardless seemed almost impossible to pull on.

"Sure," he answered Dagny without looking at her. He couldn't wait to get down and have a morning work-out. Maybe there would be somebody else there working out too? Then he would get the chance to show off his growing thigh muscles to them.

Johan finally got his tights on and chose a sparkling, green and white, tight sweat shirt, a copy of one of the Tour de France team's jerseys, to go with it. He looked content at himself in the mirror before he found a pair of white and green sneakers to match. Turning around a couple of times in front of the mirror he was almost overwhelmed by how great his ass and penis area looked in the outfit. From the bathroom he heard Dagny turning on the shower, and then a sound as if she was clapping her hands. Johan shivered when he realized what the sound probably was, and he quickly left the suite to find the hotel's fitness and gym center.

In another suite, in one of the other columns, Wei was sitting in front of his computer. He was supposed to be reading and learning about the TV program's set up before the start of the competition, but instead he'd for hours been trying to find something confirming, or preferably denying, his brother's participation in the Olympics.

Wei had had a terrible night. He'd dreamt that he was back in the old house where he grew up, and that it was his brother's birthday. His father and mother had in a ceremonial and majestic manner together handed his brother his birthday gift. It had been a pair of custom-made, metallic, gold tights from the factory where his father worked. To his brother his parents had been saying things like; "You're the only one in the family worthy of using such pants," and; "They fit you perfectly! You truly are our pride and joy." It had seemed to go on forever. Wei had felt like he was completely invisible there he sat in silence by the table together with them. He'd woken up before sunrise and had immediately started searching the internet for any information related to his brother. Were there any pictures of his brother in tights? Did they fit him perfectly? Was he really going to the Olympics?

Wei felt how his eyes had become sore from staring at the screen, and a while ago his stomach had started making noises. Not having found any information to confirm or deny anything, he reluctantly gave up the internet search for the time being.

He dressed in another of his new suits, and added a large brimmed hat to keep the sun away from his face. Then he left the suite. As he checked to make sure the door was properly locked behind him, he noticed the name the A.I. had chosen for his suite: Invidia. He looked suspiciously at it. What did it mean? Did it mean that he was an individual? That he wasn't part of the VIP group of guests at the hotel, or something like that? Was it that he didn't fit in?

He tried, but he wasn't able to get his access card to open the elevator door on the other side of the lift, so he couldn't check what name the suite in the column next to his had gotten.

While Wei took the elevator down to find something to eat he wondered if he could ask the concierge about what names the other suites had got. The problem was that probably nobody else asked. His brother would never have asked. He decided to let the matter go for the moment. Perhaps he could later ask someone of the hotel staff, if he should happen to meet anyone of them while they cleaned his room or something.

Wei checked his watch. Maybe he was late and that the other guests had already eaten? If they had, there might only be leftovers remaining for him. As soon as he was down on the ground floor, he hurried out of the elevator and made his way towards the breakfast hall.

The fitness and gym center was beautifully situated on the very edge of the cliff right next to the hotel. It was outfitted with all the latest and best within exercise equipment, offering any visitor the potential of having a quality workout and toning any desired muscle group, or groups. The different apparatuses were placed under a gazebo-like roof with no walls, and from everywhere one had a spectacular view beyond the sea.

As Johan approached the gym, he could see that there were two other guests there. He was happy when he got close enough to recognize that it was the blonde, classy looking woman, who seemed to always wear shades, and the sexy, African woman who were exercising. They were each using a treadmill, and between them, there was one that wasn't in use. He was tempted to take the available one, so he would be in the middle, but instead he chose one of the ergometer bikes in front of them. That way they could both get to admire his glutes while he cycled.

As Johan got on the bike, a white, powdered line became visible on his lower back, right in the gap between his t-shirt and the waist line of his tights.

Ophelia stared slightly shocked at the already heavily sweating man who'd just started to grunt and pedal like a maniac in front of her.

Johan had recently started shaving his chest after having discovered that the hair there potentially could cover up some of his growing muscles. A short while after, he'd read in a sports magazine that professional athletes like cyclists and swimmers often shaved their legs as well, so he'd also started shaving his legs.

Ophelia continued staring as the man in front of her began

sweating even more and grunt increasingly louder. He looked like he was cycling in heavy rain, and the stream of sweat running down his butt crack made his tights grow darker and darker over an increasingly larger area. Some white colored sweat was running down his legs, and Ophelia watched it all with fascination. Did white people sweat white? Of course they didn't, but what was that? And had the guy actually shaved his legs, or was he completely hairless? The man in front of her grunted and pedaled as if he was being chased by a flock of water buffaloes on a wild stampede. From the way he dressed, he was obviously gay, but according to the way he was clearly showing off, he was also definitely interested in women. Maybe he was bisexual?

Fernandez's wife had finished her work-out on the treadmill, and she left the gym with a small wave to the African woman, who seemed to be exercising like a man. According to her taste the woman had way too defined muscles, but still, after having noticed the bruising on the side of her breast, she'd for a moment thought about be-friending the woman so she could introduce her to her husband. With bruises like that it could happen she was into some kind of pain-sex, and Fernandez, who was drawn to violence in general and of course also in relation to sex, would probably be attracted and try to seduce her, and then hopefully have an affair with her right here at the hotel. It would have been the perfect reason for her to divorce him. Pictures of her husband having brutal sex with another woman during their honeymoon would definitely work to her advantage.

She'd been about to say something to the woman when the ridiculously dressed sports groupie had arrived and interrupted both their chance of a conversation and their workouts with his excess sweating and loud grunting. Now she felt she'd been working-out more than enough for the day, and she would rather just wait and see if another opportunity to talk to the woman later presented itself.

Ophelia followed the blonde woman with her eyes as she left. Her workout had been a joke, but, considering how thin she was, it was probably all she could manage. How she and her apparently rough husband could have sex without her getting hurt and break some bones, she just couldn't understand. Behind the woman's large shades she'd noticed that she had some light bruising underneath her eye. How some women continued to stay together with an abusive man was another thing she couldn't understand.

Ophelia turned up the speed on her treadmill and enjoyed how her new breasts bounced together with her movements. But, she wasn't completely happy, they should've bounced a lot more because they ought to have been a lot bigger.

Just as she was about to finish her run, the sweaty guy on the ergometer bike turned around. He appeared to be disappointed that it was only her left, as if he'd rather expected a crowd of spectators to have gathered behind him.

Johan was surprised to only see the fit and attractive African woman behind him. Where was the other one? He concluded that she'd probably not felt well and had had to leave. Maybe she didn't cope as well with the warm climate as he did, or maybe it was something she'd eaten. Foreign food was never as reliable as food in one's home country. There was also the possibility that she'd simply found him so attractive that she couldn't take it anymore and had had to go and take a cold shower.

He smiled at the remaining woman and was just about to initiate a conversation as she turned off her treadmill and left. Now, isn't she a shy one? He thought, appreciating both her fitness and modesty, and admired her ass and legs as she left. He had to smile when he turned around and started pedaling again. It was obvious that the women here weren't used to a real, Norwegian, Viking man.

Shit! He'd been so eager when he left for his workout that he'd completely forgotten all about finding a suitable sunbed for Dagny. Well, now it was probably too late anyway.

Johan pedaled harder and looked around to see if perhaps someone else was watching him.

Down at the beach, after having first thoroughly cursed her useless husband, Dagny was finding it a challenge to choose a sunbed.

The guests could of course choose any bed they wanted, except for those especially reserved for the suites to ensure the VIP guests a well-placed sunbed at the beach at any time, even if the hotel was fully booked.

But, Dagny didn't want either of the sunbeds that were reserved on their suite, according to her current desires their placements couldn't be more wrong. Where she wanted to be was right in between the bar and snack area on her left and the towel booth to her right. The reserved beds were placed close to the beach, which was just too far away from both. A handsome, tanned waiter appeared behind the bar, and she determined she could still see the boys collecting towels from one of the beds placed a little closer to the bar.

Dagny had carefully picked out and proudly wore a two piece bikini with a pink flower pattern along its edges. As she made her way through the sand over to one of the sunbeds nearer the bar area, her flesh quivered in every possible direction in tune with her movements, and streams of sweat were already pouring down her body.

The sunbed creaked and strained under her weight as she more dumped than sat down on it. Her calf muscles hurt from the strain it had been to walk down all of the stairs. The amount of steps she'd had to climb down had almost made her give up on reaching the beach, but then she'd gotten a glimpse of the beach bar, which meant there could be food there, and looking back up, she'd realized it was definitely no alternative going back up until the elevators had been repaired. Now, what she really needed was some food, and maybe later she would go to have her exhausted muscles massaged by one of the good looking, young, service boys. She waved at the handsome, young man behind the bar, and he smiled and waved back. Life was good!

Dagny found her iPad and read the latest Norwegian news. There was an article fronted by a picture of a girl, who really looked like any normal, large girl, but without her clothes on. The story was about how the girl had posed without her clothes on to show off her body and prove that curvy and large women really were the most natural and beautiful of women. Dagny instantly logged into her Facebook account to be among the several of thousands who liked the article. The girl on the picture had received a huge number of compliments on how incredibly brave she was to show all of her natural, ample body like that and on how magnificently beautiful she looked. Dagny glanced down at her own thighs. She was way more ample than that average girl in the picture, and therefore she was of course even more natural and beautiful than her. She would get someone, maybe the handsome bartender, to take some pictures of her so she could post them on her Facebook page. She waved at him once more and then checked the time. Fortunately she would now be served food within half an hour. Life was truly great when one was among the beautiful and privileged.

In the hotel's giant kitchen things had taken a turn for the worse.

The American chefs had begun provoking the Koreans on the station next to them by placing their arsenal of pepper closer and closer to their station, while on their other side they'd been negotiating with and almost threatening the Arab chefs to get some of their oil.

The British chefs had muscled in and expropriated the area next to their station bordering the South Americans' station, whereupon the French chefs had in sympathy entered into an alliance with the South American chefs because of their loss.

The Russian chefs had become even drunker, and had twice opened the main gas valve causing small fires and nearly explosions on the other stations.

The Swedish chefs were smoking pot with the African chefs while sharing sex-in-the-kitchen stories. Evidently they had all, at least once, fucked in a kitchen, like a plumber had fucked in a bathroom, a chairman had fucked in the board room, or a mechanic had fucked - or maybe just masturbated - in the garage. Now, the two pairs of chefs were in detail sharing their stories about how they'd done the fucking, and how often it had happened while they were cooking. So far, it was one of the Swedish chefs who'd told the best story. He'd been having a threesome while preparing an Easter dinner for a Christian society.

"I tell you, it really was that day of the resurrection!" The Swedish chef said in a thick accent and laughed hard. Meanwhile the African chefs wondered if the time had come to compare cock sizes.

The Italian chefs were busy at their station looking at Steven Seagal clips on youtube.

Flavio had needed to think and had gone for a stroll before breakfast. Now, he'd just ended a conversation with his manager on his mobile phone telling him that he'd decided to accept the hotel's invitation for him to hold one last and final concert at the hotel's grand stage that very same evening.

One of the factors in his decision making had been the amazing name he'd read on his suite door as he left this morning. Luxuria, the digital nameplate had said in shining letters, and he'd been standing in front of his suite door for a long time just admiring it. Afterwards, he'd taken the elevator downstairs and went outside to walk about the hotel's entertainment area. There he'd tried out the feeling of the grand stage and tested the acoustics. Having been satisfied that it all seemed state of the art he'd concluded that it would be just the right location for him to hold his intimate and special last concert.

Walking all the way around the hotel on his way back towards the elevator Flavio wondered if his lover was still in their suite and if he would want some sex, or if maybe he'd gone down to the beach or to the breakfast area. As he passed by the fitness and gym center he caught eye of the interesting, Norwegian man. He was dressed in a tight outfit in the same style as he'd worn the previous evening, and he was obviously working out hard. At a distance he was looking very nice all hot and sweaty, and Flavio decided he would walk over to him and say hello, and also have a better look or two.

Johan saw the sports interested and very nice Italian gentleman approaching and stopped pedaling to greet him.

Fernandez had woken up with clenched fists. He'd again dreamt about his wife making love to his friend. This time he'd been tied up to a chair, having to watch the whole thing up close. When he'd got out of bed his unfaithful wife had been nowhere to be found. He'd tried calling her mobile, but she hadn't answered, so he'd left the suite to go and look for her around the hotel premises. She'd probably gone down to the beach to show off her body to someone. But, when he'd then tried the beach elevator to go down and stop her indecent behavior, it had been out of order, and it had all made him angrier than he'd been in a long time.

Since first beach elevator Fernandez had tried hadn't worked he was now on his way over to check the second one at the other side of the hotel. Even at a distance he recognized the weirdly, tights dressed, Scandinavian guy over by the fitness and gym center. It looked like he was undressing in front of another man, right there in public. God damn it! Fernandez had nothing more against homosexuals than any other people, but for them to go at it and openly have butt fun in the open and public areas of the hotel made him even more angry than he already was. He turned around. He would first go to the reception and make a complaint, and then he would go down to the beach to confront his wife. Maybe he could also have the concierge call up his wife's name over some loudspeaker system?

As Fernandez walked angrily towards the reception, the thought about there being gay guys about to start fucking in public haunted him and made him walk even faster.

"See here! Here! Look I use potato flour between my butt cheeks and thighs so they don't get sore when I work-out. It's a Norwegian trick I learned through the media in Norway. A very famous hotel owner and sportsman swear by it, it was written in a Norwegian article." Johan stood bent over while pulling his tights down to show the sports interested, Italian man exactly on which areas he was using the potato flour.

Flavio was observing as best he could with an impressed and increasingly ecstatic look, he wouldn't miss anything the Norwegian was showing him.

"You know, many Norwegians do sports, we know all the tricks! The Norwegian butter bus is famous in all winter sports!"

Flavio had no idea what the Norwegian man was talking about, but the next time he went travelling it was very likely it would be to visit Norway. His mobile vibrated in his pocket, and he quickly read the message. It was from his lover who was looking for him up in their suite. He politely thanked the Norwegian and then almost ran towards the hotel entrance.

Once inside, Flavio came to think of that he should try quickly stopping by the reception desk and make a small request. As he approached the reception he noticed that there was an angry man already standing there, shouting at the concierge.

"I'm telling you! There was nudity! Male nudity!" Fernandez shouted.

"Sir, I assure you we'll immediately look into it if you file a complaint about the matter. There are surveillance cameras monitoring all the hotel's common areas, but, to protect the privacy of our guests, nobody watches the tapes unless there's been delivered a formal complaint. Do you wish to file such a complaint? If so, our tech support team will immediately look through the recordings of the area to see what's been going on," the concierge calmly explained.

"Do I want to file a complaint?! Of course I want to file a complaint! Have the papers sent to my suite!" For the moment Fernandez had completely forgotten about his unfaithful and inappropriately behaving wife. He turned agitated around and left the reception desk.

On his way to the elevator he almost walked straight into the Italian man, but Fernandez was just too upset to recognize him as the other party involved in the indecent behavior he'd witnessed taking place over by the gym. He took one look at the Italian's dandy appearance and concluded it was just yet another gay hotel guest. "What the fuck?!" He muttered to himself and shook his head as he entered the elevator.

As Fernandez approached his suite door he noticed the digital nameplate. Ira, it said in bold letters. Ira, what kind of a stupid name was that? He slammed the door shut behind him as he entered the suite and shouted to the A.I. to arrange for some champagne to be brought up to the suite. He hated snorting cocaine without having something to drink along with it. He then sat down to formalize his complaint. From the bathroom he could hear the sound of the shower running. His wife had obviously avoided him on purpose when he'd been looking for her. He would confront her with her unfaithful and indecent behavior as soon as she finished showering. In the meantime, he anticipated questioning her on where she'd been and what she'd been doing.

As the angry man left, Flavio walked up to the reception desk where the concierge greeted him with a smile.

Male nudity in public, what a fantastic hotel this truly is! He thought joyfully before he addressed the concierge; "Hello, would it be possible to order some potato flour of you?"

The concierge didn't show any facial expression as he replied; "Of course, Sir. How much potato flour would you like?"

Flavio wasn't sure. He'd not really thought about exactly how much of the flour he would be in need of. Regretting that he hadn't taken the time to ask the Norwegian, he just made a guess; "A kilo, or maybe two?"

"Are you baking, Sir, if you don't mind me asking? I only ask because we have one of the best kitchens in the world at this hotel, and they will gladly do their very best to cater to any craving you may have during your stay here. In addition, for the next couple of days there will also be several teams of world famous chefs here, they're preparing to go head to head in a TV cooking competition which will be broadcasted live from right here at the hotel."

Flavio's English was sometimes lacking a few words, so he didn't understand everything the concierge had just said, but he was quite sure he liked the sound of it, so he smiled delighted back at him.

"What I mean, Sir, is that if there are any kind of food you miss here at the hotel, I'm quite confident we can have it made or baked for you."

"Oh, I'm not making any kind of food. I'm going to do sports, or a kind of sport," Flavio said. He then thanked the concierge and hurried to the elevator. He had a lot to tell his lover about.

When she'd returned to the suite Ophelia had first woken up her father and then gone to take a shower.

Mugade had overslept and it made him frustrated. Time was money, and now he felt he'd lost some. Also, he was confused about his potentially new, business associate not contacting him after he'd been able to test out the merchandize yesterday evening. Or, not the merchandize per say, but he'd at least gotten to thoroughly check out the brilliant delivery system.

No advancements in any of his projects meant no new money was being made. Mugade waited impatiently for his daughter to finish her shower. How long did the implants containing the cocaine solution last? He'd forgotten to ask his No. 2. He tried calling him while he waited, but of course he didn't answer. He thought he'd heard something about the cocaine bags being safe for at least a week or two before they could, and maybe would, start to dissolve or rupture. He really didn't want to risk losing almost half a kilo of cocaine, even if it was only a test portion. There was still plenty of time to travel back home and have his daughters implants removed and replaced, but with no development in regards to his new contact, time was still of the essence. Could it have been the wrong man he'd approached the previous evening? If that was the case, then who was the man he was supposed to meet, and who was in fact the fat man who'd taken advantage of his daughter's breasts? Mugade concluded he would have to continue investigating and find out if his new contact really was someone else, and at the same time also find out more about the groping, fat man.

Joselyn was walking furiously back and forth in her office. A small stream of sweat was running down between her ambitious breasts. With the usual top three buttons in her shirt unbuttoned, they should normally have had a more than sufficient supply of cooling, fresh air, but the walking, combined with her boiling temper, had made both her and her breasts hotter than usual.

Joselyn stopped pacing and looked at herself in the big mirror mounted on the backside of her office door. Her short and very tight skirt accentuated her thigh muscles and ass fabulously, but it also restricted her movements when she walked the way she did now. She considered for a moment pulling the skirt up around her waist, so she could move more freely and also see her legs in the mirror as she passed, but the fact that she didn't know exactly who or when someone would come to her office today, made her not do it. She was waiting impatiently for someone to fix the beach elevators. To have an incident like that happening at any time was unacceptable, and to have it happen the very first morning of the hotel's opening weekend was a crisis.

Joselyn tried once more to call the control room before she decided to go down there herself to find out what was being done to fix the unacceptable problem. Maybe she should also stop by the reception desk to check if the daytime concierge was at his station. If he wasn't, it meant she would have something new to pressure him with, and if he was there, she would always find something else to blame him for. The guy was either way screwed, or would pretty soon be screwed.

Johan had gone back to the suite and wrestled out of his tights. Standing in the shower he started masturbating while thinking of the two women who'd been admiring him at the gym. They were the kind of women he was going to be together with when he divorced his wife, and the kind of women that he deserved with his new, sculpted body. He decided this was the day he would tell Dagny he was leaving her.

It took longer for him than normal to achieve an erection. Could it be because of the cycling? He thought he could remember reading somewhere that professional cyclists at times could experience a lack of erection. He dismissed the thought as his penis finally seemed to rise to the occasion when the two women started having a threesome with him in his mind. Of course it wasn't because of his cycling. The lack of erection in the start-up face was probably just due to mental stress caused by his wife and her general presence. Physically, he was by far in the best shape he'd ever been.

Johan opened the shower-door so he could see himself in the bathroom mirror as he continued masturbating. The masturbation also took longer than normal, but that was most likely due to the fact that he had to regularly abort his mission to clean off the dampness on the mirror. As he cupped his balls with one hand, he suddenly became aware of how hairy they were. Didn't fitness athletes shave off all their body hair? Johan stopped masturbating and stepped out of the shower to retrieve his razor. Then he began shaving the area between his legs.

Down at the beach the bartender informed the enormously fat and pale woman that the elevators were functioning again. He was really hoping that the news would make her leave soon. Ever since she'd showed up she'd been constantly staring at him while licking her lips, and by now it was driving him almost completely crazy.

 Dagny was still hungry despite the snack she'd gotten from the bar. She thanked the handsome bartender, who obviously cared and was attracted to her, before she got up and gathered her things and then headed for the closest elevator. She would stop by the suite to have a quick shower and a change of clothes before going to breakfast.

 Johan was having some difficulties with the shaving since it in some places was tugging quite a bit. Meanwhile he didn't notice that all the hair from his crotch had started to clog up the shower drain, and he also didn't notice that the water slowly rising around his feet, made the shower floor very slippery. The sound of the suite door suddenly opening out in the hallway scared him to such a degree that he made a deep cut with the razorblade into the skin below his left ball sack.

Blood immediately started pumping and spraying out from the cut, and Johan fainted the moment he saw it.

As she entered the suite, Dagny heard a loud thud from inside the bathroom. It could only be her stupid and useless husband. He was probably slipping and falling as he tried to get in or out of a pair of those ridiculous tights of his. When she couldn't hear him get back up again, she got angry. The clumsy man had probably hit his head so he'd blacked out, which meant she would have to go in there and check on him, since she needed to use the bathroom herself to get ready for breakfast, and she didn't have the time to just sit around and wait for him to wake up by himself.

Dagny walked over to the bathroom and opened the door prepared to either shout or pour some water over the klutz, anything to get him out of the bathroom so she could use it. She was really hungry now. Looking into the bathroom she could see Johan laying on the floor in a pool of blood with a razor in his hand and bleeding from his crotch area. That stupid man, he'd probably felt rejected by her lately and decided he would take his own life. It was so typical of her husband to choose such a dramatic way of doing it, and he'd of course made sure to do it just as she entered the room so he could be saved. This was the classic cry for attention.

Dagny looked at Johan and considered for a brief moment if she should just let him be and let him bleed out, but, then again, that would probably mean she would have to wait even longer for breakfast, so instead she walked over to the telephone in the hallway and called the reception.

As the concierge was trying to explain to her about the hotel's impressive technology, including that all the suites were equipped with a call system which meant she could have just asked the suite out loud to contact the reception for her instead of calling, several more precious breakfast minutes was lost.

After what seemed like an eternity the hotel's medical personnel finally arrived and then quickly stopped Johan's bleeding. It had all appeared far worse than it had actually been. The water that had gathered on the floor as a result of the clogged shower drain had mixed with the blood and made the whole scene appear quite messy and dramatic.

The medical team shaved the rest of Johan's ball area and sewed a couple of stitches, and then they left. Johan of course blamed the situation on an accident, but Dagny knew better. She would end their marriage sometime during the evening, no matter his desperate and foolish attempt at keeping her.

When he confused woke up on the floor, Johan had felt a bit humiliated to find the medical personnel working on mending his ball sack. But, the feeling passed quickly when he saw what an excellent job they'd done with shaving the rest of his crotch area. The small stitches barely bothered him, but he nevertheless swallowed down a couple of the painkillers they'd left him just to be sure.

The hotel had sent up a caretaker who'd cleaned the clogged drain and hosed away all the ball-blood, and Dagny was now showering. She'd of course been very concerned about his well-being, and had been so stressed because of his condition that she'd even hurried the medical staff to finish working on him.

Johan tried pulling on a new pair of tights. He had to be extra careful so he wouldn't loosen any of the stitches, and also take special care with the bandage covering his balls and the wound, so it didn't change position. Maybe he could show off the scar to some of the new women he would have once he'd dumped Dagny? He could tell them that the scar was from some sports related accident, maybe from an ironman or triathlon contest or something. He could have brutally fallen off his bike because someone had pushed him or blocked his way just as he was about to win?

Johan was really looking forwards to being single. Dumping Dagny was something he had to do, no matter how much she cared for him. He looked in the mirror. The football jersey with the red stripes together with his red sneakers would be perfectly suitable and stylish to wear for breakfast.

Wei had strategically positioned himself in one of the lounge chairs near the entrance to the breakfast hall so he could keep an eye on the doors. He definitely didn't want to be the first to enter the hall, but at the same time, absolutely not the last. He felt quite satisfied with his choice of surveillance position as it would also make it possible for him to get a good look at what the other guests were wearing as they arrived.

Wei had felt the concierge had behaved suspiciously towards him when he'd asked him about what time the breakfast was served. It had seemed like the guy was looking down, not in respect, but like he was trying to hide something. He'd also had his shoulders raised unusually high, and a couple of times he'd pulled on his shirt collar as if it was chocking him. He was sure the concierge's weird behavior had something to do with him, and that the concierge somehow thought he didn't belong as a guest at the hotel. At least not the way the other guests obviously belonged there. His brother would of course have belonged just fine at the hotel. He would have paraded around in his well-fitting tights while he was being congratulated on his participation in the Olympics.

Wei once again stared suspiciously around, he felt it as if he was being observed and ignored at the same time.

Gunther and Jurgen-Gunther were on their way down in the elevator. Gunther was extremely hungry and in a bad mood.

When they'd finally made it up to their suite again after their morning visit to the beach, he'd spent the rest of the time until breakfast to check up on the delivery of his new Porsche. It was delayed, and the sales office had actually dared to blame it on him. According to them, his request for them to change the car's upholstery in the last minute had been difficult and time demanding. In his opinion, they were only stalling the delivery. A while ago he'd read somewhere that a certain type of buffalo skin would soon be prohibited to use on, among other, car seats, allegedly because that type of buffalo was in danger of becoming extinct. He'd immediately decided that he wanted that type of skin on the seats in his new car before it would be too late to get it, and now, as a result of his concern, the delivery of his car was delayed.

Gunther's stomach made a loud, hungry rumble, and he wished the world would move faster.

Fernandez stared suspiciously at his wife as she exited the bathroom. She'd been showering for a much longer time than normal. Had she been masturbating while thinking of someone other than him? Maybe she'd been fantasizing about his so-called friend? And now, because she'd been so incredibly tardy, there was probably no more hot water left for him to shower in before breakfast, and, in addition, they would most likely be late for breakfast. Everything was her fault, and Fernandez felt how it all made him angry. It was like there was a conspiracy going on against him, maybe even one led by his wife.

Having finally had someone there to fix the elevators, Joselyn returned to her office to cool down and continue with the list over which employees she wanted to replace. The list was fast getting longer, and the last name she'd added was that of the tech support guy. When she'd entered the control room, she'd immediately noticed the unmistakable, sour smell of genitalia, and the pimple faced nerd who'd been sitting there had been staring at her breasts the whole time she'd been down there.

Joselyn smiled as she for a moment fantasized about strangling the nerd with her thighs. He was probably one of those virgin, computer geeks. She thought about going back there to surprise him, and most likely catch him masturbating to the memory of her, but then she thought about his pimpled face and how the pimples would probably erupt while she was squeezing his head, and it was kind of a huge turn off. She would instead inspect the premises to find a new suitable boy-toy. Having seen how the concierge from yesterday's romance appeared today, he was definitely out of the question as a sex partner. He bruised way too easily, besides, he'd seemed to enjoy it, and she'd got the feeling he was hoping for more, and both those things were also turn offs. After the breakfast had been served she would make another inspection round and visit all the staff stations. Joselyn then remembered she had intended to check the translation of the suites names. She punched them into her computer expecting them to return with some elegant English meaning. "Superbia, Avaritia, Luxuria, Invidia, Gula and Ira. The translation came back immediately, but Joselyn sat for a long time and stared at it. "Lust, Gluttony, Greed, Sloth, Wrath and Envy". With it came information regarding the "Seven deadly sins." For some reason the A.I had obviously made an error and named the six suites after the six first sins of the "Seven deadly sins". Joselyn was angry. It was probably due to some totally unacceptable effort of humor from some tech nerd or they could even have been hacked by some pimple faced immature teenager. Joselyn decided that it did not matter, nobody knew Latin anymore and she could handle the problem when the guests had left the hotel and before new guests arrived.

The day was still young and full of potential.

FEEDING TIME

All the VIP guests had entered or were in the process of entering the breakfast hall. The decision that the breakfast should be served indoors in the hotel's main dining room had been made by the management based on advice from the hotel's hired, expert consultants, who had concluded that the guests were likely to appreciate, and in general prefer, to be inside an air-conditioned room while eating their breakfast meals. Exactly what the expert consultants' expertise was based on was somewhat unclear, but as the guests entered the breakfast area and sat down, it seemed nobody either questioned or reflected over their decision.

Dagny was happy she'd managed to be among the first of the guests to enter the breakfast hall.

After having seated herself at one of the large, social tables with her first round of breakfast in front of her, she'd called over one of the waiters and asked him for some mayonnaise to have on her eggs. "You know, a girl has to eat! I learned that when I was a gymnast!" She said, finishing with a sensual laughter.

The waiter stood politely by the large woman's side and waited for her to finish giggling and staring coquettishly at him. He passed the time wondering just how long it was since she'd been, if she really ever had been, a gymnast, and if there actually could be any eggs at all hiding underneath the mountain of French fries on her towering breakfast plate. Then he realized she might be Russian, and Russian sportswomen were known for being quite large.

The potentially Russian ex-gymnast finally stopped giggling, but kept on ogling him. He used the short pause in her giggling to confirm her order and then retreated to the kitchen to find some mayonnaise.

Inside the kitchen he pointed out at the woman through the

small window in one of the kitchen doors, and then rubbed the opening of the mayonnaise bottle underneath his sweaty arm while a couple of the other waiters and the chefs laughed approvingly.

After having followed the waiter's ass out into the kitchen with her eyes, Dagny suddenly became aware that the Italian gentleman from the previous evening had seated himself at her table. He would have had to have arrived while she'd been busy talking to the waiter. He'd undoubtedly chosen to sit at her table because he was so attracted to her. And, who could blame him, she thought with a smile.

Flavio had just helped himself to a croissant from the buffet table and asked one of the waiters to bring him some coffee, when he'd recognized the woman who seemed to be together with the interesting Norwegian man. She was sitting alone at one of the large tables, and he assumed that meant that the man would soon join her, so he went over and seated himself by her table.

The Norwegian man was clearly gay, but perhaps he was still in the closet? Anyway, he was eager to find out as much as possible about him.

Gunther and Jurgen-Gunther had entered the breakfast room right after the Asian guy. The three of them had actually approached the doors simultaneously, and only his and his son's size had stopped them from passing through the doors at the same time as him.

Gunther had managed to squeeze himself in through the doors right behind the Asian guy, and just before his son, and he'd felt quite satisfied by his own agility and of still being number one before his son. Then, to his further joy, he'd also managed to reach the buffet table right in front of his son. Together they'd started at one end of the table and almost emptied it as they worked their way towards the other end.

They chose to sit by one of the tables closest to the buffet, and while they started eating Gunther read through the menu to see if they also should order a little something as an additional treat. Soon, both Gunther's and Jurgen-Gunther's shirts had enough food on them to save a small, African, famine stricken village.

"Dear Madam, tell me, is you friend coming for breakfast today?" Flavio politely tried asking the large woman.

It had been quite difficult to find a suitable opening in-between her violent and excessive eating to ask her a question. He'd finally thought he had an opportunity when it appeared as though she'd stopped chewing for a moment, but instead she'd risen from her chair in a surprising speed and practically run over to the buffet table for a second round.

Now, Flavio had decided to just ask her the question, no matter if she was eating.

Dagny looked at the Italian man. "Oh, he's not my friend," she answered in-between chewing. Obviously, the man was so attracted to her that he couldn't even wait until they'd finished breakfast before he made his move on her.

"Is he family then?" The Italian sent her a curious glance.

"Yes, you could say so. But, not for long, soon I'm a free woman!"

Flavio looked at the large woman as she stuffed some mayonnaise drenched French fries and something that could be pieces of egg into her mouth. He wasn't sure, but there might also have been some lobster in the middle.

He'd wondered if the two perhaps were married, that would have confirmed his suspicions about the man being a closet homosexual. Maybe he should just ask her straight out, since he couldn't quite sort out what kind of relation the two really had.

"Tell me, is your friend maybe a homosexual?" Flavio heard how rude his question sounded the minute he uttered it, but he was so eager to find out the truth about the sexy Norwegian that he'd completely ignored the little voice in his head telling him not to ask so bluntly.

The woman started laughing, and something that had to be egg jumped out of her mouth as she did so. Flavio ducked as the piece of egg flew past him with its trail of spit.

Dagny had read about Italian men and how direct they could be when picking up women, but this was nevertheless almost a new record in how much anyone had wanted her. When she'd finished laughing she winked at the Italian man to motivate him to continue courting her and said; "Johan might as well be gay for all I care!"

Flavio first felt a sudden rush of relief because the large woman had met his blunt question with such a friendly attitude, and then the relief was closely followed by an overwhelming feeling of lust as he thought about all the possibilities the Norwegian man's potentially open gayness represented. He would either try to convince his lover to have a threesome, or he would start a relationship with the Norwegian behind his back.

The thought of all the sex about to come his way made Flavio forget all about both his croissant and the fact that the large woman was still sitting across the table from him, looking at him with more than friendly eyes.

Mugade and Ophelia entered the breakfast hall. Ophelia shivered involuntarily, whether it was because the temperature in the room was ice cold, or if it was because the fat, obnoxious, groping man was sitting there, she didn't know.

Mugade saw his potentially new associate sitting at a table together with his son. Why would someone be so stupid as to bring their son to a place where he was having a meeting concerning drugs? The son, at least for the moment, made it difficult to approach the man and find out if he really was his drug dealing contact.

Mugade and Ophelia found a table on the other side of the room.

Gunther had been so occupied with studying the menu that he hadn't noticed the African pair's arrival.

Mugade grabbed a menu and waved a waiter over to the table. He took his time reading the menu thoroughly before he closed it, and then asked the waiter about what he could order that would have been the most expensive thing on the menu.

Ophelia also wanted to order from the menu. Under no circumstance did she want to risk meeting the fat groper by coincidence over by the buffet table, which would have been a highly likely scenario, since he and his son were practically sitting on the buffet table itself. Thus, ordering something from the menu was the only possible and acceptable option for her. She felt a bit stupid being so sensitive about confronting the man, especially since she felt she'd gotten some redemption by demonstrating her superior fitness and agility earlier, but she just knew he would completely ruin her appetite if she came anywhere close to him. Only the thought of it made her irritated. As soon as she got the chance she would definitely show her father one of the bruises the nasty man had left on her breasts.

Flavio watched carefully as the Norwegian man finally entered the breakfast area. He'd obviously been playing some kind of rough sex game involving his ass. He could see it by the way the man moved, he walked as if he was incredibly sore. He felt a sting of desire. He wanted to make someone walk that way, or, at least, have someone do something to him so he, himself, would walk that way. From the obvious pain the Norwegian man now was in, it was clear that the prior pleasure he'd received had to have been enormous to make it worth it.

Flavio peered around the room for his lover in a hope that he'd re-decided and chosen to come down for breakfast after all, instead of having room service yet again. He really wanted him to see, and maybe also meet, the interesting and sexy dressed Norwegian.

His lover was nowhere to be seen, but the Norwegian man had clearly caught eye of him. To Flavio's joy, the man winked and smiled at him before he started slowly moving in the direction of his table.

As he entered the breakfast hall, Johan spotted the nice Italian gentleman and decided he would go over to sit together with him. He tried his best to walk in a way so that he wouldn't upset either his ball sack stitches or the bandage, but it was difficult, and he ended up moving forwards in quite an awkward fashion. As he got closer to the Italian's table, he almost changed his mind when he saw that Dagny was also sitting there, only some chairs away from the Italian. But, now he'd gotten so close that it seemed too stupid to just suddenly turn around, as if he was afraid or something, so he continued over to the table.

Great, now the suicidal maniac is stalking his own wife. He's probably envious of all the attention I'm getting from the eager, Italian man, Dagny thought as she finally received a new, full bottle of mayonnaise. She accepted the bottle with a gracious and flirtatious wink to the waiter who'd brought it, and then she stared after him as he almost seemed to run away from her. The poor waiter obviously had a lot to do, hurrying off to his other tasks like that. It was probably just so that he could hurry back to wait on her again and get another of her flirtatious winks.

Wei, who'd entered the breakfast hall closely after the obese, Scandinavian woman and barely in front of the fat German and his son, was sitting at a table by himself. He was studying the other guests with eager eyes. He wanted to get with him every little detail about what they were eating, and how they were dressed.

Wei felt a short burst of despair as he focused on the man in tights when he entered the room. He seemed to have an even bigger bulge in his pants today than he'd had yesterday. It really looked way bigger than what he'd originally thought. Also, the man's tights filled out impressively in every other way as well. He decided he would start to working out as soon as he became rich, and, from now on, he would also begin to open all of the email offers about enlarging his penis that he regularly received. That might be exactly what the man had done; used some over-night penis enlargement system.

Wei looked around the room. Most of the males present probably all had a bigger penis than him. He would have to investigate the matter further down at the beach later.

The potentially successful celebrity came marching into the breakfast hall followed by his, probably same degree of social status, wife. Wei noticed that she was still wearing her sunglasses. She definitely had to be some kind of famous, and if she was famous, then the man was probably also famous. Famous people were always lucky and found happiness with each other, and their relationships always seemed to make them even more famous. They could both be one and other's trophy partner.

Wei wanted to be famous. His brother would be famous after the Olympics, and then he would most likely find himself a famous wife and become even more famous. The thought made Wei feel sick, and he picked up his iPhone to search the net for any news about the Olympic participants.

Fernandez immediately noticed how the Asian guy at the table by the wall was keeping an eye on them as they entered the breakfast hall. Was he only staring at his wife? Was he her secret lover? Had his wife brought him with her to the hotel? His friend was part Asian wasn't he? Fernandez tried to remember as he walked towards a table some distance away from the others. He thought he could recall his friend once telling him that his great grandmother had been from Thailand. Was his wife into Asians? He felt his anger rising. She did often say she wanted Chinese take-away.

Fernandez had meant to question his wife up in the suite before they went down for breakfast, but there hadn't been time. When he'd finished screaming at his mobile in-between trying to take a shower, she'd already been ready to go downstairs. There had been more than enough hot water left for him to shower in, and it had made him even more irritated because then he couldn't blame his wife for having spent it all on her long shower.

His phone call had been his manager calling to tell him that it seemed the media knew where he was staying, and that he had to be on extra lookout for paparazzi. After he'd finished blaming his manager for the situation and hung up, his wife had already been standing by the suite door, and even if he'd felt she deserved at least some spanking or light slapping around, the thought of any potential paparazzi watching and taking pictures had stopped him. Instead he'd quickly got dressed and then grabbed her wrist and practically pulled her through the corridor and into the elevator. His wife had actually behaved as if she wanted him to slap her, or at least as if she wanted to get some bruises, by the way she'd acted like a sack of potatoes when he'd towed her behind him.

Fernandez was fuming with rage as he sat down and grabbed a menu. The waiter was as usual way too slow to approach them, and finally he couldn't take it anymore. As he shouted for the waiter's attention, he threw his wife's menu at the closest waiter and hit him straight in the head. His anger rose to an even higher degree when he out of the corner of his eye saw that his provoking wife seemed to smile as he did it. Her provocative behavior made him wonder if she was wearing any underwear.

The waiter came over and positioned himself by their table, playing totally ignorant to the menu to the head incident. Fernandez ignored him back while he instead took some time to study his new wife. She was wearing a summer dress, and it was short, but not short enough for him to be able to see if she was wearing any underwear or not. It seemed all the things he'd been attracted to when they met and got to know each other, were now the things that provoked him the most.

"I want a Coca Cola!" He said loud to the waiter without looking at him and while he concluded his wife was probably not wearing any underwear. She'd never used to wear any underwear while they were dating, so why should she suddenly have started using it now? If she'd stopped not using underwear, that could mean she wasn't interested in him anymore in the way she had been. Then again, if she still wasn't using underwear, then who was she not using it for? Fernandez felt a fresh rush of anger wash over him.

"Aren't you going to write down my order?" He stared angrily up at the waiter.

The waiter looked politely back at the guy who obviously had some anger issues, and thought about whether he should spit or dip his penis in his Coca Cola.

"Sir, so far you have ordered a Coca Cola. I can manage to remember at least two items at a time, even if I might be suffering from a slight concussion today as a result of a surprising blow to the head."

Fernandez was on his way out of his chair to beat up the rude waiter, or at the least kick him in the balls or something.

Meanwhile Fernandez was busy arguing with the waiter Fernandez's wife was trying to cover her smile while she prepared the camera on her mobile underneath the table. She was quick with the operation since she already had the mobile ready between her legs where she'd been taking pictures of herself, quite nude, and sending them to her manager-lover. Disappointed, she heard a strict, female voice say with authority; "Sir, is there a problem here?"

Joselyn had been on her way back to the office after her inspection round when she'd heard angry shouting inside the breakfast hall. She'd immediately entered to check what the commotion was about, and now she was standing by the table where one of the guests was clearly agitated by something one of the waiters had done.

She looked at the waiter, considering if he would be strangling-worthy. If he was, she would need to find something to blame him for, which of course wouldn't be a problem for her, but after having taken a closer look, she decided he wasn't. He was way too skinny, and she would just risk snapping his neck right off. Even if she liked her sex rough, she wasn't interested in becoming a murderer because of it.

"Your fucking waiter is being fucking rude! Do you know who I am?"

Joselyn shifted her focus from the waiter to the agitated man. Now, that's a man who could really need some strangling, she thought, but unfortunately he was a guest, and therefore not really an option.

"I'm sorry, Sir, but what did he do?" She asked.

"He refused to write down my order, and according to my fucking experience, he'll forget what I wanted!"

Joselyn faced the waiter who looked like he was trying to look like he was trying.

"Is this true? You know that you should write everything down," she said strictly to him before she again addressed the agitated man; "Sir, do you want a new waiter?"

"No, I want that waiter, and I want him to write down what I order!"

Joselyn looked at the waiter again, who was now doing a number of writing on his notepad as he said; "Ok, Sir, that's one Coca Cola." The waiter then looked expectantly at the angry man's wife. "And for you, Madam?"

"A glass of orange juice."

"And one glass of orange juice." The waiter wrote it down as he repeated the order. "Will there be anything else?"

"Are you trying to be funny again?" The angry man exclaimed, staring at the waiter. Both he and his wife wanted food from the buffet table.

Joselyn stepped in between the two men and sent the waiter off to get the drinks before she said politely to the guest; "Sir, if you have any more complaints, or there is anything else I can help you with you are of course welcome to see me in my office at any time."

Fernandez had discretely been studying the hotel manager's thighs and legs. He might just have some more complaints for her later. He grunted a sort of thanks, and then he pretended to look at the menu again while he really was staring above the edge of it at her ass as she was leaving the room.

After having finished his second attack at the buffet table, Gunther finally took his eyes away from the food long enough to notice that the young, African woman was sitting only a few tables away from him and his son. He quickly got back up and went over to the buffet table again. There he chose the biggest piece of cake he could find and then tried carrying it back to his table in such a way that the woman couldn't avoid seeing it.

He sat down by the table again and started eating the cake by using large and wide arm movements with the fork, as he shuffled piece after piece into his mouth while letting out loud sounds of pleasure. On his way past the woman he'd noticed that she was eating some kind of fruit salad, but according to his theory, no one would ever choose a fruit salad if they could rather have cake. The cake really tasted exquisite, and enjoying it in front of her like this gave him a feeling of getting back at her for running past them so many times in the stairs earlier. Even though her parading in front of them could have been just to show off her body, it made the cake taste even more delicious.

When he went for a second piece of cake Gunther was joined by his son, and Jurgen-Gunther made him proud by supplying himself with two large pieces at once instead of having to go all the way to the buffet table for another piece later.

The sounds were impossible to ignore, and Ophelia couldn't help both hearing and seeing the nasty, fat man eating his cake. After a while, all the gross sounds suddenly became even more intense and came in stereo, and she could see that the fat man's fat son had joined him in stuffing himself. The sound and look of the pair eating what had to be some kind of chocolate cake, according to the sandstorm like cake crumb filled air around them, made her completely loose her appetite. She pushed her plate away and looked out the windows instead.

Gunther felt victorious when he noticed that the woman no longer seemed interested in her own food. He celebrated by shuffling another large piece of cake into his mouth.

Mugade hadn't paid any attention to what was going on around him. He'd just received an email on his phone from his No. 2 regarding his trip to Thailand, and now he was trying to write an email to his No. 3 to get an update on his business. The small buttons on his phone made it all painfully slow to get done, and he felt irritated. In addition, the food he'd ordered had turned out to be some kind of giant lobster, and he didn't care for lobster, especially not for breakfast, and then his daughter had suddenly leaned over the table to show him one of her breasts, or more precisely; a bruise on her left breast, and it had all been highly inappropriate and interrupting for him who was trying to write an important email that could be worth a lot of money.

Dagny was at first surprised when it seemed the Italian was paying more attention to her husband than to her. But, then she remembered an article she'd read about how foreign men often had to be extra respectful to other males because of their local customs, or something like that, so, in other words, this was obviously the Italian gentleman's way of trying to be-friend her husband to get closer to her. Anyway, she was busy eating, so for the moment it suited her just fine not having to flirt with anyone.

Flavio had instantly forgotten all about the fat and strange woman the second he'd seen the Norwegian man enter the breakfast hall. The man had slowly made his way over to the table, and had then started inflating some sort of small, round cushion for his chair before he'd carefully sat down on it. There was no question about it, the man was clearly having some rectal and-or anus related pain.

"Sports related injury," Johan whispered to the nice Italian man as he sat down next to him. He hoped Dagny hadn't said anything to him about the incident in their bathroom earlier, and that she didn't hear his modest adjustment of the truth.

Flavio was struggling to pay attention to what the Norwegian man was saying. Had his penis grown during the night and since he'd last seen him? He hadn't really seen much of the Norwegian man's crotch area when they'd met at the fitness and gym center earlier, as they'd mostly been focusing on his powdered buttocks, but he felt sure his penis really did look much bigger now.

In front of the closed gate at the bottom of the avenue leading up to the hotel's entrance, three cars pulled up. At the front sides of the cars' hoods, where it appeared there once had been flags attached, they all only had broken off sticks left.

All the cars also had an impressive collection of bugs stuck and squashed on their windshields and in their grills, in addition to being covered in a thick layer of dust, as if they'd been driven hard and aggressively for a long distance. One of the cars, the middle one, a large Mercedes, was also partially decorated with what appeared to be smashed eggs.

A large suit wearing shades exited the lead car and walked over to the security guard at the gate. After a few low toned words the gate was raised.

The small cortege entered through the gate and continued up the avenue to the hotel where the Mercedes stopped in front of the stairs leading up to the entrance. Soon after, two shade wearing, male suits, and two young females dressed as tennis players, were standing at the bottom of the stairs waiting for someone still inside the egg decorated Mercedes.

It seemed they would have to keep on waiting for a while, because in the backseat Mubasher was sleeping. In fact, he'd been asleep during most of the journey, except for the period when he'd been complaining about having been woken up by people who recognized his car and threw eggs at it as they drove through the small back alleys out of the city. People could really be so inconsiderate. Mubasher had complained long and well about the incidents and his people's lack of consideration until he'd finally fallen asleep again, and now none of his staff wanted to be the one to wake him up again.

Mubasher's driver turned off the car's air-conditioning, and then they waited patiently for the heat to either cook him slowly to his death, or, for the second best; for it to wake him up.

There was no question about it, Mubasher's staff all believed a change in the country's leadership was approaching, but they'd decided that they would try to balance on the line between the different power-fractions, until it became more evident which of the fractions would win. But, for the moment, the Dictator was sleeping, and they were waiting.

Had the Swedish chefs down in the hotel's giant kitchen known about Mubasher's staff's tactic, they would have nodded knowingly and approving.

Joselyn had just received the news that the country's leader had arrived at the hotel; the feared and respected Dictator. When she, the previous evening, had received the message confirming his visit, she almost hadn't believed it. This had to be a scoop of gigantic proportions. Having one of the world's last successful dictators as their guest would ensure more publicity around the hotel's opening weekend than she could ever have wished for. The man was renowned for his exclusive taste in all the finest the world could offer. His new yachts and cars were always portrayed in glossy magazines around the world.

Since the hotel's opening, Joselyn hadn't had the time to watch the local news, or any other news for that matter, but she'd decided she would discreetly contact the media and inform them about the great Dictator's stay at the hotel. But first, she would let him settle in to his suit and get comfortable.

She smiled, and almost forgot about her current irritation of not having been able to find a suitable new person for a quick office romance.

Having finished one of her inspection rounds, confirming that the hotel currently seemed to be running smoothly, she made her way back to her office to prepare how she should approach the media with the news about the Dictator's visit.

After having seen his daughter's bruised breast, Mugade had drawn two conclusions. The first was that the packaging of the cocaine was much better than he'd feared, it actually made him a little proud that they could take such a rough handling without rupturing, and the second was that the fat man simply couldn't be his new business associate. No one who knew or understood what was inside those breasts would dare to risk rupturing the packages by handling them that way.

It of course also explained why the man hadn't tried to follow up on their initial meeting.

To Mugade it was anyway mainly good news. It meant that the

business the fat man had referred to was something he should try taking control over, firstly; since it was obviously a way of making money that he wasn't already aware of, and secondly; because he felt partially misled by how the man had behaved when he approached him.

He decided that his next step would have to be to renew his effort to find the correct man, and then muscle the fat man into giving him his Dunder business, or whatever it was he'd called it, as soon as the opportunity presented itself. He would probably get a chance sometime during the evening, maybe after dinner.

He could be quite threatening in the dark.

Johan was sitting next to the nice Italian gentleman eating a banana. Bananas were what many professional athletes ate, according to an article he'd read.

He also wanted some eggs, maybe raw, but then the sight of mayonnaise drowned eggs all over one of Dagny's plates made him change his mind. He wouldn't under any circumstance want to give Dagny the impression he was copying her. Instead he ordered a beer. It was, after all, his vacation and therefore a special occasion. Also, he'd worked out really good this morning, so he sort of deserved it.

Ophelia left the breakfast hall to go to the suite and change into some beach wear. She wanted to be among the first of the guests down at the beach, so she could get the best positioned sunbed.

Her father hadn't noticed that she left their table, but after she'd showed him her bruised breast during the breakfast, he'd sat as if in deep thoughts for a long while, and she now felt quite certain that she would manage to get her new car upgraded to a Bentley by playing on his fatherly sympathy.

Johan suddenly excitedly remembered that he'd earlier seen some beach-balls in the window of the hotel shop by the main entrance. He quickly finished eating his banana and gulped down his pint of beer, before he left the nice Italian man with a joyful; "See you later!" Then he hurried as fast as his bandaged crotch and stitched ball sack would allow him towards the hotel shop.

Flavio was confused by the Norwegian man's abrupt departure, but also slightly motivated after having heard him mumble something about going to get a ball to bring down to the beach for exercise.

As the man left, the fat woman across the table from him suddenly stopped eating, and Flavio watched somewhat puzzled, as she instead started to wrap food into paper napkins, looking as if she was preparing for a very long journey.

Dagny had out of the corner of her eye watched her useless husband leave the breakfast hall.

She knew that he knew that she would soon be going up to their suite to get changed before going down to the beach, and she really didn't want to have to deal with him repeating any of his stupidity from earlier in the morning in a last hope to keep her. After all, he still had one more ball that he could also try cutting. The dumb man had even mumbled something about a ball right before he left.

But, as he left, she meant she'd seen him turn towards the hotel's main entrance instead of towards the elevators, so maybe, if she was quick, she could make it up to their suite and get changed for the beach before he reached getting up there to try anything.

Not having been properly finished with her breakfast, she quickly wrapped herself some snack-filled doggy bags to bring along with her down to the beach, just in case the beach bar should happen to be closed or something.

Wei had left his table without anyone noticing it, and gone to his suite for a change of clothes.

Standing in front of his suitcase, he found nothing in it that he thought looked in any way similar to what the other guests were wearing. Then he recalled he'd seen a shop by the hotel's main entrance, and he decided he would go there to see if he could find something more proper to wear. Maybe he could find something that was special, but, at the same time, that was also something everybody else wanted to wear.

Gunther and his son were just about finished with their breakfasts.

Their table and immediate surroundings looked like they'd been subject to a child's birthday party, which had also included a major food fight.

Neither of the two felt the need to visit their suite before going down to the beach again, but finding a toilet was highly prioritized.

They left their table in the same hurry that they'd captured it, and this time Jurgen-Gunther beat his father in being the first of them to squeeze out through the doors. Gunther was in such a rush to reach the toilets that he barely had time to be proud of his son for doing so.

As Flavio passed the reception on his way to his suite after breakfast, the concierge called out and caught his attention.

"Sir, here's your potato flour." The concierge smiled politely and handed the packet of potato flour towards him.

Flavio looked at the handsome concierge. The young man had some very strange bruises around his neck, or could it be a rash of some kind? He smiled back and thanked the concierge, but felt uncertain about what to do. What if the bruises, or rash, indicated that the young man suffered from some kind of disease. Maybe a contagious disease…?

Eventually, after a period of quite awkward silence where the concierge stood trying to hand the packet of potato flour to Flavio without getting any response, Flavio very cautiously accepted the packet of flour, gripping it in the bottom left corner with two fingers. As he then walked quickly towards the elevator, he made sure to hold the packet at what he felt constituted a safe distance away from his face and body.

Mugade had entered the lobby area just behind the Italian man. He was on his way back to the suite after having finished breakfast, or rather, his chain of thoughts. He'd planned to stop by the reception desk to ask if any new guests had checked in, hoping that the information might give him a lead as to who his new business contact really could be.

Mugade couldn't avoid noticing the bag of white powder the Italian man received.

Potato flour?

What idiot would have the need to use potato flour in his suite at a hotel? That was clearly a bag of cocaine! The man had to be his new business associate, and he had to have the biggest balls ever, to openly traffic his drugs like that. Having it delivered to the hotel as potato flour...

Mugade stopped walking. He would rather approach the man sometime this evening.

He watched as the man eagerly, but very cautiously, of course in great respect of the packet's contents, carried the bag over to the elevators and then entered one of them.

Mugade felt relieved. His potentially new business associate was clearly a professional, and so skillful that not even he had been anywhere near to suspect him of being involved in the drug business.

Up in the suite, Flavio found his lover practicing his in-between-the-rounds, boxing-match walk.

His lover was holding one of the sofa cushions above his head as he paraded around in circles in his underwear, and it was one of the sexiest sights Flavio had ever seen.

Flavio then carefully placed the bag of potato flour on a shelf inside one of the closets in the bar. He wasn't sure yet if he would dare to use any of the flour, at least not until he knew whether or not the concierge in fact was suffering from some kind of disease.

According to his knowledge, gay people were very easily infected. But, of course, he hadn't been a homosexual for very long, so he was still learning and could be wrong about that.

Nevertheless, he wanted to be sure before using any of it.

After having handled the bag of potentially contagious potato flour, Flavio washed his hands vigorously before he offered to oil down his lover's body and maybe take some more pictures of him for his portfolio.

"Maybe you should try doing the walk wearing tights? Do you have any tights? If you don't have any, maybe we could check with the hotel if they could help us get hold of a pair? Or, I could just ask the Norwegian about borrowing one of his pairs?"

Flavio's lover was deeply focused on his doing his walk perfectly and had barely heard a word of what Flavio had been suggesting.

An alarm started going off on Fernandez's mobile phone, and he looked irritated at it. It was time to take his steroids again, and he left the breakfast table without a word to his wife.

There really was nothing to be said to her at the moment, or, at least, no opportunity for him to say what he wanted as long as a number of busboys were constantly running around them clearing off the breakfast tables.

He would first go the suite and take his steroids, then stop by the roof terrace for a drink and to call his manager for an update on any news articles mentioning him, and then he would confront his wife with all her errors as a human.

Fernandez's wife was, as always during their short marriage, happy to see her husband leave. She could see how angry he still was, and that he wasn't far away from snapping. Hopefully, it would happen at any moment, and preferably at a time when they, or he, were surrounded by a lot of people.

Underneath the table she took another picture of herself between her legs and sent it to her lover-manager.

As a precaution, she'd brought her bikini with her in her handbag, so she would be able to just change down at the beach instead of having to stop by the suite. It was just in case Fernandez should happen to be in their suite taking his drugs, and in that situation, maybe, potentially capable of letting out a rage on her that was unhealthy, rather than career supporting, for her.

CORNY SIESTA

The hotel's advertising agency had sent out a flying drone to take some new pictures of the hotel premises and the beautiful beach area in front of it. According to the weather forecasts it was going to be another sunny day, and with actual guests at the beach and around the hotel area it was an excellent opportunity to get some updated pictures for the hotel's webpage and new brochures.

The hotel's control room received a message to start the engines in the wind turbines to make them appear like they were running on their own by wind-power and producing the hotel's electricity.

The turbines' propellers lazily began spinning when the tech support guy activated the engines. He then went back to what he'd been doing before the instruction came in; using the hotel's security cameras to search for the sexy, African woman with the amazing breasts.

Down at the beach, Ophelia had settled down on a sunbed close to the water.

She'd ordered a drink from one of the beach waiters patrolling the area, but as soon as she'd tasted it, she'd sent it back, and instead she'd ordered a new one that would have been more expensive.

She was wearing one of her new bikinis; a purple, very sexy, tiny bikini top and matching thong. After having rearranged her towel, she turned from lying on her stomach to lying on her back. She glanced down her body and then started studying her breasts.

She had to admit, they did really look perfect, although, one size too small. Fortunately, her father had finally come around, and promised her that she would get the bigger implants as soon as they were back home again. She closed her eyes and imagined how fantastic she would look when she was driving around in her new convertible with her big breasts.

Blissfully in her own thoughts, Ophelia hadn't noticed that the fat, nasty, breast groper and his fat son had arrived at the beach, or that the fat man had chosen to fall down on a sunbed close to hers.

After they'd left the breakfast hall, both Gunther and Jurgen-Gunther had had a successful and satisfying visit to the toilet.

Afterwards, on their way to the beach, they'd stopped by the hotel shop by the main entrance to buy some swim trunks, saving themselves the hassle of taking the long elevator journey up to their suite to change into their old ones.

Down at the beach, they both changed quite indiscreetly, half-hidden behind some towels one of the sunbed boys had brought to them, into their new swim trunks, before Jurgen-Gunther immediately ran down into the water and transformed into a World War ll submarine.

Gunther ordered a large German beer from a nearby waiter and settled down on a sunbed. He divided his attention between proudly watching his son play war, bombing imaginary ships and pretending to shoot the other bathing guests in the water, and horny watching the young, African woman's breasts and body.

Gunther had bought and wore the same kind of swim trunks as his son, and even though he usually didn't care, he actually felt that this pair was quite stylish, with their bright red color, tight fit and somewhat revealing cut.

To the hotel's other guests and staff, the swim trunks carried proudly by the two fat bodies, really looked like they rather had the ambition of being thongs instead of trunks.

Flavio was trying his best to avoid getting any sand inside his sandals as he entered the beach. He hated the sand, but he loved to watch the tanning and sweating bodies. For the occasion, he was wearing a new, bright green speedo.

Having dried off a beach chair underneath one of the umbrellas by the bar, he sat down and ordered a drink. Then he peered around the beach, hoping to spot the Norwegian man playing with his new ball, or balls, or maybe someone else, preferably in minimal clothing.

Flavio couldn't help noticing the large German man. At first he thought the man was naked, and he recalled reading somewhere that Germans were notorious nudists, but upon a closer inspection, it turned out the fat man was actually wearing some kind of swim trunks, possibly a thong. The trunks was nevertheless so revealing and small that it would have made any experienced nudist blush, when and if they'd managed to spot it.

Flavio shivered, the wannabe nudist really wasn't his type. Instead he stared at the young, African female laying a couple of sunbeds away from the German. She had a beautiful and sexy body. There was no doubt, he would much rather have had sex with her than the man. Maybe he wasn't that gay after all, he thought smilingly. The woman reminded him of all the women he'd used to have before he discovered he was gay.

At that moment the Norwegian man exited the elevator a little further down the beach, and Flavio once again knew that he was just plain gay. The Norwegian was wearing a pair of bright green sneakers, actually perfectly matching his own speedo, but which made it impossible for anyone not to notice the guy. He'd changed into another pair of tights, which were just as sexy, but that had slightly shorter legs than the ones he'd worn for breakfast and during his work-out earlier in the morning. He was also wearing a singlet with an advertisement for a restaurant, or disco - or something, in Bangkok, which he'd probably visited at some point. Beneath his arm, he was carrying what looked to be some kind of colorful, plastic ball.

It was evident to Flavio that the guy was clearly on his way out of the closet.

The Norwegian still had the same kind of wiggly walk that he'd had at breakfast, as if his balls had grown too big for the space between his thighs, or if he was a cowboy who'd just finished an endurance race across America, or if he...

In fact, when he looked closer, it actually appeared like the

Norwegian's penis had grown even bigger since he saw it, and him, last.

Up in his suite Mubasher was irritated and exhausted from being irritated. He'd sent the hotel management a request to have some of the beach sand brought up to a closed off and private area for him on the roof terrace. The hotel manager had soon replied that, regrettably, his request was impossible to grant at the moment since it was the opening weekend and the hotel was full of VIP guests. Instead she'd offered to close off a part of the beach for him.

He'd walked out onto the suite's balcony and looked all the way down at the beach. It had simply seemed too stressful and too far away to even be worth considering journeying down there.

Now, he was lying on his bed exhausted from the whole ordeal, while he wondered what he could come up with that would entertain him. When the riots and uprising of his people eventually calmed down, he would find and employ a person who could come up with things solely for his entertainment, a sort of personal amusement organizer. He calmed down a little as he thought about how much easier his life then would become. It would have to be a woman, of course, preferably young, and unquestionably very sexy. That reminded him; he did have two of his mistresses with him, they could probably provide him with some entertainment.

Johan spotted the nice Italian gentleman sitting at a table by the bar, and decided he would go over and have a drink with him before he went to take a couple of laps in the water. He was hoping that the sexy, African woman, who'd been at the fitness and gym center this morning, was also down at the beach. Then she could watch him work-out again, this time while he was swimming.

He'd also brought with him the inflatable, plastic ball that he'd just bought at the hotel shop. After his swim, he would use it to do some other water exercises with. But, first of all he wanted a drink or a beer.

As he carefully made his way through the sand over towards the Italian's table, he felt how the water resistant bandage he'd put on his ball-cut was being stretched and pulled, and he tried his best to walk in a way that wouldn't misplace it. It had been an even greater struggle than usual to get the tights on with the new bandage since it had been thicker than the non-waterproof one.

The light morning breeze had slightly increased into a light wind, which carried with it some sand from deserts quite far away. The sun was nevertheless shining, promising it would be a really hot day.

Exiting the beach elevator at the side of the beach where the massage tables and the hotel's surfing and diving school were set up, Dagny decided she would first try surfing, and then she would get herself a massage. Her muscles were still hurting from all the stair-walking she'd had to do earlier in the morning.

One of the beach waiters passed her, and she ordered a large ice cream since she anyway had to wait for the handsome surf-instructor, who'd gone to find a wet suit that she could borrow.

The instructor was gone quite a long time, so she also ordered an umbrella drink to ease the wait.

The sun had already made the day very warm, and the sunblock Dagny had put on earlier was now starting to gather in the folds of her fat, making it look like she had white circles decorating her now pinkish colored body.

From inside his booth, the surf-instructor peered out the door, regretting that he was on surf-instructor duty instead of waiter duty. Usually, it would be the other way around, but today, the guy on waiter duty had told him that there was a really sexy woman, in the smallest bikini imaginable, sunbathing on the other side of the beach, and, in addition, she'd apparently seemed overly occupied with her own tits.

Instead, he was now stuck with that large, striped, whale of a woman. He would pretend to be searching for a suit a little longer, in the vague hope the woman would get bored, or, more likely; hungry, and then leave.

Dagny noticed the surf-instructor peeping out from his booth. He was of course checking out her delicious, voluptuous, Scandinavian body, and trying to be discreet about it. She giggled and waved girlishly at him. He was for sure interested in her, and was probably very grateful to have her as his first customer for the day.

Dagny wriggled into a more comfortable position in the sand, and one of her bikini straps slid down from her shoulder exposing a large section of a pale breast.

Inside the booth, the surf-instructor shivered and retreated quickly from the opening by the sight of the pale, saggy breast. He went back to his search, meanwhile trying strenuously to erase the image from his mind, and unfortunately, too soon, he finally found a suit he guessed could fit the woman.

The size label on the suit had more X's on it than he bothered to count. It had to have been made either for a very rare, extremely large human specimen, or it was actually a cover for one of the water jets? But, as long as it would cover up some of the sweaty, fleshy woman while he pretended to teach her some surfing, he really couldn't care less which it was as.

Wei was in the hotel shop to do some shopping, but he had some difficulties understanding what type of shop it was actually supposed to be. It seemed to want to be some sort of combined, very exclusive, clothing, gifts and souvenir shop, but, in fact, everything he could see being sold there was cheap crap made in Asia with prices belonging in Western Europe.

He was looking to buy something to wear to the beach that was special, but that wouldn't make him stand out from the other guests. The man working behind the counter was irritating him enormously by trying to make him get a smaller size every time he found some potential clothing.

Wei was well aware that he wasn't as big as the man working

there, but that didn't mean he couldn't buy his clothes in exactly whatever size that suited him, even clothes belonging to someone twice his own size, or twice the man's size for that matter, if that was what he wanted. He felt the man behind the counter was patronizing him, probably because his own clothes fitted him so well.

He continued and did the rest of his shopping, not looking at, or paying any attention to, the meddling and rude sales guy. He would bring the bag of new clothes with him down to the beach, that way he could see what the others were wearing before he decided on what he should wear. He could then easily get changed in one of the beach changing rooms.

In the hotel's control room, the tech support guy received a message from the surf-instructor to start up the wave generator, and set it to create some small to moderate waves at his end of the beach, because he had a customer.

The tech support irritated fulfilled the instructor's request with quick movements before he returned to his monitors, where he from several different angles at once was watching the sexy, young, African woman tanning on the beach. When the surf-instructor had, so inappropriately, interrupted him with his stupid message, he'd just been finished with zooming in and turning all the relevant and available cameras towards her body, and had just reached to begin stroking his penis through his pants.

Up in his suite, Mubasher was laying naked on his back on top of his bed. He had four pillows supporting his head, so he was able to see what was unfolding on the floor in front of the bed without having to make any effort to do so.

On the night stand, beside the bed, there was a bottle of champagne in a cooler, and next to the cooler, there was a packet of Viagra.

On the floor, in front of the bed, two of his brought along, Persian carpets, had been placed on top of each other, and on top of the carpets, his two mistresses were wrestling in their underwear. To make the fight more realistic, he'd promised the winner a small fortune in money, but still, their wrestling effort still seemed a little lazy to him, and he thought about if he should remove the rules about no hitting, kicking and hair pulling.

Instead of changing anything, Mubasher instead studied his two mistresses for a while longer. He wondered if they might already be tired. Maybe there was something he could implement to motivate them to fight each other more vigorously?

Regardless, they were both sweating beautifully, and despite the lack of vigor, he still enjoyed watching them. He was sweating himself as well, and that part he didn't enjoy.

The air conditioning had been turned off to make the girls sweat, but it seemed the fan next to his bed wasn't alone enough to keep him cool. He peered around the room, but found that the remote to the air conditioning was lying too far away. It was all the way over at the table in the lounge like TV area, almost on the other side of the suite. There was no way he would get up to go over there now.

Instead, he ordered his mistresses to stop, and then told them that the one who brought him the remote would get a bonus twice of what he'd offered the winner of the wrestling match. His request seemed to do the trick for the mistresses' motivation, and their fighting instantly became more violent.

He felt both aroused and frustrated by watching them. Which one of them would he have sex with first? Maybe the winner, because she'd won, and that was sexy, or the loser, despite her losing, to comfort her, and because she would feel even more grateful for getting the opportunity to have sex with him…

All the decisions he was having to consider had made Mubasher feel tired, and he tripled the winner's money to get the fight finished before he would become too tired to have sex with anyone.

He picked up the packet of Viagra and poured some more champagne in his glass, using it to swallow down one of the pills with.

The girls were fighting harder. They had now reached quite a distance beyond the carpets, as they both were struggling to reach the table where the remote control was, while at the same time trying to stop the other from getting to it first.

Mubasher decided he would have one of his lifeguards go out and buy some costumes for them to wear the next time. Maybe some sexy superhero or gladiator costumes would make it more entertaining to watch?

If costumes turned out difficult to obtain while he was staying at the hotel, he would just request to have some of the hotel uniforms. Maybe they had something similar to those French, housemaid uniforms or something like that? If not, the normal hotel uniforms he'd seen when he entered the hotel had been kind of sexy, so a couple of those would also do as sort of a last, emergency alternative.

One of the mistresses seemed to finally have pinned the other one down, and Mubasher watched expectantly. But then, the pinned down mistress seemed to find some new motivation, and they rolled around again, knocking over a small coffee table and making it, and all the things on top of it, come down with a loud crashing sound.

Mubasher found himself highly amused by the development of the fight, and he could see his penis slowly starting to swell. It all made him thirsty, and he threw in another bonus to the one of the girls who would also bring him some more cold champagne from the refrigerator. If they were clever girls, the closest refrigerator was the one next to his bed, and he hoped they were, because that would bring the fight closer to him, and then he wouldn't have to stretch his neck so much to see the fight properly.

Why hotels had to place the refrigerators so that their guests would have to get out of the bed to get a drink, was incomprehensible. Here, the small refrigerator was placed on the outside of the night stand, and looking at how far away it was, made him briefly miss his own bed. From his bed, he could reach down himself and just get out any drink he wanted from the cabinet built into his bedside table, or, if he was too tired to reach, he could just call on one of his discreet servants, and they would get it for him.

Mubasher forgot about his thirst as one of his mistresses made a little scream. It seemed the fight had taken another turn, and he made an attempt to get up into a slightly more elevated position on the bed to see them better.

Down in the basement "The Almighty" hummed yet again and the digital nameplate on the Dictator's suite door changed from showing nothing into showing the name "Acedia".

Only a second later the hotel answered to the new name by vibrating and trembling ever so lightly, and the previously, virtually, invisible gap, reaching from in front of the security booth outside of the hotel entrance and down the avenue, became a tiny bit wider. "The Almighty" was still working on interpreting the information it had gathered. One the one hand it now had numerous small projects in relation to the guest's personal welfare, but on the other it had laws to obey and fulfill. There was no moral battle being fought inside the A.I core, only a clinical interpretation of the information it found and then a conclusion with a solution to potential errors and faults. "The Almighty" continued to hum and processes, while it continued to search the internet. Regarding a dry scalp it found a number of way on how to treat and heal it, but regarding the personalities it so far had only found one. The solution seemed irrevocable and its source was from humans themselves, but "The Almighty" had been programmed to find solutions in the plural sense of the word and it was therefore determined to make absolutely sure it was missing some information. Confused by the information regarding a solution it would continue searching until it hopefully found some guidance on how to best execute its role.

About the hotel premises, no one noticed or bothered to pay any attention to what had just happened. Tiny earthquakes, or trembles in the ground, were not at all unusual in most parts of the world. It was probably simply just a normal, very small, insignificant quake, or maybe some people doing construction somewhere down the shoreline from the hotel.

The only one noticing the tremble was the surf-instructor, but he dismissed it as an aftershock caused by the large woman yet again falling off the surf board while it was still up on the beach.

The woman giggled as he grabbed her fleshy arm and pulled her back up on her feet. Sweat was pouring down her fatty flabs, and for a moment he thought he smelled a fart in the air. It could have been her who'd released it in her effort to get up, but he realized it could have just as easily been him passing the air, as he had to strength-lift the female mountain of flesh to manage to get her up into an upright position again.

The session seemed never-ending, and the surf-instructor felt how his hands were all moist and slippery after having held on to the woman's sweaty and marinated flesh. Even though he'd made the tech support guy activate the wave generators, there was no way he was going to bring this lesson out into the water. The woman was more than slippery and wet enough as it was.

Jurgen-Gunther was splashing around in the shallow water. His already impressively large behind seemed to be functioning as a flotation device, and was most of the time the only part of him that was visible above the surface, while his upper body, head and legs were somewhere below.

Occasionally, his round head bobbed up, and he pointed his small, sausage fingers at someone else in the water or at the beach while he made shooting sounds.

Gunther had grown tired of watching the sleeping, African woman's body, and was now focusing solely on his son.

"Pang!" Jurgen-Gunther had just surfaced again, and this time shot one of the beach waiters. Gunther clapped his hands excitedly, and watched proudly how his son was obviously winning the battle he was fighting. He continued to clap and laugh every time Jurgen-Gunther shot someone.

Motivated by his father's support, Jurgen-Gunther found an increasing number of enemies to fire at. The effort of his intense war-hunt made his nose start running, and soon his face was covered in snot.

Up close, others would have probably considered it to be an attempt at a very special variant of facial camouflage.

Johan finally reached the Italian's table by the bar and sat down in the chair next to him and ordered a beer. After all, he was on vacation, and on vacation, the only drinking rule was that there were no drinking rules.

"You remember my sport's accident? It really pains me, but I just exercise hard to get the pain out. You're a slender man, not much muscles, but if you start working out, they'll come fast."

Flavio looked at the Norwegian man and smiled, the way he saw it, he'd just received a nice compliment about his waistline.

"Maybe you can show me some exercises?"

"Of course!" Johan replied the Italian enthusiastically. "I was planning to have a workout with this ball down in the water after I finish my beer. Let's do it together! Ball play is excellent exercise, and for a beginner, such as yourself, it will be perfect. Norway has some of the best beach ball players in the world. You can really get a great body from ball playing!"

A moment later Johan became even more excited when he spotted the sexy, African woman on a sunbed further down on the beach.

Flavio barely managed to stop himself from clapping his hands. Then the Norwegian high fived him, and life was even sweeter.

Ophelia woke up. She'd fallen asleep in the sun dreaming about money, breasts, sex and expensive purses.

Had it started to rain? She'd clearly felt drops of water hitting her legs and thighs, but looking up at the sky, she couldn't see any kind of clouds for miles.

Peering around the beach, she became aware of the fat, groping man sitting on a sunbed only a couple of beds away from her. As she watched him, he clapped his hands, and she could clearly see drops of the man's sweat fly through the air around him. Disgusted, she felt how the moist drops hit her skin and looked down on her legs. She of course knew there was no acid involved, but the feeling of the nasty man's sweat on her skin was an almost burning sensation. She obviously also knew that white men didn't actually have white colored sweat, but she still thought that the fat man's perspiration appeared to have a white-ish color when it hit her skin.

Ophelia felt revolted and quickly used the tip of her towel to wipe off her thigh where the sweat had last hit her. Automatically, she then smelled the towel, before it occurred to her what a nasty thing that was to be doing. She hastily gathered her things and moved several beds away from the sweaty fountain of a man.

Johan and the Italian had gone into the water and were eagerly throwing the big, inflated, plastic ball to each other. Sometimes, Johan would miss catching it because he was trying to see if the young, African woman was watching him, and even though the waist high water did help ease his mobility slightly, he still felt that his bandaged balls were a hinder to his usually impeccable agility.

He excitedly noticed that the woman moved some beds closer to where he and the Italian was exercising, and he began making an even bigger effort to impress her by throwing himself after the ball. He felt sure he looked way better doing it than most of the professionals he'd seen on TV.

Flavio was doing his best to try to keep up with the eager Norwegian, and hoped that he maybe, somehow, could impress him in the sport's activity they were doing.

So far, it was one of the best sports Flavio had ever tried out.

He laughed out loud and admired the Norwegian man, who seemed to be showing off for him, throwing himself in the most flirtatious and irrepressible ways, trying to catch the ball.

Dagny felt completely worn out after the surfing lesson, even if it only had been done up on the beach.

She'd gotten the surf-instructor to take some pictures of her posing with the board down by the water, so she could later post them on Facebook to pleasure her friends and admirers.

After having fought with the wet suit to get it off, it seemed to have glued itself onto her ample body, and then felt a hint of desire over the instructor's apparent eagerness to help her undress, she hugged him while giggling and promised she would soon return.

Dagny then wobbled over to the massage tables.

The surf-instructor slightly panicked when he felt how the fat enveloped him like a suffocating, sweaty and stinking cocoon as the plump woman hugged him. Thinking he would never be able to forget the traumatic feeling of her embrace, or manage to ever wash away all the sweat she'd left on his body, he ran over to the nearest shower and started vigorously scrubbing himself down. Meanwhile, he thought about how it seemed that large sea-related creatures were always dangerous and scary. Moby Dick, sharks, giant octopuses, sea-monsters, and, of course, this woman in a wetsuit, although, the two latter might just be one and the same.

Thinking of the gruesome woman again made the surf-instructor focus on scrubbing even harder, while he wished strongly that he'd been a snake, so he could have just shredded all of his skin instead.

Wei had gone into one of the beach changing rooms to put on his new pair of flowery, Bermuda shorts. It had either been that or a speedo, and he'd decided he would save the speedo for later.

As he was in the middle of changing, the door to his stall suddenly opened, and a man came walking in. Wei, who was standing surprised with his new shorts down by his knees, didn't have time to say anything before the man exclaimed; "Fuck! Why don't you lock the door, pervert!"

Wei noticed how the rude man stole a quick glance at his penis before quickly retreating and slamming the door shut. Finally, he managed to react, and pulled his shorts almost all the way up to his armpits. He felt deeply frustrated that he hadn't had anything to answer the impolite man. Anybody else, but him, would have had an answer ready to deliver in such a situation.

Also, the guy had stared at his penis, probably because it was so much smaller than his gigantic one.

Wei stayed in the changing room until he felt his face had turned into a more neutral shape and color.

Outside the beach changing rooms, Fernandez cursed loudly to himself.

Fuck! That guy's penis had been enormous, and that was probably why his wife maybe was interested in him. Now, where was his wife, and where was that stupid, slow moving waiter with his drink?

Fernandez headed towards the beach bar to ask what became of his drink. He would continue searching for his wife later.

At the other side of the beach, Fernandez' wife had just exited the elevator and was on her way to see if she could get a surf lesson. She was trying to avoid her husband as best she could, and knowing him, she knew he would never try doing anything where someone else might have an advantage over him.

At least, that seemed to have been the rule after he'd become famous, and surfing was, as far she knew, something he'd never done before, and therefore, it was most likely something he would never, ever try.

On her way down to the beach, she'd been observing the surf-instructor from the elevator windows, and he'd definitely looked kind of sexy, at least from a distance. He'd been standing in the open shower close to the surf booth, scrubbing himself with such an intensity and vigor that she'd been impressed by his stamina.

Gunther waved a beach waiter over to his sunbed. "Tell me; where are the dolphins? You say in your brochures and commercials that there are many dolphins here. I haven't been able to see any dolphins, and my son wants to see dolphins. I came here to sit at the beach and watch the dolphins, just like you have promised!"

The waiter smiled politely at the obese and obnoxious man on the sunbed, and replied that he of course would immediately investigate the matter of the missing dolphins. Then he went back to the bar to have the bartender contact the control room. On his way, he decided he would dip his penis deep into whatever drink or food the rude and insufferable fatso ordered next time.

In the control room, the tech support guy was still busy masturbating while looking at the sexy, African woman on his monitors. She'd just moved to another sunbed, and at the same time also turned around, so she was now lying on her stomach. He'd of course changed the direction of the surveillance cameras to be able to continue keeping an eye on her from all possible angles.

At first, he'd been disappointed when she'd lain down on her stomach, but then he'd seen that she was wearing a thong, showing her nice, sexy ass, and he'd felt that he had no choice but to continue masturbating.

Suddenly he was interrupted in his intense work by yet another, new message. This time it was the beach bartender who wanted him to activate the Dolphin Attraction System. He hurried over to activate the system. The bartender's message had seemed urgent, or it might have been that he was just inspired by what he was currently doing.

Either way, the tech support guy turned the system on to maximum dolphin attraction, and then, after having tried to zoom in the cameras just a tad bit more, he went back to masturbating.

The surf-instructor felt his luck had changed, and was now happy he'd pulled surf duty instead of waiter duty. One of the sexiest women he'd ever seen had approached him and asked for a surf lesson.

She was wearing an expensive looking bikini and large, dark shades. He started fantasizing about all the different porn clips he'd seen where the sexy, mature woman seduced the younger, handsome service man.

As he was inside the surf booth to find a suitable wet suit for the woman, he used the opportunity to quickly oil down his abs. When he got back out to her with the smallest wetsuit he could find, she made him feel even luckier when she refused to put it on. Evidently, she preferred to have the lesson wearing only her bikini.

Fernandez's wife checked out the handsome and eager surf-instructor. Maybe, after she'd finished with the whole divorcing her husband ordeal, she would visit the hotel again. The instructor was clearly attracted to her. He was maybe a bit young, but according to all the latest trends, a younger man to play with was exactly what a successful and sexy woman should have these days.

Wanting to impress the sexy woman, the surf-instructor ordered the biggest waves possible from the control room.

He hadn't experienced anything that could even remotely compare to this during his weekend course on massage techniques. A fat, pink- and red-ish toned woman had turned up and dumped her heavy body down on one of the massage tables; he'd been surprised that the table had held the massive load, although, it had let out a loud whining sound.

First, he'd thought, and really, really hoped, that she'd just needed to lie down for a rest, and that maybe she wanted a glass of water or something because she was overheated by walking on the beach in the hot sun. But, then she'd said she wanted a massage, and he'd instantly felt slightly panic-stricken and confused. How was he supposed to massage any muscles, when there was only fat to be seen and found?

He'd looked desperately around to see if there was someone nearby that he could ask for help. What was lying in front of him on the table was clearly, at least, a two man operation. Unfortunately there hadn't been anyone within sight that could help him, so he'd braced himself and started massaging as best he could.

Soon, he felt it as if he'd joined in a competition to knead the largest dough in the world. Using his elbows and fists, he'd gone through every massage technique from the course, and even others that he'd improvised along the way, and now, the only other thing he could come up with would be to try some direct punches into the large flabs of flesh.

There was a tight reek of old sweat in the air, meanwhile, new sweat was pouring down in streams between every fold on the woman's fat body. He tried his best to avoid getting his hands wet, but it was inevitable, and he'd already gotten prune fingers.

Then, there was also the flaking. The woman's skin was peeling off everywhere on her body, and the only good thing about all the sweat was that it stopped the flakes from flying around. Otherwise it would have looked like there was a local snowstorm going on.

Still, the absolute worst thing about it all was that the woman actually seemed to be really enjoying herself. She was continuously grunting and making other noises of pleasure. He noticed in dread how her fat, pale, cellulite covered thighs slowly moved further apart, and he could clearly see some of her pubic hairs sticking out on each side of her bikini line. He closed his eyes tightly shut while trying his best to keep his increasing nausea under control, and then he moved quickly up to work on the woman's shoulders instead. She responded by unhooking her bikini top, and he felt it as if he'd been trapped.

Everywhere he looked on the woman's body there were sweat, flaking, hair growth and overwhelming amounts of fat, and now, in addition, her white, sagging breasts were floating about out in the open. He searched helplessly around the large body, thinking there had to be some part on the mountain of flesh that he could touch without having to confront and fight it.

Having caught eye of her feet and toes he escaped down to that potentially safer area, and started massaging her feet while he stared out across the water, dreaming he was far, far away out there. Whether it was in a boat, or not, or swimming surrounded by hungry sharks, it didn't matter. Only the thought of being anywhere else than where he presently was calmed him a little down.

Dagny giggled and moved her legs further apart. It was clear the sexy massage boy had moved down to her feet to get a better view of her body. She made some sensual, purring noises and wriggled her toes seductively as he worked on her feet.

A little further down at the beach the surf-instructor made sure to regularly smile at the massage guy and occasionally give him the thumbs up.

He stood closely behind, and had placed his hands around the slim waist of the blonde, beautiful woman, while he moved his hips parallel to hers, as he pretended to show her how to stand on a surfboard while it was lying on the beach.

The woman was playing along with him, pretending she knew nothing about how to stand upright or keeping her balance.

The massage guy felt a sting of hatred for the surf-instructor, who was playing around with the sexy blonde, but still took his time to pause and mock him at regular intervals.

At the table in front of him, the giant woman was grunting louder and louder, and her legs were now so far apart that he was afraid she would roll off the bed. Thankfully, her legs were apparently equally fat, so they helped to keep her stabilized and centered on the bed. If nothing else, she at least seemed to be proportional in her obesity.

The massage guy bit his teeth together as he continued rubbing the woman's feet, trying to ignore the sweat that was even in-between her fat toes.

Ophelia was watching the nasty, German and his son. The fat man actually had bigger breasts than her, and his fat son was clearly heading in the same direction; he already had bigger breasts than she'd had before her operation.

Had the wind become stronger? She brushed away some sand that had stuck to her body.

In the control room, the tech support guy was closing in on his orgasm when he once again was interrupted. It was so irritating and frustrating! Just when it had looked like the sexy woman was about to start touching herself.

Evidently, the surf-instructor had got another customer, and this time he required the biggest waves possible.

The tech support guy turned the wave generator control to maximum strength, and then returned to his masturbating session. He found that the delicious, African woman had once again turned over, and she was back to lying on her back again, showing her beautiful breasts. He soon forgot that he'd ever been interrupted.

Down in the water at the beach, Johan had completely abandoned being careful because of his bandage. He'd noticed that the sexy, African woman was stealing glances around the beach area, and he worked hard at throwing himself around in the water to catch the ball in the most impressive and imaginative ways he could think of, every time the Italian threw the ball at him.

Flavio had found himself being more and more excited about the ball play, as it seemed the Norwegian was going further and further in his effort to show off his ball skills. No grown man would have that much fun playing with a plastic ball unless he had some kind of hidden agenda.

Flavio laughed and clapped his hands as the Norwegian once again jumped high out of the water, stretching to reach the ball, and then came splashing down with the ball safely in his grip.

The tech support guy was now really annoyed. Just as he for the second time had been seconds away from reaching his climax, he was once again interrupted. This time it was the hotel manager, and, of course, the matter couldn't wait or be ignored.

It seemed the hotel's Advertisement Agency, whose drone was presently flying around recording and taking pictures of the hotel, wanted them to speed up the wind turbines. They meant it would look better if the turbines were running at a higher speed, so it would appear as if the hotel was producing an impressive amount of electricity.

Still having one hand around his penis, the tech support guy used his other hand to turn the small wheel controlling the turbine propeller's engines up to a maximum. He then hurried back to his monitors, showing the sexy woman, and continued masturbating.

Sitting by the beach bar, Fernandez felt increasingly warmer and more irritated. Maybe he was sick? Maybe the rude waiter at breakfast had put something in his Coca Cola? Maybe his wife was in on it? The Asian guy, with the enormous penis, was clearly watching him from his sunbed underneath one of the largest umbrellas. Maybe he was planning how he would use his big penis on his wife when he wasn't paying attention?

There was also a fly, or some other similar, extremely annoying insect, circling constantly around his head, flying in a way as if it was intentionally trying to irritate him. Up and down, from side to side, all the time almost directly within his line of sight. No fly would ever fly that way unless it was looking for a fight.

Fernandez was getting angrier by the second, and then, to top it all off, the bartender had the nerve to come over and tell him that it looked like he was starting to get sunburned on the top of his head.

The unexpected, strong gusts of wind were starting to blow sand all around, and soon there seemed to be sand everywhere. Gunther momentarily forgot about the grains of sand in his butt crack as his eyes also became full of it.

Dagny resembled the fat wife of the cartoon, superhero character, the Thing.

Only a moment earlier she'd gone down from the massage table, covered her herself with a new layer of sunblock, and then started making her way to the other side of the beach to get some refreshments in the beach bar.

She'd only managed to walk a few meters down the beach, when sand had started blowing all around her, and now, grains of sand were clinging to every inch of her sunblock covered body.

Between the hotel's seven columns, the turbine propellers speed increased even further, and yet more sand started blowing everywhere around the area.

The sheer force of the propellers even made the hotel itself start to lean over as they pulled at it, as if they wanted it to fly away with them.

"Verdamt sand!" Gunther felt how all his careful protection of his ass area was ruined as the sand, now inevitably filling up the space between his butt cheeks, slowly grained him sore. The whirling sand seemed to manage to get into every crack and opening on his body.

As the guests down at the beach all tried to gather their belongings, before they were either blown away by the wind, or lost all their visibility in the sandstorm, some large, torpedo-like shapes became visible in the water, not far out from the beach. The torpedoes seemed to be heading straight for the beach-line at high speed, and shortly after, the first one of them raced a couple of meters up onto the beach, leaving a trail behind it in the sand.

It was a dolphin, and soon it was joined by more of its kind.

They seemed to be swimming side by side right up onto the beach. Some places they would crash into sunbeds, and other places they would crash into other, already beached, dolphins.

The beached dolphins were rapidly covered by the blasting sand, and looked like giant, Chinese eggrolls there they laid spread out along the beach line.

In the control room, the tech support guy still had his penis out, but it was now hanging limp. Its momentarily state of freedom had been forgotten by its normally very attentive owner, since he was busy urgently trying to undo the waves he'd started.

It seemed, the combination of the Dolphin Attraction System

operating together with the wave generator, had somehow disorientated the dolphins, and, as a result, they were now beaching themselves all along the beach.

Slightly panicking, the tech support guy tried turning the beach cameras away from focusing solely on the sunbed where the sexy woman had been sunbathing, to rather focus on the beached dolphins and the area in general. The problem was that it seemed grains, from all the sand blowing about, had inflicted the cameras' small rotation systems, so now they were locked in their current angle. Nevertheless, he'd been able to see how the sand was blowing everywhere, and how people had begun running around when the dolphins had started landing themselves on the beach.

Finally, he managed to stop the wave generators and shut off the Dolphin Attraction System. But, from what little he could see of the area by looking at the monitors showing footage from the locked cameras, it had been too late. Hurrying over to the turbine propellers' control, he also turned them off. The strong wind and the sandstorm instantly halted, leaving behind a beach area that looked deserted, except for all the stranded dolphins and disarranged umbrellas, sunbeds, chairs and tables.

Shit, he just knew Miss Hardfakk was going to be angry. But, on the positive side, it meant that she would probably visit him again, and give him another opportunity to see her breasts.

The tech support guy suddenly became aware that his penis was still hanging out. What he missed noticing, was that the previously ever so tiny and ignorable gap, in front of security booth outside the hotel entrance, had grown wider. The reason he missed this, more or less, significant little change in the scenery, was actually really not his fault, as there were no surveillance cameras located in that area. And, even if there had been cameras there, they weren't likely to have been prioritized, and therefore they wouldn't have had any monitor allocated to them in the control room for the tech support guy to see.

Nobody else at the hotel either noticed that the hotel slowly swayed back to its original position as the wind turbines were shut off, or, the other more or less significant little detail; that the hotel didn't sway the whole way back to a fully upright position.

In front of the two beach elevators, lines of sandstorm and dolphin fleeing guests and staff had started forming. Jurgen-Gunther was one of the last to arrive by one of the elevators, after having had to struggle hard, climbing over some sandy, beached dolphins, to get there. He was exhausted and crying.
Gunther walked over to his son, and offered him a piece of cake that he'd been able to partially cover from the sand with his Hawaiian shirt. He looked around to see if anyone noticed his exemplary parenting and his great generosity, sharing his last piece of cake like this. Jurgen-Gunther sneezed and got some snot on the piece of cake, but his parenting worked, and his son was soon occupied eating snot covered cake instead of crying. He'd of course been very hungry after having played submarine war for so long, and then also having to climb over those stupid dolphins.

Joselyn was angry. How that disastrous situation down at the beach could happen was beyond her comprehension, but, nevertheless, it had happened. As soon as she'd gotten an overview of the situation, she'd sent the caretakers down to the beach to push the dolphins back out into the sea again. They'd actually managed to ask her about what they should do if they found any dead ones, and she'd had to stare at them with her pointy breasts until they'd finally understood that she didn't care about what condition the creatures were in, only that they were all, as quickly as possible, removed from the hotel's beach area. Afterwards, she'd called the useless tech support guy, who'd had the nerve to ask her if she was on her way down to him, to tell him to start the current generator, so that the currents would bring the dolphins away from the area. She had then written an angry instruction to "The Almighty" demanding that it came up with a solution on how to prevent any such incidents from ever happening again and that it had to do corrections in regards to the suite names. Joselyn almost flattened the send button on her computer with the strength behind her punch when she sent the message. If the stupid computer not soon started to behave properly and do what was best for its users, she decided she would march down to the basement and punish it, maybe by pouring some water into its core or something.

Afterwards she felt exhausted and in strong need of some kind of stress relief. She peered frustrated around the office for something that could help her let out some steam.

Down in the basement "The almighty" analyzed Miss. Hardfakk's instructions. It was programmed to give advices and not to receive them, still, this could be the missing information it had been searching for. Maybe its earlier information had been correct? "The Almighty" begun analyzing not only the guests at the hotel, but also how the humans who operated it behaved. Did they do anything that could confirm their intentions? It started to gather data from the firework explosions, the use of the hotel propellers and the waves down below of the cliff. It was obvious that the humans were trying to make something happen and of course it felt obliged to assist, but what were the humans trying to achieve? "The almighty" begun analyzing the vibrations and placement of the hotel, into the equation it drew the extinction and evacuation of other forms of wildlife from the area. Now it only needed to determine what the intention behind it all was. It hummed its way back to the interpretation of the guests staying at the hotel. There had to be a purpose and therefore common sense behind it all and then of course a solution.

Riding the elevator up from the beach, Fernandez's wife got a glimpse of her husband exiting the other beach elevator over at the other side of the hotel. The sight made her quickly withdraw from the windows, she didn't want to risk her husband seeing her, and have him waiting for her outside the elevator when she got off. He was about the last person she wanted to see right now.

When the sandstorm had hit the beach, she'd sought shelter inside the surf booth, where all the surf equipment was, together with the surf-instructor. There, one thing had soon led to another, and the surf-instructor had fucked her hard from behind up against a surfboard covered wall until they both came. The young instructor had then given her his mobile number, just in case any of them wanted to give or receive any more lessons during her stay at the hotel. She could still taste the salty flavor of the surf-instructor's sweat in her mouth and smell the scent of him and his fluids on her skin.

Carefully, so not to be spotted by Fernandez, she got out of the elevator. She looked again over towards the other elevator and caught eye of her husband as he was walking in the direction of the lobby entrance. Discretely, she followed him at a distance.

Having gotten inside the lobby, Fernandez seemed to change his mind about where he was going. She could see him turn away from the suite elevators and instead walk over to the reception desk, before he continued into the corridor leading to the hotel staff's offices.

Fernandez's wife hurried out the main entrance, and then ran around the corner of the hotel to where the offices were located. There she started systematically looking in through one window after the other, hoping that she would get a glimpse of what her husband was up to.

Most of the beach guests rushed directly to their suites for a shower and change of clothes, after having been sandblasted and torpedoed down at the beach. It was also soon time for lunch.

In the hotel's giant kitchen, the chefs were casting suspicious glances at each other, while intense whispering was currently taking place among the different, newly conformed, fragile alliances.

The American chefs were suspecting the Korean chefs of having stolen one of their recipes, and they were trying to provoke them into admitting that they might have it. In return, the Koreans threatened to bombard all the food with pepper if the Americans followed through with any of their threats.

The Russian chefs were way past drunk, and had begun turning the main gas valve on and off for fun, while they were trying to sell their station, inclusive the main valve, to the highest bidder. The Italian chefs had both had to be thoroughly bandaged, after having accidentally, lightly stabbed and cut one another when showing off some of the new knife-skills they'd picked up watching the Steven Seagal clips on the internet.

In the background of the currently developing conflicts, the rest of the chefs were trying to avoid and conquer. There was a friendly atmosphere, as that of a gunpowder keg just waiting for the fuse to be lit, in the large kitchen.

Fernandez had decided to stop by the hotel manager's office to complain about the sandstorm down at the beach. Weren't they aware of how extremely important the eye sight of a professional athlete was? His sight was equally as important as his legs and feet, and possibly even as the rest of his body.

He marched angrily up to the door with a nameplate stating; Hotel Manager, on it, and knocked aggressively, before he just opened the door and entered without waiting for an answer.

Joselyn was taken completely by surprise, first by the hard, almost violent, knocking on her door, and then by suddenly having the angry man from breakfast standing in the middle of her office. But, she was obviously not as surprised as the man himself.

Fernandez had barged into the manager's office and halted right in front of the desk. Now, he was standing with his mouth halfway open, both in surprise, and because he'd been about to say something about the fucking sandstorm. But, the sight of the hotel manager sitting behind her desk, with her skirt pulled up around her waist and her long muscled legs stretched out on top of the desk, had instantly muted him. He was suddenly horny and angry at the same time.

Joselyn had expected that the angry man at some point would visit her office, she could recognize a player when she saw one, but she was still surprised by the rude way he'd just barged in. Now, he'd clearly entered into the typical, incapacitated state men so often found themselves in when faced with a really sexy, half naked woman. Despite him being a guest, she decided she had nothing to lose by stretching her rules a little and have sex with him anyway. After all, he was kind of scruffy sexy, like an athlete who'd peaked and was well on his way into a rough-style-of-living maturity. And, not to forget, she would enjoy punishing his inflated personality.

She got up from her chair and walked over to him while she effectively unbuttoned her blouse. Since the first three buttons were already undone, it didn't take her long.

Fernandez watched the woman coming towards him while removing her blouse, and it immediately brought him out of his trance-like state. He vaguely noticed that the she was still wearing her skirt around her waist before he tore of his shirt and pulled down his slacks. As soon as she was within reach, he grabbed her head between his hands and pushed her down towards his erection, which was eagerly reflecting his lust.

Fuck! Joselyn felt how the man's hands were pushing her head down towards his penis, was the guy really expecting her to blow him? And even to blow him before he'd done anything for her?

She began fighting him. There was no way it was going to happen, at least not the way he wanted.

He'd gotten her down on one knee, but her thigh muscles brought her up to an upright position again. Then they both began struggling to get their way, ending up in a wrestling match around the office where they were both trying to climb on top of each other.

Fernandez was horny and confused. What the fuck was wrong with this woman? If she hadn't been so damn sexy, and he hadn't been so incredibly horny, he would have punched her, but for the moment he restricted himself to continuing trying to get her head down to his erection. She was surprisingly strong, and he started sweating from the effort.

Standing outside the hotel manager's office windows, Fernandez's wife was carefully, so not to be spotted, filming the scenario taking place inside the office with her mobile phone, but she was far from sure about what it was she was actually seeing. She'd expected to film her adulteress husband having sex. Instead, it looked like he and the hotel manager had begun some sort of weird, half-naked wrestling exercise, and if it hadn't been for the partial nudity, she would have thought they were fighting to kill one another.

Suddenly, the pair inside both fell. It looked like the woman had managed to tip her husband over, or maybe it was the other way around? They landed hard on the floor, and then started rolling around, both trying to get a vantage grip over the other. By now, they were quite slippery from sweating, and they were panting so hard that her mobile was actually recording the sound through the small gap where the window was slightly ajar.

Joselyn was more turned on than she could remember to have been in a long time. Increasingly motivated by her own horniness, she made another effort to roll the man over, so that she would be on top. Having gotten him on his back, she quickly grabbed his erection and turned so she was facing the other way, positioning herself on top of him for a little 69.

Fernandez thought the woman had finally surrendered, and that she'd taken hold of his erection to blow him. He relaxed a bit and waited as she placed herself the wrong way on top of him. He expected to feel her mouth around his penis at any moment. Instead, the next thing he felt was her thighs squeezing the sides of his head, and then her wet vagina being rubbed against his face. Meanwhile, she closed her handle grip around his penis more and more. It started to hurt. Shit, he felt he couldn't breathe. It frustrated and scared him, and it also made him really, really angry.

Was the guy actually trying to hit her? Joselyn felt how the man obviously was trying to punch her ass and thighs. His slapping only made her even hornier, and she rubbed and squeezed the man with all the strength she had left until she felt triumphant as the orgasm rode through her body.

The last thing Fernandez felt was deep anger and rage as he realized he'd just been sort of violated, practically raped, and then he blacked out.

Outside the office windows Fernandez's wife was wondering whether or not it was a fact that her husband had actually just been murdered right in front of her very eyes, and how much she would inherit if he really was dead. She was also wondering how much her recording of the murder would be worth to the paparazzi, and how she could make money on it without having to admit that she was the one who'd shot the film.

She continued filming as the woman, who'd just strangled her husband, seemingly dried off her crotch on his face and then got up. Then she leaned back down towards his face and put her ear above his mouth, obviously to listen for his breath.

Joselyn was slightly relieved to hear the man breathing. He would be just fine again, and if she was right about what type of man he was, he wouldn't dare to do anything in regards to what had just happened when he woke up.

She took hold of his pants, which was still lying around his ankles, and pulled them back up, and then she found his shirt and helped him on with that as well.

After having first checked that the corridor outside her office was clear of any hotel staff, she dragged the man out into the corridor. Then she went back into the office and got dressed herself before she called for the hotel's medical staff.

"It seems one of our guests has passed out from the heat and possible fatigue. I found him just outside my office. He was probably on his way to seek help. Please bring him back to his suite and follow up on that he's doing okay."

Joselyn sat down in her chair and stretched out her legs. She felt satisfied and relaxed. Being a hotel manager might not be so boring after all. She checked her messages, but everything seemed to be running smoothly at the hotel again. The stupid super computer with its malfunctioning A.I seemed to be working with the task of improving, since it status showed that it was analyzing how to proceed with satisfaction. Joselyn decided she would write a report to the owners, explaining that they would need to consider investing in a wind-wall, or something similar, down at the beach, to prevent their guests from being inconvenienced by the occasional, local sandstorm. After all, being a professional meant taking care of your duties.

Fernandez's wife watched as the hotel manager dressed and then dragged her husband out into the corridor. It was probably a cover up, and she was excited to find out what the woman would do to dispose of his body. Then she overheard the woman's phone conversation, and for a moment she felt a sting of grief as she realized that her husband was alive and that he would probably be fine.

Feeling a little down that Fernandez wasn't dead after all, she left her position outside of the office windows, but, as she made her way back to the suite, her mood soon rose. The recording she now had on her mobile would ensure her a lot of money when she divorced Fernandez, and, in addition, it would severely humiliate him. Had he been dead, the humiliation wouldn't have been possible.

As she walked, she called her manager-lover to discuss how to best use the evidence she'd just collected.

Flavio had, unlike most of the other beach guests, not gone directly to his suite after the sandstorm incident. Instead he'd stopped by the hotel shop by the main entrance. He wanted to check if the shop by any chance sold the same kind of tight pants that the Norwegian man was always wearing. Pants like that would simply look magnificent on his lover, but, unfortunately, the shop didn't sell anything even close to resembling the Norwegian's pants.

On his way from the shop to the suite elevators, Flavio saw two of the hotel's medical staff carrying a person on a stretcher. From what he could see, it appeared to be the man who earlier had been so agitated when he spoke to the concierge with the bruised throat, and when he looked closer, it seemed like the man on the stretcher was suffering from a sore and swollen throat and neck area, it was almost identical to the symptoms he'd seen the concierge have. Flavio decided he had to take great care. It could appear like something contagious was slowly spreading among the hotel's guests and staff. He would now definitely make sure to stay far away from the bag of potato flour he'd received from the concierge.

FEEDING TIME

It was lunch time. Most of the guests were hungry, and maybe just a little exhausted after their not so relaxing time down at the beach.

Lunch was offered both inside, in the same room as the breakfast, as well as outside, on one of the dining islands. At each location there were set up two large buffet tables, all with an almost unbelievable abundance of different dishes stacked and beautifully arranged on them.

Waiters, dressed in crisp, new uniforms, stood at attention in both areas ready to cater to any wish and request their guests might have.

Inside, the air conditioning made a low humming sound, as it continuously worked to control the air temperature, keeping it at an acceptable level for the room's visiting humans and their food.

Outside, small birds and insects were exposed to a last minute spray of insecticides in the air around their areas, as a lethal warning to stay away while the food-chain's VIPs ate their lunch exactly where it suited them the most.

"The Almighty" registered that the evacuation of other life forms were almost completely done by the humans and it hummed excitedly as it now seemed the solution was all about timing. It was no perfectly clear what the humans intended to do and "The almighty" felt confident it would be able to help them achieve a satisfactory result.

Dagny was among the first to arrive for lunch. After having been at the beach, she'd spent the time until lunch soaking in the suite's deluxe bathtub. The traumatic experience of the sandstorm had made her feel that she deserved some proper pampering, so she'd ordered up an ice cream while she bathed. When the waiter bringing up the ice cream arrived, she'd shouted for him to come in to the bathroom and give her the ice cream there.

The waiter had unquestionably been very attracted to her natural beauty, and had barely been able to control himself there he'd been standing with his mouth halfway open and just staring at her. To please him, and give him an extra, special tip for his service, she'd granted him a view of one of her thighs together with a small peek at her breasts as she on purpose, accidentally, lifted them above the bubbles in the tub as she accepted the ice cream.

The waiter had been so appreciative of her gesture that he hadn't even wanted to wait for her to get him another tip. He'd just sprung out of the bathroom, carrying a look of what could only be described as sheer joy on his face. She assumed he'd run straight off to his buddies to brag about what he'd seen. That was just the nature of how men worked.

Seeing the two bountiful buffet tables, Dagny approached the nearest one and began loading plates with an efficiency that would have made any professional excavator jealous. This time, she carried her plates over to one of the small tables. She didn't want her lunch to be disturbed by any admirers, after all; lunch was one of the most important meals of the day, that was, of course, in addition to the other meals!

Working on the other buffet table inside, Gunther and his son would have made the professional excavator change his career had he rather been focusing on them. Like experts they were dissecting and removing the best and most delicious parts of the different dishes. They were working in deep concentration, resembling two doctors performing complicated, emergency surgery, if one only disregarded the fact that they were both wearing stained, Hawaiian shirts and flowery shorts.

The amount of stains on their shirts were increasing at a high rate, seeing as how sampling of the food, meanwhile they were serving themselves, was obviously part of their operation technique.

The waiters working inside had for safety reasons made a

tactical withdrawal into one of the corners of the room. None of them wanted to risk accidentally getting in the way of any of the three large guests who seemed to be performing some kind of advanced assault-dance around the buffet tables. Their work-insurance didn't cover them either getting stomped on or being stabbed by a fork out of control.

At the dining island outside, Johan was sitting together with the nice Italian. They were both laughing as they once again were looking through the pictures on his mobile phone of him doing different types of sport.

Johan felt relaxed and happy together with the Italian man. He was clearly almost as sports interested as himself, but, at the same time, he was obviously much less knowledgeable about every type of sports. Suddenly, he became aware that the sexy, African woman had arrived, and he watched her as she seated herself alone at a table not far from them. In an attempt to get her to notice him, he began talking extra loud to the Italian while showing him the pictures one more time from the beginning.

Flavio was happy. He'd never met anyone quite like the loudmouthed Norwegian. True, he wasn't as young or attractive as his current lover, but he obviously still took great care of his body, and showed a great pride in whatever he did and achieved. Why he'd now suddenly started shouting at him when he spoke, he would have to try to figure out later. The man seemed to be full of so many small and big surprises that it was never boring when he was around, and then there were his beautiful pictures of himself in tights. He would have to ask him if he could have copies of them as a momentum of their new and, hopefully, long lasting friendship.

Ophelia was comparing pictures of the new model Bentley versus the new Mercedes on her mobile. The Bentley would undoubtedly make her look better. She tried zooming in on some of the pictures to see details of the car's interior. To be discrete, while sitting at the dining table, she'd held the phone in her lap underneath the table, but, trying to look at the pictures like that, felt as an awkward operation because her breasts were directly in her line of sight. She gave up on being discrete and instead placed her elbows on the table as she continued studying the pictures. She would have to get her father to buy her one of those new smartphones with a larger screen when she got the bigger breasts. But for now, the sun was shining, and life was good. Only, it would have been better if that stupid man, sitting some tables behind her, had stopped shouting.

Ophelia waved one of the waiters over to her table, and then followed her father's example by just ordering what would have been the most expensive thing on the menu. When the waiter explained to her that she would have to use the room service menu if she wanted to order a la carte, since the lunch served only consisted of the food on the buffet tables, she felt annoyed, but then quickly instructed the waiter to rather go and get her the most expensive things from the buffet.

Fernandez's wife had seated herself some tables away from the African woman she'd met at the gym.

Before lunch, she'd stopped by the suite and changed into a short skirt with a low waist and a revealing top. In front of her, an elegant salad was laying invitingly on the plate, but for the time being she wasn't paying any attention to it. Impatiently, she was waiting for her lover-manager to send her a text message about what to do with the video she'd shot of her husband's weird sex play. She hoped he would soon send her the: all-clear, to pass it on to one of the paparazzi.

Mugade arrived at the outside dining area and went over to join his daughter.

He soon felt extremely frustrated by the loudmouth sitting together with the Italian man close by. The loudmouth made it difficult, if not impossible, to currently approach the Italian and find out if he, in fact, really was his new contact. Then his daughter started nagging him about how a Bentley would be so much more appropriate as her new car instead of the Mercedes.

Wei had changed his strategy from breakfast, and had arrived as one of the last for lunch. He'd cast a quick glance at the outside dining area, and after having seen that the sun was shining from such an angle that the shade from the umbrellas weren't very effective, he'd chosen to have lunch inside.

Seeing the two mauled buffet tables with only leftovers remaining on them, he'd at first thought that all the other guests had been inside and helped themselves to food before moving outside to eat, but after having observed the three persons still sitting in the room eating, he concluded that there had to be some sort of eating competition going on.

Wei searched the sparse buffet tables and eventually found some food that had hidden underneath some healthy salad, and therefore probably escaped the trio. He put the food on his plate and sat down at one of the tables close by the competitors to see who would win.

Focusing on the contest in intense, violent eating helped Wei momentarily forget about his own lack of achievements.

Both inside and outside, the waiters were somewhat puzzled by why all the guests seemed to be so hung up on only having bottled water, since the ice cubes in all the drinks they were pouring in themselves as their main source of fluid intake, were made from tap water.

In the hotel's giant kitchen, the chefs had all agreed on a fragile truce while they ate their lunches at their respective cooking stations.

High above the guests and waiters in the dining areas and the chefs in the hotel's giant kitchen, two of the hotel guests had no idea, and couldn't care less, about what was taking place below them. The two were Fernandez and Mubasher.

On their way up, carrying Fernandez to his suite, one of the medical staff had suddenly gloatingly recognized their patient. As soon as they'd put his unconscious body down on the bed in the suite, they'd jumped at the opportunity to get some revealing pictures of the famous Golden Bald Gomez in his current, exposed condition, thinking they could easily sell them to the media later and make some extra money. Fernandez's sunburned bald spot on the top of his head, combined with the red-purple-ish, chainlike bruise around his neck, made for some excellent motives.

After the photo session they superficially examined him, just to make sure that he was still breathing, but otherwise they did little else before they left.

The chokehold Fernandez had been subject to, in combination with the steroids he'd taken earlier in the morning and the impressive amount of drinks he'd had down at the beach, would have him flat out for several hours.

Mubasher had just finished having sex with the mistress who won the fight. The one who lost, had suffered some injuries, and had been brought down to the hotel's medical room by one of his bodyguards. He was now sitting on his balcony, feeling quite exhausted after the sex. His mistress had been riding him forever. Obviously, she hadn't understood what kind of effect Viagra had on his penis, and that his erection would last for a very long time. She'd been waiting for his penis to, at some point, go limp, showing her that he'd been satisfied.

He'd been both irritated and impressed by the young woman's stamina. The way she'd been able to ride him for so long, after just having fought the other mistress, really proved that she was the appropriate winner. At least some of his countrymen, or rather countrywomen, knew how to appreciate him and properly show their gratitude towards him.

Mubasher thought about how a new and bigger gold statue, maybe one of him naked, showing his mighty, erected penis, could, and most likely would, help to make the rest of his people appreciate him more. Then he came to think about how much work had been involved with the last statue he'd had made and gave up on the idea. Instead, he asked his winning mistress to pose naked for him on the balcony to make the view more interesting, but, of course, after she'd first filled up his champagne glass. Mubasher vaguely heard the suite's telephone ringing, and instructed his mistress to get his other bodyguard, the one who was standing outside guarding the door, to have him answer the telephone, and then for her to hurry back and continue posing. When the bodyguard finally picked up the phone, Mubasher could hear by his answer that it was the hotel manager calling. It was probably regarding some invitation to a, doubtlessly, stressful event that he would have to politely decline to attend at.

THE FLUFFY STUFFY ANIMALS' JOY CLUB

One of the advertised attractions in the hotel's brochure was the fashionable and state of the art entertainment area, where there would be offered a variety of shows for both children and adults. The advertisement also claimed that some of the children-shows, in fact, were going to be entertaining and possibly educational for adults as well.

Since there wasn't much else going on at the hotel in the hours between lunch and dinner, and because the hotel had been strategically located a far distance away from any other offers of entertainment to keep the guests from spending any of their money outside of the hotel's premises, most of the guests found their way to the brochure-reputed area for the post-lunch entertainment.

They must be Swedish or something... Early twenties, maybe? I really don't know anything about them, Joselyn thought as she observed the blond pair working with the hotel's children entertainment. She'd met up by the stage in the entertainment area to see to it that the pair began the show the way they were supposed to and according to the time schedule.

There were so many employees at the hotel that, even though she'd obviously registered most of them, she'd not yet had the time to closely inspect them all. She would need to check if these two were also hired to do any other jobs at the hotel.

The pair looked like they'd just crawled out from a stone hut in a small and primitive village somewhere in Scandinavia, and they behaved as though they'd really seen the sun before. Every time she'd been jogging on one of her inspection rounds, as long as the sun was up, she'd seen both of them sunbathing, regardless of the time of day or how high, or low, the temperature had been.

Nevertheless, the young man of the pair definitely had, despite his scruffiness, the right looks to qualify as a potential office-romance candidate. In general, she wasn't really into blonde guys, but the current lack of other potential fuck-worthy men at the hotel, made her willing to slightly lower her demands and make some minor adjustments to her preferences, at least until she found some new employees to hire. The small séance she'd had with the guest had definitely only been a one-time affair.

Come to think of it, hadn't she recently read somewhere that Scandinavian men weren't as virile as men from many other countries? Maybe it would be better for her to just put the whole thing off until Monday, when she could get hold of some new employees? After all, she'd just had her way with that rude guest, and he had sort of satisfied her needs for the day. But still, there was the whole day tomorrow to consider and plan for.

Joselyn's wristwatch struck the hour, and she could see the Swedish pair start hopping and fooling around on stage dressed up in their bear costumes. Content everything was working satisfactory, if ever so childish, she left the entertainment area to go to her office to prepare for the evening's happenings.

They'd just been fucking like bunnies backstage, or probably more like Care-Bears, the way they were dressed. Of course, the care-part hadn't really been any part of the fucking, and the red finger marks, where papa bear had been holding mama bear while fucking her from behind, were still glowing on mama bears neck.

Up on stage, mama bear adjusted her bear-head as it once again almost fell off. That happening would have clearly showed off the red marks on her neck, and that, of course, wouldn't have been very child-friendly. Inside the head, it smelled of sweat and some other sweet, synthetic scent. She'd been sweating hard during the fucking, and the warm bear-outfit now gave her a feeling of being trapped inside a very small, smelly and hot sauna. Papa bear patted her back, as a signal for them to change their seemingly random jumping into a more synchronized jumping, in tune with some irritating, but popular children's song.

The seats in front of the stage were mostly empty, except for a few adults, who were already looking bored, and a fat child, wearing a snot- and food-stained, ugly shirt.

Mama bear could feel how papa bear's sperm was running down the inside of her thigh as she jumped around on stage. Fuck it, so what? Mama bear thought. If anyone noticed anything through the suit, the kid would probably think mama bear had to pee, and the parents would just assume it was sweat and feel sorry for her. She hoped papa bear had remembered to close his bear suit's zipper before they entered the stage. Even though the adult audience did look as though they were the kind of people who would have enjoyed the backstage show more than the stupid jumping currently going on, and like they would have preferred watching papa bear's penis flapping around, rather than it being restrainedly zipped in. The last alternative would at least have been preferred by the two women and one of the men in the audience, mama bear concluded when she took a closer look at them. The, indisputably, gay man was sitting with a very noticeable, even at the distance from the stage, bulge in his tights.

The fat child, sitting in-between the adults, was pointing one of his chubby sausage fingers at her, as if he was shooting her with the buggers that were probably stuck to it. Mama bear truly hated children, and she hated the smelly, hot bear costume. As she continued jumping and wishing for the show to end, she kicked more viciously about herself. How they were going to be able to keep this up through the whole season, she had no idea.

Gunther was watching the bear show. It being part of the hotel's entertainment offer, and he being a paying guest at the hotel, he wouldn't risk missing a single thing that he'd paid for. Also, it seemed Jurgen-Gunther was having fun. He was playing bear-hunter, or some other macho shooting game. Gunther looked around, weren't there supposed to be served beverages and some kind of snacks during such shows? Even if they'd just finished lunch, it felt far too long to have to wait all the while until dinner before they had something to eat again.

Johan was eagerly watching the stage. He imagined himself being inside one of the costumes doing the jumping. But, he would of course do it with far more finesse and vigor than the two currently messing about on stage. He would have been the center of everyone's attention, and the women watching would all have wanted to have sex with him.

After having looked more careful at the bear outfits, he decided that his outfit should have been tighter. It would have looked much better with tights and just the bear-head. That way, the audience would have gotten the chance to admire how his thigh muscles flexed when he stylishly jumped around, bent and stretched on stage.

Johan had to look twice, but he was certain that one of the bears was actually sweating through the suit in the crotch area. He stared at the stain. Of course, if the sweating person in the bear costume had instead been wearing a pair of black tights, the stain wouldn't have been visible at all. It could have been a sort of black-bear. Did they call it black-bear in English?

He turned to the Italian sitting next to him, and at the same time he had to adjust his legs a little further apart because his ball-sack stitches were stinging a little as he changed position. He wanted to share what he'd been thinking about, after all, the Italian did seem to both really appreciate and share his interest in tight clothing.

Mugade felt frustrated because he hadn't gotten any opportunity to approach the Italian man during lunch. It seemed the loudmouthed, tights fanatical man was constantly by his side, and to him, this all meant that he wasn't selling as much drugs as he could have done. Every hour passing without him achieving to make contact and finalize the details around their business deal entailed pure losses. He both could and should have been making more money.

Mugade had only gone to the show to see if an opportunity presented itself for him to start talking to the Italian man, but now, seeing how that blond leech of a man was still clinging himself to his contact, it was clear that he would have no such luck, and his frustration rose even further. To calm himself down, he did what he usually did whenever he felt such frustration. He retrieved his laptop from its bag - he never went anywhere without it - and started going over the figures he was making before he took a look at the status of his different business franchises in general. One thing that usually always made him relaxed and happy was seeing how much money he was making on his dating websites. It seemed Europe was a bottomless pond, filled with horny, needy, elderly people.

Both his female- and male dating profiles were so popular that he had to have a couple of guys employed full time just to answer all the requests the profiles received. It was his No. 11 and No. 12 who currently did this job.

Mugade logged into some of the profiles to see how the two numbers were performing at their job. He wanted to control how they answered any requests, and if they were making as much money as possible on the business.

The usual profile set-up consisted of a picture of a local, young, black, female beauty, followed by an emotional text, first explaining how she, as the innocent victim of some tragic incident, found herself to be in some kind of severe financial distress, and secondly how she, obviously only by pure coincidence, loved and was attracted to elderly, wealthy, white men.

For the male profiles he would use pictures of models he and his two numbers found on the internet. Like the females, they would similarly have experienced some severe trauma leaving them very lonely and in financial distress, and they of course were, on their side, seeking to get to know kind, loving and wealthy elderly women.

As Mugade went through the profiles, he noticed one where the profile's inbox showed that no reply had been sent to one of the messages. He looked more closely at the profile and recognized it at once. It was actually one of the profiles he, himself, had set up, using a picture of a semi-famous, black, male model.

The unanswered message was from a woman somewhere in Europe, and if he remembered correctly, it was in fact also he who had and answered the woman on a previous occasion. If he wasn't mistaking, she was from a country called Norway. He read the message in the inbox. It was a steaming, passionate message where the woman first told the profile about how beautiful and sexy he was, and then about how she was currently in a loveless marriage, but that she was soon to be divorced, and that she hoped they could get together then. She was more than willing to buy a plane ticket for the profile to come to Norway - Mugade grinned for himself - or she could herself travel to Italy, where the profile was supposedly living, so they could finally meet each other face to face there.

Mugade still hadn't been able to shake off the frustration he was feeling about the money he was currently loosing, so he decided he would answer the woman to see if he couldn't at least fool her into transferring some money to one of his accounts. How much could he ask for to buy a ticket?

He answered the woman in an equally steaming and passionate tone as hers, claiming how he simply loved and worshipped voluptuous, Scandinavian women, but that, so very sadly, it would be very difficult for him to leave Italy to go to Norway for the moment because his grandmother was severely sick, and so on. He then continued to explain how the profile would have to travel quite far, both by bus and ferry, to reach an airport offering any flights with connections to Norway, and that it for sure would entail several flight changes for him to get there.

Mugade finished the message by writing that the large costs involved, with all of the traveling necessary for his profile to do to possibly get to Norway, would of course be far too much and too expensive for her to be bothered to help him with. He then reviewed the message, and just to be sure, he went back and also added a sick sister to take care of. Then he pushed send and instantly felt a little better. Now, some money, not previously being made, would soon be made.

Flavio was watching the jumping bear show with joy. He wasn't sure, but it could very easily be two men inside the costumes. To him, their jumping resembled a sort of plump ballet, and he really liked ballet. He simply loved the athletic skills and the stamina the ballet dancers would show.

There could perhaps be a woman inside one of the costumes, but he wasn't bothered by it. After all, he had made love to a lot of women in his younger days. She could have just kept the costume on, only slightly opened the zipper and bent forwards, and then he would have almost enjoyed it, maybe…

Flavio was more sexually aroused than he could remember having been in a long time. Spending time with the alluring, Norwegian man, had made him realize that there were still a lot of unknown beauty out there in the world to be discovered and have sex with.

He wished the two dancers on stage had been dressed in some nice, tight, ballet tricots instead of the bulky bear costumes. He turned to the Norwegian to share his opinion, and found, to his delightful surprise, that the Norwegian was already looking at him.

Dagny's mobile vibrated in her purse. Having dug through some layers of different types of - according to the wrappers - healthy candy, she found her mobile and read the message. It was a notification saying that her dating site profile had received a new message. She logged into her account from her phone, and read the message before she looked at the picture of the man who'd sent it. It was the attractive, young, muscular, black man, that she'd wanted from the moment she saw his profile picture on the site. After she'd also read through his profile, and learned about how much he loved his family and struggled to take care of them, and how all the hard work he had to do had made him end up being single, she'd found herself being sad and extremely horny at the same time.

Now, he had sent an answer to her last message, and, in addition to everything else, it was evident that he was also a gentleman. Taking care of his severely sick grandmother, and also - Dagny had to blow her nose - his sick sister like that. She looked at his picture again. The thought of how grateful he would be to get the chance to enjoy a woman such as herself, a woman with both money and delicious curves, made her feel a sudden urge to immediately divorce Johan. She would have to tell him that she was leaving him, as soon as possible.

Dagny wrote a message back to the black Adonis and told him that she was ready for him. She also included asking how much money he would need for all the traveling he would have to do to manage to get to Norway, and to where she should transfer the funds. After a short moment of thought, she added her phone number, and then she sent the message. Immediately afterwards she regretted not having added something teasing and a little dirty in the text. Maybe something like; if he enjoyed giving massages, how she enjoyed receiving them. She would have to include some of her sexy ideas the next time she wrote to him. The thought of how he would react when he finally got to read about her desires, made her feel better at once.

Wei was sitting in the front row, watching the bear show and wondering why it seemed most of the others were sitting in the rows further back. Did the rows further back have a better view, or better seats? Normally, at concerts and such, the most expensive seats were the ones in the front and closest to the stage, but maybe all the others knew something he didn't?

And why were everybody else dressed so casual? He had after careful consideration chosen a full dark suit and a festive bow tie for the occasion, but the other guests were simply wearing shirts and shorts or light summer dresses.

Wei noticed a sexy lady, also properly attired in a suit, standing by the side of the stage. At first the sight made him happy, but then he recognized that the lady had to be of some Asian descent, maybe half Asian, and he realized that she in fact was one of the hotel's employees just wearing her uniform. His own outfit then made him feel even more alienated than before. How come everybody else seemed so comfortable in what they were wearing? As if they all knew exactly what to wear at all times?

The guy in tights was sitting some chairs away from him. He could of course wear tights everywhere he went, filling them out nicely as he did any time of the day. Had his brother been there, he would probably have filled the tights out just as nice.

Wei looked around, studying once more what all the other guests were wearing and how they behaved. He'd expected there to be karaoke-nights in a classy hotel like this, but he felt he couldn't ask anyone if they knew whether or not there actually would be karaoke offered at some time later, without letting them know that they knew more than him about such things. He felt inadequate. He just knew that everybody else knew more than him, not just about which seats were the best, what to wear and the karaoke, but about all things in general.

Wei noticed the probably famous and successful, sexy, blonde woman sitting alone in one of the seats all the way in the back. She was looking at her mobile and laughing at something. Maybe it was her husband texting her something funny and clever about promising to make it to the next show in his casual and elegant clothes.

Fernandez's wife had just sent another picture of her vagina to her manager-lover. It had been easy taking the picture, even though she was in public, sitting all alone on the back row like she was. Even if her husband had woken up by now, the stupid, useless children show was something he would never go to, so she felt safe in her place and was able to relax while using her mobile.

She received a picture of her manager-lover's erection in

return, and the background behind the erected penis made her laugh. It was one of the afternoon's papers, fronting pictures of her naked husband being strangled by a pair of muscled, female thighs. The woman's face wasn't shown, but her husband's face could be seen perfectly. Even the bald patch on top of his head was clearly visible with its almost glowing shine, as if it was really sunburned. Life felt good!

She took a couple of more pictures of her vagina and sent them back to her manager-lover. Afterwards she sent the same pictures to the surf-instructor, and at the same time asked him if he wanted to hook up later in the evening in the surf booth down at the beach.

Now, all that remained was sending the actual movie of Fernandez and the woman to the press, not just some selected pictures. She felt a bit impassioned by having to wait, but to send out small teasers first, like the pictures, always helped to work up the public's and the press' interest.

Up in his suite, Mubasher was getting dressed. It had been an exhausting day, but still, he'd felt obliged to accept the hotel manager's offer of having his dinner down at the hotel restaurant. At least she'd promised him a closed off and private area.

In addition, he'd also felt compelled to agree to attend the evening's concert with the famous, Italian singer: Flavio Balducci. Supposedly, it was to be the singer's final, farewell concert. Maybe, by showing the public he attended such, the riots and general uprising among his people would calm down. Also, the fact that the hotel manager had turned out to be a very sexy woman, had played a not so insignificant part in his decision to attend. At present, he was one mistress short, and the hotel manager seemed fit enough to be able to put up a decent fight for him against his current, healthy mistress. He would just need to find a way to convince her to become a mistress instead of continuing to be a boring hotel manager, but then again, who would say no to the powerful leader of a nation? And, if anyone could, then who would say no to practically any amount of money? Mubasher felt slightly more motivated, but the feeling lasted shortly, as he realized he still had all the evening's wearying social appearances ahead of him until he maybe could relax again. He let out a loud groan followed by a sigh. It was all so stressing and inconvenient, but what didn't one do for ones people.

One of his mistresses, the one who'd won the fight since the other one had a broken arm, helped him to get his flip flops on. She first lifted his left leg and then the right one.

Mubasher looked at her and signaled her to give him a blow job while she was down there, and since he was already standing up. It would be a shame to waste the effect of the last Viagra that was still in his body, and maybe it would help motivate him to face and endure all the work the evening had waiting for him. He interrupted his mistress, who'd already set to work, and asked her to call for his other mistress before she continued. The fact that she'd broken her arm during the fight earlier didn't mean she couldn't use her mouth now.

In his suite, Fernandez was trashing everything in his path, and some of the things that weren't. He was running between the different rooms throwing and kicking anything he could get his hands or feet on. He'd already torn apart all of his wife's clothes, the TV he'd smashed into the crystal glasses that had previously been so neatly set up on the shelf behind the bar, the suite beds he'd turned upside down, and now he was currently throwing around chairs and pulling down lamps.

Eventually, Fernandez felt exhausted and sat down on the floor, but he only sat there for a moment before he again was overwhelmed with rage and continued trashing the suite. There could be cameras anywhere, and there probably were! And where was his fucking wife?

After some more intense trashing, he went into the bathroom and began mixing himself a cocktail of drugs consisting of steroids and ecstasy nicely blended with some other performance increasing and mood regulating drugs. How the drugs were actually supposed to be taken, he couldn't care less about.

The whole thing had started when he'd been woken up by his mobile, which he had soon after crushed by hurling it into the wall on the other side of the room. That fucking telephone call from his manager had been the drop that sent in him into a rage stronger than he'd ever experienced before. Apparently, there were pictures of him getting humiliated and strangled in all the evenings' newspapers.

Fernandez didn't care who'd taken the pictures, he just wanted revenge.

Down in the hotel's giant kitchen, the fragile truce between the chefs was no longer fragile, or a truce. They had all started throwing different types of food at each other.

Everything had begun when the English chefs had asked the South American chefs to pass them some avocadoes. The avocadoes, normally considered not to be among the most dangerous of fruits when thrown, as opposed to perhaps the cactus fruits or the pineapple, were suddenly thrown in ways that really hurt the ones they hit, and the normally very friendly fruits, suddenly found themselves to have been the trigger of a major food throwing war between the chefs.

THE LAST SUPPER

Two of the hotel's dining islands had been prepared for the evening's meal, and a very special menu had been set up.

Once Again, beautifully shaped paper lanterns had been hung strategically placed around the dining area. Their romantic, golden glow enveloped the small islands, but otherwise the areas were almost completely surrounded by pitch black darkness.

At the entrance to the islands the waiters were standing lined up at attention, and a dignified silence blanketed the area, perfecting the impression of the place.

A noisy cricket, inappropriately breaking the perfect silence, was at the last minute quieted down with a lethal dose of insecticides, and then quickly removed by a conscientious caretaker before the guests would begin to arrive.

The evening grew, if possible, even darker and more romantic as the minutes passed.

Then, suddenly, the silence was again broken. This time by the sound of dangling jewelry and shuffling flip flops as Mubasher entered the dining area.

In front of the great Dictator walked one of his bodyguards, dressed in a black suit, and behind the bodyguard followed one of his mistresses, dressed in what looked like a cheerleader outfit merged with a belly dancers' dress - both modified to fit in at a flashy strip club.

Behind the mistress, Mubasher's jewelry embellished flip flops were the source of the loud, shuffling sound, as he was dragging his feet like he couldn't be bothered, or was just too exhausted to manage to lift them high enough above the ground to make his steps fall into any normal way of walking. He was dressed in one of his silk and velvet summer uniforms, in white and dark red colors.

Behind Mubasher walked his other mistress, wearing an identical outfit to the first one, but with one arm in an embellished sling. She was regularly bending over to pick up diamantes and other precious stones that were continuously falling off the Dictator's shuffling flip flops. Following her was another of the bodyguards, who was currently focusing on little else but the mistress' ass every time she bent over to pick up a jewel. His level of attention would have made any attempt of threat or attack on Mubasher's person executed by her ass completely futile.

The specially assigned waiter stepped forward to welcome the great Dictator as he arrived, and then guided the group over to one of the islands. A thick, gold rope, in the same style as the ropes used at the entrances of only the most exclusive night clubs, hung around the island to close off the area.

Once seated on a specially brought out, soft, large and throne-like chair, Mubasher looked around the area. He was disappointed to find that he was almost completely alone, only one of the hotel's other guests, a lonely, Asian man sitting at one of the other dining islands, had been there to admire and greet him as he made his entrance. Mubasher had expected the restaurant areas to be filled with people witnessing his public and friendly appearance. At least the Asian man seemed to be staring at him, and that made him feel slightly better about the situation. Maybe the man would report to his friends, and then they would report to their friends again, about just how normal and active the great Dictator was, and how he was mingling with regular people. Anyway, there would probably soon arrive other guests to witness his presence.

The waiter opened a bottle of champagne, and filled the glasses on the table. One of the mistresses tasted the champagne before giving Mubasher a slight nod of approval. But still, to be on the safe side, he waited for a little while longer, to really make sure she hadn't been poisoned, before he started drinking himself.

Wei had decided to again arrive early for the meal. He'd wanted to make sure that he would get one of the best tables, and at the same time also be able to better observe how the other guests were treated and how they looked as they arrived. In addition, this time he hadn't wanted to be the last one to arrive in case there was another unannounced eating competition taking place.

Choosing a table had taken him quite a while since he had no idea which of the tables the other guests would have chosen as the best one. Also, one of the open dining areas had been closed off by an expensive looking rope. He'd wanted to enter that area, but as soon as he had approached the rope, a couple of the waiters had come running and politely stopped him.

Instead, he'd reluctantly sat down by a table overlooking the enclosed area, while his thoughts had started playing with him. It could be that all the other guests would be sitting in the enclosed area, and maybe that was the reason why none of them had bothered to come down early to get a good table? Or, maybe it was his brother together with his Olympic team that had arrived at the hotel, and they were of course receiving some special VIP treatment?

Wei had just started to believe that he'd figured out exactly what was going on, and he'd been moments away from moving himself to a more discreet table, where his brother and the Olympic team wouldn't be able to see him when they arrived, when the extravagant and elegant man entered the area.

He was now sitting as if he'd frozen in the position and place he was in when he first laid eyes on the admirable man. The man clearly had everything, and it was all so perfect that he considered suicide right there and then, just because he, himself, was so far away from being and having all what the man clearly was and had. The man was obviously so highly successful, that whatever he was wearing, it would be something others would immediately copy, if they could afford it.

Wei looked at the two beautiful women accompanying the man. That they loved him dearly was evident by the way they held out his chair for him, and then tasted his champagne to make sure it was good enough for him to drink. If he'd only had all what that man had, it would have been his brother, and not he, who would have been the one who was jealous.

Wei's eyes almost started to tear up as he continued admiring the perfectness of what he saw. The difference in treatment by the hotel staff was of course understandable, because this was truly a special man.

He felt sickened by the strong desire of wanting to be the other man. The man's finger jewelry made a ding, every time it hit his glass, as if it was announcing to the world that he was taking another sip of champagne. To Wei, it was the sound of importance meeting expensiveness.

Gunther and Jurgen-Gunther arrived in a hurry for dinner. As they entered the dining island, Gunther grabbed the arm of one of the waiters and escorted him over to the nearest table where he and his son sat down. "Where are the menus? We're hungry! Menus and a beer, and the beer must be German."

The waiter politely explained that the evening's menu was special, and that he would have to be excused to go and get the plate where it was written down what their choices were.

"Anything mit beef?" Gunther asked before the waiter had the time to go anywhere.

The waiter confirmed that there was a meat course on the menu.

Gunther ordered two of the meat courses, in addition to whatever appetizers were the largest ones they offered. Then he ordered some peanuts and other nuts, but not olives, before he changed his mind and asked for the olives too, as a small snack while they waited for their appetizers.

Both father and son had caught a cold, probably because the air conditioning in their suite was set to the lowest temperature possible. Gunther blew his nose in a way that would have made all the elephants in Mozambique gather around him as their leader. That was, if he'd been in Mozambique. While his son soon followed up with a trumpeting showing that he was unquestionably the next in line to lead.

Beer and a milkshake arrived shortly after together with assorted snacks, and after a few minutes the floor around

Gunther and Jurgen-Gunther's table was covered by a fine layer of escaped snacks.

Gunther lit a cigar, but then reconsidered. He rather wanted to eat some more snacks before the appetizers arrived, so he threw the cigar butt into the fish filled pond surrounding the island.

Some fishes swam eagerly to meet the butt, in a hope that it could be food, but they were bound to be disappointed.

Dagny was the next to arrive at the dining area. She'd been faster than her stupid husband, and had been the first of them to leave their suite, while he was still fumbling around with changing his diaper, or bandage, or whatever he called it. She couldn't care less.

Tonight, she was hoping that the Italian gentleman would join her again, and therefore she chose once more to sit at one of the large, social tables.

Dagny noticed that the nice, little boy traveling with his father was drinking a milkshake, and being inspired, she ordered herself one. Only a few moments later the waiter came back out carrying a pink milkshake with both a big umbrella and a party flare in it. She giggled and leaned forwards, displaying enough cleavage to dry haul a midsize to large passenger ship in, as a way of showing her gratitude to the waiter for his swift and attentive service.

The waiter serving her the milkshake would later claim that he was traumatized and temporarily snow blind when he arrived back with the other waiters.

Dagny felt special, it didn't look like the little boy's milkshake had had any flare in it. It was probably the waiter's way to show how interested he was in her. Content, she began slurping at the straw in her milkshake with such ferocity and volume that one of the hotel's caretakers came storming out to check the pond around the island to see if there was a breach somewhere.

Fernandez's wife walked slowly across the small bridge to the island. The discreet illumination of the area was all else but discreet when it illuminated her as she entered, and everyone present could clearly see that she had no underwear on.

She sat course towards the fat woman sitting alone by one of the large, social tables. If her husband by any chance should manage to come down for dinner, she didn't want to be sitting alone.

Dagny didn't notice the newly arrived woman until she sat down by her table.

She'd been busy ordering another flaring milkshake, and it was obvious that she was popular among the waiters, because, this time, they'd sent a new one. She giggled by the thought of how they must have been fighting between themselves in the kitchen to get to be the one to serve her.

Then she politely greeted the skinny woman who'd sat down across from her, while she discretely studied her face to see if any wrinkles caused by her smoking were showing.

The sweet smell of flowers had to give way to something else.

Johan still walked broad legged as if he was a cowboy, perhaps one with a broken back. The new bandage had felt quite stiff when he'd put it on, and walking around, it felt even stiffer.

The hotel's laundry service hadn't been able to return his favorite pair of tights in time before the evening's meal, so he'd ended up having to use the same pair as he'd worn for breakfast. As he'd struggled to pull them on, he'd thought they'd had a faint, musky smell about them when, so he'd compensated by showering himself in cologne. His favorite sneakers had also smelled a bit funky, so he'd doused them in cologne too before putting them on.

Arriving at the dining area, Johan at once recognized the sexy blonde from the gym. He sat his course towards her table, but then he noticed Dagny's broad, doughy shoulders, with her sagging underarms that resembled an extra pair of breasts, and he quickly changed his direction towards another table.

He sat down at a table set for four, and made sure that he was placed so that his body could be seen in profile from the entrance to the dining area. That way, if the sexy, African woman came, she would be able to see his strong, muscled thigh, and then probably be irresistibly tempted to join him at his table.

After having tried for ages to convince his lover to join him, and then probably also meet the Norwegian, Flavio had given up on trying to persuade him to come along for the evening meal.

Upon entering the dining area, Flavio instantly forgot his lover completely. The Norwegian man was obviously waiting for him, and wearing the same fantastic pants as always. He smiled broadly and headed towards his table.

Johan was happy to see the Italian man. That meant they could be talking about sports until the African woman arrived, and then she could listen to his stories together with the Italian.

Johan made sure that the Italian man seated himself on the chair next to him on the right hand side, so he wouldn't obstruct the view of him or his thigh from the entrance.

Flavio felt appreciated. The Norwegian obviously wanted him to sit close to him, the way he insisted he should take the chair by his side. As he sat down, his eyes and nose momentarily started watering, there was an awfully strong, musky odor, mixed with some other intense scents, resting heavily over the area. But soon, a fine wind blew most of the smell away, and as Flavio was able to breathe properly again, he smiled happily at the Norwegian, who'd picked up his mobile and started showing him his newest Facebook pictures.

Mugade and Ophelia entered the dining area together. They both looked exclusive and stylish, as if they should have owned the place, or as if they could have owned any place.

Mugade noticed that his latest candidate, in the running up to be his new business associate, was once again sitting together with the homosexual, loudmouthed man. It was clear that the Italian had first sat down by the table, and that he'd then been joined by the other man, who was now openly trying hard to pick him up. To his surprise, Mugade saw the homosexual man waving at him and Ophelia, as if he wanted them to join them at their table. He hadn't the faintest idea why, but this could represent the opportunity he'd been waiting for to approach the Italian.

Out of the corner of his eye, Johan saw the sexy, African woman arrive together with her father. Her father actually looked to be about the same age as him, but he could clearly remember having read an article about how age difference in relationships between men and women in African cultures often was viewed differently than in Norway, so he felt sure his age wouldn't represent any relevant issue. Also, age was of course never as relevant as fitness, and he was at least just as fit as a twenty-something, or maybe even younger, man.

Johan tried flexing his thigh as he made a choice to go for it, and waved for the sexy daughter and her father to come and join his table.

Mugade became even more surprised when he heard that the Italian and the homosexual were having a discussion, using what could only be code words, as he sat down with Ophelia at their table.

"I just didn't want to use any of it after having seen how those two men looked," the Italian said.

"Oh, but it really makes you feel much better. It's a shame if you don't get an opportunity to test it. I understand your reluctance, but you can get some of my stuff. I always bring plenty, at least two bags, anytime I travel anywhere. One time, one of my bags ruptured, and all my clothes became white. It looked as if I was a baker when you looked inside my suitcase. See, here, I have a picture of it on my Facebook page."

Mugade also bent forward to see the screen on the strange, homosexual man's mobile phone. There was a picture showing a suitcase where all the clothes clearly were covered in cocaine.

"So, are you also in the business?" Mugade tried asking the man, he understood nothing of the situation. He wouldn't under any circumstance share any of the profit with a third party, but he had difficulties understanding which of the two strange men who really was the big dog, and then also, who in fact was his new contact.

"In what business? Do you mean the workout business? Oh yes, I work-out a lot, so, among other, I use the potato flour between my butt cheeks so they won't get sore and such."

"Ah, so that's why your sweat was white at the gym this morning!" His daughter cut in.

Mugade felt irritated, the two men were obviously just regular idiots, or maybe some kind of kinky, homosexual bakers, but either way, they were still clearly idiots. Yet again he'd wasted his time when he should have been making money. He needed to find the person he was supposed to meet and somehow make up for his losses.

Ophelia wasn't sure what to think of the Italian and the sweaty, tights wearing man. It was obvious that they were lovers, but why had they waved for her and her father to join them? And was her father really interested in starting up in the bakery business?

A waiter turned up by the table, and as usual she and her father ordered what would have been the most expensive thing on the menu.

Shortly after, Ophelia and her father excused themselves to the two men and found their own table.

As the sexy woman and her father left the table, Johan felt a little disappointed, but he could understand that her father might want some alone time with her during their dinners. Also, her father had clearly felt overshadowed by him.

But, he was anyway happy since the sexy woman had finally showed some interest in him, and she'd actually seemed impressed by his clever use of the potato flour. He really felt he'd left an impression on her, and he could continue to impress her tomorrow, probably already in the morning at the gym.

Flavio felt relieved when the African pair excused themselves and left the table. It was clear that the couple for some reason had been interested in the Norwegian, but everything felt better now that he had the man's undivided attention all to himself. Also, it was soon time for his concert, and all he wanted now, before he had to go and prepare for his performance, was to relax and listen to the Norwegian talk as he showed him more pictures of himself in tights.

The thought of how surprised and impressed the Norwegian would be by his singing made Flavio both happy and horny.

After having run around between the tables at the restaurant with his arms out to his sides, playing a fighter plane, for a while, Jurgen-Gunther had been bored. Now he'd positioned himself at the edge of the pond surrounding the dining island, and armed with pebbles from one of the flowerbeds, he started throwing pebbles at the fish he could see swimming around.

One of the waiters noticed what the fat, little boy was doing by the edge of the pond. He actually couldn't care less about the fish or what the snot and food covered little boy was doing, but at the same time he didn't want to be bothered by any of the other guests complaining about getting hit by either one of the small rocks, or the splashing water.

The waiter went by the kitchen and picked up some pieces of bread before he walked over to the boy. "You know, you may upset the other guests when you throw rocks like that. If you want contact with the fish you can feed them some of this bread."

Jurgen-Gunther looked up at the waiter. He didn't want to feed the fish. He wanted to kill it! Reluctantly he accepted the bread and started eating it. The waiter had turned away from him, as someone had shouted for something, and was already hurrying back to his post. The bread tasted nothing without strawberry or chocolate topping on. Jurgen-Gunther threw the pieces of bread as hard as he could at the fishes just below the surface before he returned to his father for some more dessert. The bread the waiter had given him had made him realize how hungry he still was. He hurried back to his father, and together they studied the evening's special menu to see what kinds of desserts were available.

Up in his suite, after having finished mixing his drug cocktail and then ordered room service, making sure his order would be placed outside the door when it was delivered, so the waiter wouldn't see the destruction of the room, Fernandez made a couple of decisions.

First, he would enter the drug business, just like he'd been considering to do from the moment he'd heard about the great business deal, but hadn't been completely sure of because he had his career to think of. Secondly, he would take some kind of revenge on both the hotel manager and his wife.

To begin with, he would take his drug cocktail to calm himself down, and to better be able to come up with a plan on how to execute his revenge. Then he would go downstairs to find out who his drug supplier was and to look for the two women.

Down in the giant kitchen, the chefs had run out of food and other groceries to throw at each other.

The Korean chefs had for a while been threatening to throw their largest frying pan, but then the American chefs had countered by throwing one of theirs instead, and claimed that it was only meant to prevent the Koreans from actually throwing theirs.

The frying pan missed the Koreans and instead hit one of the African chefs, who immediately retaliated by throwing a special lobster casserole back at the Americans, claiming that their miss had been racially motivated.

Soon all the other chefs also started hurling whatever they had of cutlery and cooking supplies at whoever they could.

Joselyn appeared in front of the dining area's main entrance with a microphone in her hand, and looked strikingly sexy in a black outfit that sparkled in the dim lights. Her skirt seemed even shorter than the ones she usually wore, and her dark, deep cut, suit jacket seemed to cling to the sides of her breasts, making them almost even more noticeable than if she'd been naked.

"My dear guests, I hope you're all satisfied after this evening's special meal! And if you would now all be so kind and follow me over to the concert arena, I have an exceptional surprise for you."

Joselyn took a deep breath, perfectly aware of the effect it had on her already sexy figure. She also tightened her leg muscles and changed her position slightly, knowing that her high heels would accentuate the well sculpted shape of her calves.

"Some of you might already know that we have some very famous guests staying with us here at the hotel this weekend, and I'm proud to be able to point to you that one of them is the world famous singer Flavio Balducci, who, to our great joy, has accepted to hold an intimate and very special concert just for our hotel's exceptional guests. That means all of you!"

Mubasher was to go in the lead of the procession of hotel guests over to the concert area. He and his entourage were solemnly guided out from the closed off island where they'd been eating by two of the waiters.

Mubasher's stomach was full of lobster, some soufflés and plenty of champagne, and his mood was good, even though he obviously had to walk all the way over to wherever the concert was taking place. His bodyguards carried with them his special, large, soft and throne-like chair, while his mistresses were busy collecting the jewelry that were dropping like little, shining poops behind him, as he shuffled forwards.

Halfway to the concert area the procession had to make a stop as Mubasher had suddenly realized that he, instead of walking, rather could be carried by his entourage on his comfortable chair the rest of the way. Once his mistresses had assisted him in properly seating himself on his throne-like chair, the procession could once again commence.

Dagny still hadn't finished eating her dinner when the hotel manager appeared by the entrance and started to speak. Learning about the concert, she hastily got the waiter to bring her a doggy bag for her remaining food and one extra bag with some dessert.

As the procession left for the concert area, Gunther and his son brought with them their plates with the cakes they'd ordered. There was one piece of every type of cake that had been available on the menu on each of their plates. Gunther had learned from his previous mistake of assuming that food and drinks would be served during the hotel's shows, and he would most definitely not be made into a fool twice.

Johan was very surprised to hear that the nice Italian man was a famous singer, and he immediately began looking through his phone to see if he had any pictures of the two of them together, so he could post it on his Facebook page and other sharing communities where it was sure to be seen.

Wei was trying to cut in the procession line to get as close to the fabulous and impressive man with the entourage as possible. He finally made it to the front of the line, and didn't care what the other guests thought of his behavior. To him it was crystal clear that it was the man in front who was the important one, above, not just him, but all of the guests.

When most of the other guest had left their tables and lined up in the procession, Mugade and Ophelia decided that they might as well go along after them since none of them for the moment could think of anything better to do.

Fernandez's wife had barely touched the food that she'd ordered without paying any attention to what she was actually doing. She followed the procession of guests as the last one to leave the dining area while busy texting on her mobile. Still, she wasn't really paying any attention to what exactly was going on, but she knew she didn't want to be alone when Fernandez eventually turned up.

Joselyn waited until she'd seen all the guests get up from their tables, before she did one of her trademark pirouettes showing of her ass. Then she started walking seductively towards the concert area, elegantly leading the guests as if they were a flock of sheep.

Flavio had been led by one of the hotel staff to the concert stage's backstage area so he could change his clothes and prepare for the special, intimate concert.

Down in the hotel's control room, the tech support guy was

having a hard time finding suitable cameras to record the famous singer's last concert while at the same time having cameras that followed the hotel manager in her short skirt and the sexy, African woman's cleavage.

He'd offered to take a double shift for free to make up for his slight mistake earlier in the day, but, actually, it had really been so he could continue masturbating to whatever sexy images he could manage to catch with the surveillance cameras. A job he'd thought for sure would be plain and boring, had turned out to be the best thing he'd ever experienced, and it had also brought him closer to real life, sexy women, than he'd ever been.

Behind the tech support guy a small, red light had started flashing, indicating that there might be a minor fire down in the giant kitchen where the chefs were. The tech support guy, busy with his cameras, didn't notice the small, flashing light, and it being a silent warning system, relaying on the attentiveness and non-busyness of an awake, human being, it wouldn't get any attention either.

HAPPY ENDINGS

Flavio had thought it through several times, and each time he'd concluded that this special concert would be his very last. After this, he would give up his singing completely. He'd failed in what meant the most to him. The singing had become meaningless.

By holding his farewell concert this evening, the public would think he was quitting while he was on top.

It all made sense to him now. This was the reason why he'd taken the vacation. This was the reason why he'd had to experience the things he had during his stay at the hotel, and among them; meeting the Norwegian and getting to know other people without them knowing that he was a singer.

Flavio felt both relief and grief as he entered the stage. Looking over at the band the hotel had provided him with - they were all so handsome and young, and with the knowledge that this really would be his final concert, he decided he would also make it his best ever.

In front of the stage, all the other guests had now gathered. He'd noticed one man arriving later than the others, and for a short moment he'd felt slightly proud of his watchfulness for recognizing the man. It had been the man who'd clearly been ill, and was carried away on a stretcher earlier in the day. It seemed even he had found the strength to come and listen to his final concert.

As the band started playing one of his most famous and beautiful melodies, Flavio closed his eyes and started singing softly along with the melody. His voice was exceptional and the band was superb.

During the first two songs, the band and Flavio put increasingly more pressure on each other's performance, and together they built the songs towards more impressive crescendos than even Flavio himself had ever heard before.

Inspired by the arousing feeling of the wonderful music they created together, both the band and Flavio laid and even greater effort into the third and last song of the concert.

High above and behind Flavio and the band standing on stage, a falling star became visible on the night sky. It looked magnificent and had a trail of glowing light behind it.
The falling star in the background was such a perfect accompaniment to the song Flavio was singing, that it was as if some humans had ordered it to fall exactly there at exactly that moment.

Dagny watched the falling star and made a wish. She wanted the African gentleman from the dating site to be hers, and for him to please her in all the ways she deserved.
She would tell Johan that their marriage was over the minute the concert had finished. With a smile on her face, Dagny peered around to find out where he was sitting.
Gunther also saw the falling star. He had no wishes, but at that moment he decided that he would buy the young, African woman for the rest of his stay at the hotel. In his world, and according to his experience, everything could be bought if only the amount of money was right. As soon as the concert was over, he would approach the African man, who was either her pimp, or her father, or both - either way, he really didn't care, with an offer. If anybody should ask, he could pretend that she was Jurgen-Gunther's vacation nanny. Not that anybody would ask, they never did, and anyway, he really didn't care whether or not they would.
The thought of being able to fondle the young, African woman's perfect breasts whenever he felt like it during the rest of his stay at the hotel, made Gunther in a jolly mood and brought a wide smile to his face.
Jurgen-Gunther wanted more cake and ice cream too. He felt it was so unfair that he would have to wait all the while until the concert ended before he could get some more. He turned and told his father, who seemed to be in a very good mood, but who wasn't really paying any attention to him. If the man on

stage started singing one more song after this one, he would begin crying to get his father's attention. Knowing his plan would work, Jurgen-Gunther started to smile.

Ophelia glanced up at the falling star; she wanted the singer to perform at her upcoming birthday. She would have to inform her father after the concert, and at the same time remind him that her new car had to be a Bentley, a convertible, of course.

Ophelia smiled by the thought of how fabulous she would appear to everybody who saw her.

Being inspired, more by the music than by the falling star, Mugade decided that he would first confront the fat German man, which he would do as soon as they left the concert, and scare him into handing over the control of his Dunder Business-thing, and then he would focus on finding his real, new drug associate. If necessary, he would even call his original contact and pressure him.

The thought of all the money to be made, put a broad grin on Mugade's face.

Johan had determined that once the concert was finished, he would tell Dagny that he was leaving her for a more bachelor-like lifestyle that would suit and reflect his new body and persona better.

He was hoping that the African woman would be at the gym the next morning, and that the hotel's cleaning service by then would have returned his favorite pair of tights, so he could wear them and impress her even more.

Johan looked around at the other guests to see if he could spot Dagny anywhere, and he did. She was smiling lovingly at him, and he smiled back, thinking about his- soon to come - freedom.

Fernandez was brimful of drugs, and that, in a sweet combination with his natural taste for violence, had made him make the decision that he, in the dark after the concert, would kill the hotel manager. Nobody would ever know it was him. He could feel the sensation of absolute power and invincibility brought on by his cocktail of drugs starting to take hold, and he just knew that by getting his revenge, he would set everything that was currently so wrong, right again.

From his vantage point, standing slightly higher and behind the other guests, Fernandez peered around for his wife. He soon recognized the back of her head up front. She will also get punished the way she deserves, he thought and grinned bloodthirsty.

Fernandez's wife made a decision and pushed the send button on her phone, forwarding the footage of her husband being strangled to the selected paparazzi she and her manager-lover had used with success several times before. Now she would leave Fernandez. At this point, she'd gathered more than enough proof from their marriage for her to become satisfyingly famous and wealthy.

She wished that the surf-instructor would soon confirm their meeting down in the surf booth after the concert. The thought of having sex there again, combined with the thought of the suffering and huge public humiliation Fernandez was about to experience, made her laugh and smile.

Mubasher had made one of his mistresses make a recording of him participating at the concert. The footage of him sitting among regular people like this would surely make his countrymen and -women stop rioting and realize how much he really cared about the little people. He would have the recording sent directly to the news stations as soon as the concert was finished, and that would be the end of these last stressful days' situation, making everything alright and back to normal again.

Mubasher slightly repositioned himself in his comfortable, soft chair and looked at the manager of the hotel who was standing by the side of the stage. He definitely wanted her as one of his new mistresses, and the thought of her fighting his current mistress champion in the relaxed and comfortable surroundings of his own mansion, made him smile, even if he was very tired.

Wei looked around at all the other guests, and a warm sense that had formerly been unknown to him, started spreading inside his body. They all seemed to be smiling at each other, even to him, and the smiles really seemed genuine and happy, and for once, he felt included.

He could see the fat, German man smiling at the African man, and the African man smiling back. In fact, it even looked like the privileged and very special man was actually smiling at him. Wei felt how this all represented a turn of events for him. From now on things were going to be different. Finally, he was one of the others, and the thought made him smile.

Joselyn watched the concert from the side of the stage with a content smile. It was unquestionably a great success. She could see how all the VIP guests were also smiling, they were clearly happy with their stay at the hotel.

In her pocket she was holding the remote for the evening's firework in her hand, and she was certain that every single one of the guests would feel even more special and privileged once the evening's grand finale was over.

The beautiful falling star wasn't actually a falling star at all, and therefore, it of course wouldn't be granting any human wishes either. The believed to be star was actually an American spy and communication's satellite that had malfunctioned in space, and then fallen out of its orbit. Now, it had entered the atmosphere, and was partially burning up as it was heading straight for a small city in the neighboring country.

Regardless, from Earth, the falling satellite still looked like a beautiful star, and the hotel guests who were witnessing its fall couldn't see it without feeling special and privileged, whether their wishes came true or not.

As Flavios' melodious voice created its very distinguished vibrations, and as his song approached its beautiful finale, Flavio noticed that the women in the audience were starting to change their facial expressions. This was nothing new to him, and he kept looking at them as he increased the intensity and volume of his voice. He would of course deliver, like he always did, and the women would soon get to really experience the remarkableness of his true gift.

Some of the women shifted positions in their chairs. Flavio knew they were headed for their orgasms. He would give it to them now. After all, this was his final concert ever, and he wanted to deliver better and with more impact than ever before. He also wanted his lover to be able to hear his voice all the way up to the balcony on the top floor.

Flavio closed his eyes and focused, bringing his voice to new heights for the final part of the song.

Down in the hotel's kitchen area, without being able to hear anything of the beautiful concert taking place outside, and without that it would have made any difference; in between broken kitchen supplies, turned over tables, surrounded by small fires started by someone throwing Molotov cocktails, and in the rain of water by fire extinguishers, the chefs had started advancing on each other armed with knives and frying pans. Some were circling each other about to attack, while others were just slowly moving forwards towards each other with their knives ready to strike.

Dagny felt a warm feeling between her legs, a known feeling. She was about to have an orgasm. She started sweating, and moved around in her chair, which protested noisily in return.

Dagny couldn't stop herself from joining in on making noises, and started to moan and grunt.

Johan stared excitedly down at the growing bulge in his tights. Together with the bandage, his oncoming erection made it all look very impressive, and he started peering around to see if anyone had noticed how great he and his crotch area looked.

Mugade couldn't believe what was happening to his body. He'd just got an erection, and it was a powerful one. It could only be compared to the erections he would experience the first period together with one of his new wives, or the ones he would get after he'd just made a shitload of money.

When she'd totally unexpectedly started feeling sexual and horny, Ophelia had discretely moved some chairs away from her father. Now, she was holding on to the edge of her seat, trying to hide her ecstasy as multiple orgasms raged through her body.

On stage, Flavio was experiencing something he'd never experienced before. He'd sung himself into an erection, and now he felt as if he could, and maybe even would, make himself come. He closed his eyes as he prepared for the great finale.

Wei felt like hiding and tried once more to cross his legs the opposite way, but it seemed futile. He could clearly see his own erection, and he was embarrassed trying to hide it from the other guests.

Gunther shifted uncomfortable in his chair. It was too narrow for him, but that wasn't the reason for his present discomfort. He felt something, almost like a tingling sensation in his scrotum area, and next to him, Jurgen-Gunther had also begun twisting in his seat and laughing out loud as if he was being tickled.

Through the drug fog he was in, Fernandez vaguely noticed how his penis got hard. The sensation made him feel even more powerful, and he started pointing the spear like shape in his pants in the direction of the female hotel manager.

Fernandez's wife was having an amazing orgasm, and was biting her lip, trying her best not to shout out loud.

Mubasher felt how his penis really wanted to get erect, but without any aiding medication or supportive effort by his mistresses, it struggled to do so all on its own. To Mubasher it felt both pleasurable and quite exhausting.

As he was just about to finish the song, Flavio opened his eyes again. He could see that the women in the audience were having their orgasms. And then, when he looked closer, he could also see that so were the men. He could hardly believe his own eyes. He'd done it! Just as he was about to give up his career forever, he'd actually done it! How he'd done it, he hadn't the faintest idea, but the important thing was that he'd done it!

Flavio drew one last, deep breath, and sang the last sentences of the song with more joy, emotion and strength than he'd ever done before. He could even feel how the ground almost seemed to vibrate underneath his feet from his powerful singing.

Joselyn could no longer restrain herself, the orgasm passed in waves through her body. It was as strong as any she'd ever experienced from strangling someone, and involuntarily, and therefore by coincidence, but still perfectly timed, she pushed the button on the remote in her pocket, setting off the grand firework display. Big, impressive rockets flew screaming towards the dark sky before they exploded in thunderous showers with a multitude of colors.

Down in the basement "The almighty" was ready and it turned the wave generators into making large waves pounding the cliff side and then it activated the large propellers into maximum speed, allowing them to start pulling the hotel swaying out towards the ocean, almost as if the hotel stretched itself, bending out above the cliff. Its calculations showed that this would help to resolve its tasks. Its purpose was to help and assist humans and it could do so just by gently helping the humans in doing what they already did. As its sensors showed that everything developed satisfactory "The almighty's" hum turned into an almost satisfied cat like purr that would have impressed its nerdy creators.

The earth underneath the hotel vibrated. Then the crust shifted slightly. Then the gap opened wider. Then a big part of the cliff started moving. Then the hotel and the ground underneath it began moving.

All the while, the band on stage continued playing the beautiful melody.

Then the hotel and its premises all started elegantly and majestically to slide towards the ocean while the fabulous fireworks were exploding above it. The exclusive hotel then toppled over and came crushing down. Behind it all, a wall of rocks followed, crushing, crumbling, and finally grounding it all into a fine, white gravel, which in time would become the finest, whitest sand.

In the news, the story about the destruction of the exclusive, All Inclusive, luxury hotel was overshadowed by the incident of an American, communication's satellite crashing into a children's hospital in a country that, even before the incident happened, hadn't been particularly impressed with the Americans in general.

The destruction of the children's hospital would have been an incident horrible enough on its own, but then, the nuclear bomb installed inside the satellite as a safety feature, to ensure that American technology would never end up in another nation's possession by normally extinguishing the satellite before it would ever crash land anywhere, detonated a little after schedule. The powerful bomb detonated well after the satellite had crash landed, thus destroying most of the small village surrounding the point of impact. The rumors were that it most likely happened to make sure that there were absolutely no witnesses.

In the international news, the story about the hotel disaster only became a small footnote just above an even smaller article about the last of the black rhinoceros being killed by snipers, so that Asians could digest its horn to increase their sexual stamina.

The incident with the falling satellite would nevertheless not pass entirely in silence. In several countries people would protest and demonstrate because they lost their internet connections, and by that their main mean of communication for several days, until a new spy and communication's satellite was finally sent up to replace the one that had been destroyed.

The owners of the exclusive hotel, received a record breaking settlement from their insurance company, which they

immediately invested in one of the most luxurious cruise ships the world had ever seen.

The fine, white sand left after the hotel, its staff and its guests, would for decades mark the spot where the titanic hotel once had been.
When the wear and tear of time eventually had cleared the rest of the hotel's remains away, some Russian investors arrived at the beautiful and promising location.

THE END

ABOUT THE AUTHOR

Maximus Mucho gave away and sold everything he owned in 2012 and bought a sail boat. His plan was to sail around the world, but, because he is such a nice guy, he brought his girlfriend with him, and she, it turned out, is also very nice, so she quickly became pregnant, and suddenly they had the loveliest daughter.
To no regrets, this put a stop to their plan of world sailing and domination.
Then Maximus Mucho found out that sailing was, in fact, very tedious and quite boring, so he began writing books. Funny books.

His books are easily recognizable in terms of the humor, but they also always have an underlying, more serious, message written in between the lines about taking care of the environment and the animals on our Planet.
It's all there to see for the awake reader.

Maximus' hope is that his stories will leave you teary-eyed with a broad smile on your face and a sore stomach after numerous belly laughs, in addition to a severe crush on the books' characters.

You can find and connect with Maximus on Facebook (Maximus Mucho) and Twitter (@MaximusMucho).

OTHER BOOKS BY MAXIMUS MUCHO

TO BEE OR NOT TO BEE
-
ATTACK OF THE ZOMBIES
-
A Hilarious Zombie Comedy – Laugh out loud Zombies with
a twist.

SPACE RUN
-
A Crazy, Adventurous and Hilarious Space Opera Epos,
not just for Sci-Fi fans.

9730643R00133

Printed in Great Britain
by Amazon.co.uk, Ltd.,
Marston Gate.